A NEW SENSATION

Sarah was caught up in the most amazing dream she had ever had. She was in a large, soft bed and somehow her warm flannel nightgown had vanished. But she wasn't cold. No, she was actually warm. Very warm. There was something large and hot next to her. She was pressed up against it. It felt sinfully wonderful. She breathed in the warm scent of brandy and linen.

She felt a delicious pressure on her lips. Firm yet soft. Like velvet. Seductive. Her mouth moved to explore the new sensation and was rewarded with a moist heat.

Wake up, a small voice said. Something this good cannot be right.

Sarah silenced the voice.

BOOK YOUR PLACE ON OUR WEBSITE AND MAKE THE READING CONNECTION!

We've created a customized website just for our very special readers, where you can get the inside scoop on everything that's going on with Zebra, Pinnacle and Kensington books.

When you come online, you'll have the exciting opportunity to:

- View covers of upcoming books
- Read sample chapters
- Learn about our future publishing schedule (listed by publication month *and author*)
- Find out when your favorite authors will be visiting a city near you
- Search for and order backlist books from our online catalog
- Check out author bios and background information
- Send e-mail to your favorite authors
- Meet the Kensington staff online
- Join us in weekly chats with authors, readers and other guests
- Get writing guidelines
- AND MUCH MORE!

**Visit our website at
http://www.kensingtonbooks.com**

The Naked Duke

Sally MacKenzie

ZEBRA BOOKS
Kensington Publishing Corp.
www.kensingtonbooks.com

*To Mom and Dad
who share my addiction to Regency romances,
and to Kevin, Dan, Matt, David, and Mike
who are a trifle disconcerted
to have a romance writer in the family.
Also with thanks to Nancy and Robert
for reviewing some of the many drafts of this book—
You helped me find my way.*

Chapter 1

The devil was still asleep.

Sarah Hamilton squeezed closer to the stagecoach window. The farmer next to her grunted, shifting his considerable weight to take over the small space she'd made between them. The movement sent yet another fetid blast of yesterday's fish and sweat her way.

She glanced again at the man seated across from her. Even in sleep, his long, pale face and high-bridged nose were arrogant. She shivered, remembering his icy blue eyes when he'd climbed aboard the stagecoach in London. He looked just like the picture of Satan in her father's copy of *Paradise Lost*. This, she felt certain, was her first specimen of the British *ton*—a lazy, useless, drunken, conceited, womanizing, degenerate product of years of inbreeding.

She swallowed. Her uncle was an *earl*, for God's sake. What if he were as cold as this fellow?

The coach lurched around a corner and clattered into an inn yard. Sarah bounced off her neighbor's ample thigh and cracked her elbow sharply on the wooden panel beneath the stagecoach window.

"Ow-mmmp!" She shut her lips tightly, but it was too late. She'd woken the sleeping man.

Anger flickered in his cold blue eyes. He glared at

her, his hard gaze traveling slowly from the wisp of red hair she felt straggling across her forehead down to her dowdy, colorless dress. His upper lip crooked into a sneer. She wanted to vanish into the upholstery. Even the fat farmer held his breath.

Fortunately, the coach door swung open at that moment.

"Green Man!" the coachman shouted. "Best get out and stretch yer legs."

The man gave Sarah one last glare, then shrugged and turned to push past the coachman. Sarah's seatmate exhaled a long breath that echoed her own. They watched the man saunter across the inn yard and disappear inside the building.

"Thank Gawd," the farmer muttered. He squeezed his bulk through the coach door.

Sarah inched across the bench after him. She'd been sitting all the way from Liverpool, and her hips and knees felt as if they would never straighten again. When the coachman offered his hand, she took it gladly. She staggered as her feet touched the cobblestones.

"Ye all right, miss?" Small brown eyes, warm with concern, peered at her from under thick graying brows.

"Yes, thank you. I'm fine." She released her grip on his hand and reached into her reticule, bringing out two coins. They vanished between his beefy fingers.

"I 'spect someone's coming to meet ye?" he asked, pocketing the money.

Sarah looked down and fiddled with the strings on her reticule. "I have relatives nearby."

"That's good." He touched the brim of his hat. "Well then, good night, miss." He leaned closer, saying in a low voice, "I'd steer clear of that cove ye was riding with—the swell, that is."

Sarah nodded. "I certainly intend to."

"The fat bloke, he stinks of fish. But the swell . . ." The man shook his head. "He stinks of . . ."

"Evil. I quite agree. I do hope I never see the man again."

She smiled at the coachman and turned toward the inn. It was a sturdy, welcoming building. Light and sound spilled out from its windows. She heard the clatter of mugs and silverware, the raucous laughter of men in the common room. The scent of ale and roasting meat drifted past her, but her stomach rebelled. She was too tired to eat. All she wanted was a room with a bed.

The innkeeper pushed back his greasy hair as she approached the front desk. His lips squeezed together as he examined her wrinkled dress and crushed bonnet. He could not have looked sourer if he had chewed a barrelful of lemons.

Sarah sighed and straightened her shoulders. "I need a room for the night, please."

"Got no rooms."

"You must have something!" She swallowed and took a deep breath. She could not appear on her uncle's doorstep at night, exhausted and filthy. "I'll be gone in the morning. I'm visiting my uncle, the Earl of Westbrooke."

The man snorted. "Yer uncle's the earl? And mine's Prinny hisself. Get on, girl. I know what yer trade is and ye'll ply it somewhere else."

Sarah blinked. "You can't think I'm . . ." she squeaked. She swallowed and tried again. "That I'm . . ." No, she couldn't say it.

The innkeeper could. "A whore, a doxy, a tart," he sneered. "I'll thank ye to get out of my inn."

Just as he spat out his last words, a tall man with reddish hair stepped into the hall.

The troll behind the desk bowed immediately. "Yes, my lord? Did ye be needing something?"

"Sounds like you're needing a little milk of human kindness, Jakes," the man said, his words slurring slightly. He barely glanced at the innkeeper; his attention was all on Sarah. "You wouldn't really throw this poor damsel in distress out into the night, would you, old man?"

"Ye know this woman, my lord?" The innkeeper shot Sarah a worried glance. She smiled vaguely. *She* certainly didn't know her potential savior.

"Well, we haven't met, but I've been expecting her." The man stepped closer, bracing himself against the wall with his hand. Sarah could smell his words. This red-headed lord had found the bottom of a brandy bottle.

She should have been terrified, but there was something oddly familiar about him. She studied his slightly glazed hazel eyes and lopsided grin. Perhaps he reminded her of the fervent young men who'd gathered in her father's study to argue politics and drain tankards of rum punch.

"Come on," he said. "The room's this way." He lurched toward the stairs and grabbed the railing.

He must have confused her with another traveler. She followed him as he stumbled up the narrow steps and weaved along the corridor. Her conscience urged her to speak up, but her exhausted body told her conscience to shush. She could not go another step tonight. Surely the woman her redheaded escort was expecting would not arrive tonight, and if she did, she would understand. Any woman would be willing to share accommodations in such a situation.

The man finally found the room he was seeking. He opened the door and stood aside to let Sarah pass through. She paused on the threshold. There was one point she should clarify.

"This is not your room, is it, sir?"

The man propped a broad shoulder against the doorjamb and grinned. It was impossible not to respond to the twinkle in his eye, even if it was a drunken twinkle, and the deep dimple in his right cheek. Sarah smiled back. He leaned closer.

"Oh, no, mine's farther down the hall."

"Ah." Sarah tried not to choke on the brandy fumes that enveloped her. "Well, then, thank you." She stepped into the room. The man remained on her doorjamb. She could not close the door without catching his fingers. She looked at him uncertainly. "I do appreciate your help."

He nodded. "Water," he said. "I bet you'd appreciate water to wash with as well."

"Thank you, that would be wonderful." Washing off her travel dirt sounded almost as heavenly as sleeping. "But I don't want to be a bother."

"No bother." The dimple deepened. "James will thank me, too. I'll have some water sent up directly."

"Who's James?" she asked, but her new friend had already vanished down the stairs.

Sarah shrugged and closed the door. The mysterious James was a puzzle to be solved in the morning, when her poor brain was up to the task.

In a moment, a young girl appeared with a large pitcher and a towel. Sarah waited for her to leave, then stripped off all her clothing. The fire warmed her skin as she rinsed the sea salt off her body and out of her hair. While she toweled herself dry, she eyed her discarded clothes. She had lived in them for three very long days—she could not bear to put them right back on. She shook each garment vigorously and hung them all up to air. With luck, they would be acceptable by morning. She did not want to reek of the sea when she met her uncle.

Her stomach clenched. *Why* had her father insisted that she come to England? She couldn't begin to count the number of times he had railed against the aristocracy, calling it a cesspool of idiots, the fatal infection of England. Yet when he had been dying, he had insisted that she go to his brother, the earl.

"Go home, Sarah," he'd said, his voice thin and whispery, "to England." He'd gasped and struggled to sit up. "Promise me . . ."

Sarah swallowed sudden tears. She would never forget her father's smile at her promise. When his last breath had whistled out moments later, she truly believed he had found peace.

She sighed, pulling her comb through her wet mass of hair. If only the promise had given *her* peace. The Abington sisters had badgered her to change her mind from the time she'd told them she was leaving to the moment she'd finally stepped onto the *Roseanna* bound for England.

"How could David ask you to go so far away?" Clarissa, the short, stout sister, had said yet again as Sarah had closed the door to her father's house for the last time.

"It was the fever talking." Abigail, the tall, thin sister, said, patting Sarah's hand. "It's not too late to change your mind, dear. We'll just send word to the docks."

Clarissa nodded so sharply that her gray ringlets bounced over her ears. "Your father is dead, Sarah. Now you need to do what's right for you."

"What will happen if you go to England and the earl repudiates you? You'll be alone, at the mercy of all those unscrupulous men." Abigail shuddered, her hands clasped so tightly their knuckles showed white.

"It's true, Sarah." Clarissa's pudgy fingers dug into Sarah's arm. "You've lived a very quiet life here in Philadelphia. You have no idea! Why, you've hardly spoken to any American men—and American men are leagues different from those corrupt Englishmen. As different as house cats from man-eating lions."

"Woman-eating," Abigail whispered.

"Too true. Those dukes and earls and whatnots—they think women are theirs for the taking—and discarding."

Sarah shook her head, banishing the uncomfortable memory. It was too late for regrets. She was here. She hoped her uncle would welcome her. If he didn't . . . No, she wouldn't think of that. She wouldn't let worry spoil her first chance in two months to sleep in a real bed on terra firma. No matter what happened with the earl, she did not intend to cross the Atlantic again.

With that vow, she snuffed out the candles and climbed into bed.

James Runyon, Duke of Alvord, looked up from his contemplation of the fire as Major Charles Draysmith stepped into the private sitting room, leaving the door ajar.

"I believe I saw your black-hearted cousin Richard in the common room, James," Charles said, running his broad hands through his curly brown hair. "He must have come in on the stage. God, how I'd love to smash that beak of his back into his brain box!"

"Richard is here?" James lifted one golden eyebrow. "I wonder what the devil he means by showing his face in the neighborhood."

"Devil is right." Charles joined James by the fire. "I

expect to see horns and a pitchfork every time I look at the man. You really should do something about him."

James poured Charles a glass of brandy, then stretched his booted feet toward the hearth and watched the firelight glow through his own glass. "What do you suggest? Murder, even if justified, is still generally frowned upon in England."

"Call it extermination." Charles took a sip of his brandy. "You'd be ridding the country of vermin."

"I wish everyone shared your opinion." James's voice was bitter. "No one will believe Richard poses a threat to my existence until he drops my corpse on Bow Street's doorstep."

"I can't believe it's as bad as that."

"Believe it." James ticked the events off on his fingers. "My horse's girth suddenly goes loose and I fall going over a jump. An incompetent groom? The man swears the girth was tight when the horse left his care, and frankly, I believe him. A stone falls from Alvord's tower and misses me by inches. The place *is* hundreds of years old. Mortar doesn't last forever. I get bumped on a London street and almost fall into the path of an oncoming carriage. An unfortunate accident. The walkways are so crowded, don't you know?" James swallowed a mouthful of brandy.

"Too damn many accidents if you ask me," Charles said.

"Exactly."

"And no one suspects Richard's hand in this?"

"Richard is never nearby. There's nothing pointing to him as the villain. I've made what inquiries I can, but no one can connect him with any of my 'accidents.' There are some people in London who think I belong in Bedlam. The last time I tried to hire a Bow Street Runner to help investigate the matter, I was reminded that the war was over and I should relax and get used to civilian life."

"Damn!"

"Precisely." James leaned back in his chair. "So I confess, now that you've spotted Richard in the environs, I'm more amenable to Robbie's notion that we spend the night here at the Green Man. I've concluded nighttime travel is not good for my health—it gives Richard too many attractive opportunities to send me to the hereafter." James shifted to look directly at Charles. "Speaking of Robbie, I don't suppose you met him in the hall, did you?"

"No."

"Regrettable. He is much too drunk to be left unattended."

"Who's too d-drunk?"

James turned to survey the redheaded man snickering in the doorway. "Ah, Robbie. We were wondering where you had got to. Come in, if you don't need that doorjamb to keep you upright."

"Course I don't, James." Robbie walked carefully across the room and lowered himself into a chair. "Have you been discussing the luscious Charlotte while I've been gone?"

"Please don't refer to my future wife as 'luscious,' " James said.

"Well, you're right there. Charlotte is about as luscious as a frozen prune."

"Robbie . . ." James's brows snapped into a frown and he started to rise. Charles put a hand on his arm.

"I hate to say it, James, but Robbie's right this time. Good God, man, why do you think the wags call her the 'Marble Queen'? She's as cold as stone."

Robbie drunkenly patted James's shoulder. "Listen to

Charles, James. He's smart. War hero like yourself. If he says steer clear of Charlotte, do it. It ain't as if she's the only female who'll have you. All the unmarried girls—and half the married ones—would leap at the chance to be the next Duchess of Alvord."

"I doubt that." James raised his hand as Robbie and Charles both protested. "No, I've seen all the girls on the Marriage Mart. God, I've been hunted by them since my father died. I'm sick of it. Charlotte will do. She's been out a few years—she's not some young girl in her first Season. She's a duke's daughter, so she'll know how to run my household." He looked pointedly at Robbie. "And I'm sure she's quite capable of carrying out her other wifely duties."

"Well, she *is* female, I'll grant you that, so she must be *capable* of giving you your heir," Robbie said, "but don't you want to *enjoy* the process?"

James felt himself flush. "I'm sure Charlotte and I can rub along quite well."

"But what's the rush?" Charles asked. "Blast it, man, you're only twenty-eight! I'm thirty and I'm not scrambling to get myself leg-shackled." He leaned closer. "You made it through the war. What's the hurry to get an heir now?"

"We've just been discussing the hurry, Charles—my ambitious cousin, Richard. He's just a shade too anxious to become the next Duke of Alvord."

Later, James deposited his drunken friends in their rooms and turned to his own door. Unfortunately he was still much too sober. No amount of brandy was capable of drowning the thoughts churning in his mind.

The room was dark, with the only light coming from

the embers in the fireplace. He yanked off his boots and stockings, and then shrugged out of his shirt, dropping it on the floor. He wasn't exactly looking forward to asking the Duke of Rothingham for his daughter's hand in marriage. Not that Rothingham would be surprised or displeased. The man had certainly dropped enough hints the last time they'd run into each other at White's. James was confident he'd get a positive response.

He shed his breeches and drawers. Wedding Charlotte wouldn't be the tragedy Charles and Robbie made it out to be—he'd never expected to find love at Almack's. He had to marry sometime. Charlotte would do. He just hoped Richard would concede defeat once the knot was tied.

He padded naked over to the wash basin. The water was tepid, but he was used to few comforts after the Peninsula. He closed his eyes, picturing Charlotte Wickford. Blond hair, blue eyes—or were they green? Brown? He wasn't sure. Petite. Her head came about to his mid-chest. He had a lovely view of her coiffure when they waltzed. Her lips—well, she never said much of interest. He had not quite gotten around to seeing how they tasted.

He swiped at his face with a towel. He didn't *want* to marry Charlotte. He'd rather marry a girl he liked, but he hadn't found one yet and he couldn't see that he would anytime soon. He rubbed his eyes with the heels of his hands. God, he felt trapped. Time was definitely running out. That carriage wheel in Richard's last attempt on his life had come within a hairsbreadth of splitting his skull.

"Hmpzm."

James spun around. Bloody hell! There was someone in the room with him. How could he have been so damn careless? He hadn't expected trouble at the

Green Man, so of course that made it the perfect place to lay a trap. He lunged to grab the iron poker by the fire and saw the laundry spread out there. He paused. Stockings, shift, dress. A woman's laundry? Now he knew why Robbie had been sniggering. He'd smuggled a whore into his room.

He left the poker by the fire and cautiously approached the bed. The girl was asleep, a blanket pulled up to her chin. James lit a candle. She muttered and moved, the blanket slipping slightly to uncover her neck and shoulders.

She was beautiful. Her long hair was unbound, spread across the pillow in a fiery ribbon. Her features were as fine as her clothing was coarse. James studied the high cheekbones, long eyelashes, and elegant neck. In the gentle glow of the candle she looked young and innocent.

"Come on, love, time to get up." He touched her shoulder. Her skin was smooth and warm. His eyes followed the line of her collarbone to the hollow at the base of her throat. He imagined tracing that line with his lips.

He hoped the girl didn't awaken now. Whore though she undoubtedly was, she still might be taken aback by the unmistakable evidence of his interest in her. Standing there naked, he had no way of hiding his admiration.

The girl twitched her shoulder and burrowed deeper into the pillows. Who was she? Could Robbie have imported her from London? James didn't think so, but she obviously was wasted at a backwater inn like the Green Man. She looked fine enough to be some rich man's mistress. His mistress? He tested the idea and was surprised to find that he was tempted.

He would decide in the morning. It was clear that the girl was exhausted. He'd never really thought about it, but he supposed simple whores didn't get a lot of sleep.

They had to work on their feet during the day and on their backs at night. He'd let her sleep and see how things stood in the morning.

He climbed into the other side of the bed. He could feel the heat from her body and hear the steady tempo of her breathing. He smiled as he closed his eyes and tried to find a comfortable position. He was definitely looking forward to the morning.

James noticed the sweet scent first. Delicate, clean, feminine. He drew a deeper breath and felt a soft weight on his chest. And a delicious warmth along his side. And something round and smooth on his upper arm. The warmth nestled closer and a slight exhalation tickled across his neck.

The girl. She was still in bed with him. He swallowed, trying to tame the blood surging through his head and another part of his anatomy. *Don't jump on her like a hungry animal,* he told himself. Savor the moment.

He opened his eyes slowly. The covers had blessedly slipped down to his waist during the night. The girl's slender arm rested across his chest. He followed the delicate curve of her wrist and forearm, the tender angle of her elbow. A curtain of long, reddish hair hid her face and the small breast he felt resting against his side and arm. He wanted to see them, too. He wanted to see all of her.

He raised his free hand carefully—he didn't want to waken her just yet—and touched her hair. It was soft, shot through with threads of gold. He tangled his fingers in the silky strands, lifting them so he could study the girl's face. Her skin was peach-tinted, not freckled like the skin of some redheads. Her nose was a little blunt and her lips a little thin. Perhaps once she opened her eyes—and her mouth—the illusion would be broken, but for now she looked like a fairy tale princess. Certainly the most beautiful whore he had ever seen.

He let his eyes wander down to the soft, pale weight resting on his arm with its slightly darker tip just peeking out against his side. Exquisite.

He didn't know where Robbie had found the girl, but at the moment, he didn't care. He had much more interesting subjects to occupy his mind.

He smiled as he put his lips against the girl's mouth.

Sarah was caught up in the most amazing dream she had ever had. She was in a large, soft bed and somehow her warm flannel nightgown had vanished. But she wasn't cold. No, she was actually warm. Very warm. There was something large and hot next to her. She was pressed up against it. It felt sinfully wonderful. She breathed in the warm scent of brandy and linen.

She felt a delicious pressure on her lips. Firm yet soft. Like velvet. Seductive. Her mouth moved to explore the new sensation and was rewarded with a moist heat.

Wake up, a small voice said. Something this good cannot be right.

Sarah silenced the voice.

She heard a funny little growl and the pressure left her lips. She whimpered, wanting it to come back, and it did, but on her neck this time, just under her ear. She raised her chin to give the lovely pressure more room. It moved down her neck in small nips and licks, stopping just short of her aching breasts.

Something warm and strong kneaded the back of her neck, then followed her spine down to her hips, skirting the parts that most burned for its touch. Her body was on fire. She twisted, panting.

"God, you're good, sweetheart."

A male voice.

Her eyes flew open. She looked up into warm amber eyes, golden hair, and sculpted lips . . . now heading down to sample the tip of her breast.

She screamed and shoved against a very naked chest. She screamed again, pulling back her hands as if burned.

"What the . . ."

The man sat up, frowning. Sarah took the opportunity to grab the pillow under her head and swing it at him.

"Get back, you, you—lecher!"

"Lecher?"

The man ducked. Sarah swung again and hit him solidly on the ear.

"That's what I said. Get out of my bed. Get out of my room or I'll scream the place down."

"You're already screaming, sweetheart."

"Well, I'll scream louder." She sat up, lifting the pillow high in both hands, ready to knock him onto the floor if he wouldn't climb out on his own.

His eyes got an odd, intent expression. He was not looking at her face. She dropped her eyes to see where he was looking.

"Ack!" She slammed her pillow down to cover her chest.

That was when the door banged open and another woman screamed.

"James!"

"Damn," the man muttered. "Aunt Gladys. Why the hell is she here?"

Chapter 2

Sarah stared in horror at the crowd of faces at the door.

The nasty innkeeper, alternately sneering and wringing his hands. A pair of sniggering footmen. The drunken lord from last night trying unsuccessfully to muffle his laughter. And two elderly women, one tall, one short, their wrinkled faces and bright, inquisitive eyes framed in stylish bonnets.

"James," the taller one said again, this time without screaming. She and her companion stared at Sarah's pillow; it was all that stood between her and complete exposure. She flushed and slid lower in the bed, pulling the thin blanket up to her chin.

"Aunt, how delightful to see you. Pardon me if I don't get up." James could feel a hot blush surge over his face. He wouldn't be surprised if his entire body was red, including the unruly part that was making an unseemly tent in the thin blanket. He shifted position.

"James . . ." His aunt appeared lost for words.

He smiled slightly as he surveyed the people at his door. Lady Gladys Runyon, his father's older sister, tall and angular with over seventy years in her dish, stared at him, her deep flush echoing his own. Lady Amanda

Wallen-Smyth, her constant companion, was beside her.
Lady Amanda, who was in her mid sixties, was small and
delicate looking. An illusion only. Let the slightest scent
of gossip waft her way and she was after the details like a
ferret down a rat hole. Now her shrewd brown eyes darted
around the room, taking careful note of everything—the
girl's clothes by the fire, his breeches on the floor. Finally
they latched onto the girl herself. He swore he saw the old
Ferret's nose twitch. The girl crept even lower under the
blanket.

Robbie had finally mastered his laughter. Now his
face bobbed up above Aunt Gladys's head. His mouth
moved like that of a beached fish, but no sounds came
out. He was making slashing movements with his hand
across his throat. James wasn't sure what he was trying
to convey, but cutting someone's throat, preferably Robbie's, seemed like a very good idea.

"Robbie, kindly show Aunt Gladys and Lady Amanda
downstairs. And close the door when you leave."

"James . . ."

"Yes, Aunt. I'll be down directly. Now please go
along with Robbie."

James sighed with relief as the door finally shut. He
turned to the girl. She was still clutching the blankets to
her chest, eyeing him warily. She certainly was a very
odd whore.

"Please don't scream again," he said. "My poor ears
have suffered enough."

"Then don't do anything to make me scream." Her
eyes strayed down to his chest and then skittered back
to his face. "Do you have *any* clothes on?"

He grinned. "No, do you?"

All the skin he could see turned as red as her hair.
He wished he could see if her blush extended as far

as his had, but there was no time. Aunt Gladys would not be waiting patiently. If he wasn't downstairs quickly, she would be back upstairs hauling him out of bed, naked or not.

He frowned slightly. Now that he didn't have a pillow attacking his ears, he could focus on the girl's voice. It was very nice, soft and educated. She certainly didn't sound like a local whore or even a higher-priced London demi-rep.

"You sound American."

"I *am* American." The girl was being very careful to keep her eyes on his face. For a whore, she was amazingly embarrassed by his bare chest. "From Philadelphia."

"That's a long way to come to visit the Green Man, sweetheart. We're quite proud of the place, but I'm shocked that its fame has spread across the Atlantic."

"I did not come here to stay at the Green Man," she snapped, "and I can't say I'm much impressed with an inn that lacks locks on its doors."

James chuckled. "True, so if you didn't come to enjoy the questionable hospitality of the Green Man, why are you here?"

"To see my uncle. The stagecoach got in too late for me to go directly to his home last night."

James thought he knew all the people in the neighborhood very well, but he hadn't heard of a villager who had an American niece. "Your uncle? Who's your uncle?"

"The Earl of Westbrooke."

James felt his jaw drop. "*Westbrooke's* your uncle?"

"Yes."

James swore he saw golden flecks of fire flash in the girl's hazel eyes.

"My name is Sarah Hamilton, and my father was the earl's younger brother."

"David. He did go to America." James nodded. "So you are here to see the Earl of Westbrooke." He smiled. Then he grinned. Then he collapsed back on the pillow and howled with laughter.

"Oh, God," he gasped. "The Earl of Westbrooke! I can't believe it!"

Sarah clutched the blanket tightly to her chest and stared at the man convulsed with laughter on the bed. This morning could not get any more bizarre. Was the man a lunatic? Naked or not, she should have thrown herself on those ladies' mercy while she'd had the chance.

"I don't see what's so funny."

"No, you wouldn't." The man sat up and grinned. "In fact, I should be crying, not laughing. But I'm not unhappy. This unusual incident may prove to be the best thing to happen to me in a long time."

Sarah tried to keep her eyes on his face. It would have helped if he would show the least embarrassment about his naked state, but now that the older ladies were gone, he seemed quite comfortable in his skin. It was very nice skin. The blanket had slipped down to pool at his hips, revealing a fine dusting of golden hair, slightly darker than that on his head. She felt the shocking urge to use her fingers to trace its path from his collarbone to his navel, over the planes of his chest and the muscles of his flat belly. She flushed, looking up to find his eyes on hers.

"Sweetheart, I would love to let you do whatever it is you're thinking of, but if I don't get dressed and downstairs promptly, Aunt Gladys will be storming back in here to help me."

"I have no idea what you are talking about."

"No? Well, perhaps it's just my dirty mind that's

imagining all the lovely things we could be doing if I didn't have to be downstairs—and if you weren't a lady, of course."

He turned to swing his legs off the bed. Sarah admired the ripple of muscles in his broad back before she dove under the covers. She heard him laugh, then move around the room.

"Coast is clear," he said. "I'll be right outside the door when you're ready."

Once she heard the latch click, she pulled the blankets off her head and took a deep breath. Well, at least now she knew who the mysterious James was. That is, she knew what he looked like. She burst into a hot blush. She knew what quite *a lot* of him looked like.

Still, she didn't know his surname. What was she to call him? Not James. She had never addressed a man by his Christian name. But then, she had never slept with a naked man before. Naked with a naked man! If her face got any hotter, she would set the bed aflame. She slid out from between the covers and darted over to the fireplace to retrieve her clothing.

If she had to find a man in her bed, she had certainly found an excellent specimen. She knew the Abington sisters would tell her that she shouldn't notice such things, but she wasn't blind, and only a blind woman would not have found this man wonderful with his dark blond hair, broad shoulders, and amber eyes. And his voice! It made her think of warm honey. Mellow and deep and magical. It had certainly cast a spell over her.

She pulled her dress over her head and dug a comb out of her reticule. She surveyed her hair in the mirror. She should have braided it last night, but then it wouldn't have dried. Well, she had paid the price. Now it was a mare's nest—a red mare's nest. She started to tug her comb through the mess, remembering how the Abington sisters had bemoaned its unfortunate hue.

"Maybe it will darken as you get older," Clarissa Abington had said when Sarah was thirteen, "and look more like your father's."

"Just keep your bonnet on, dear, and no one will notice," Abigail whispered.

"Sometimes, Sarah, men think girls with red hair are *fast,* so you must be especially careful." Clarissa waggled her stumpy index finger under Sarah's nose. "Red hair is a curse—it's that simple. Men will assume you are a whore."

Sarah's hand stilled. Had the man in her bed this morning thought she was a whore? Heart pounding, she leaned against the wall for support. Exactly what had happened last night?

She took a deep breath and tried to suppress her rising panic. Was she still a virgin? Certainly she would know if she wasn't, wouldn't she? She would feel . . . different.

Well, she had certainly felt different when she awoke this morning. Was that enough? She did not know. No one had ever bothered to explain the mechanics of procreation to her. Was being alone with a man sufficient? The Abington sisters had always been so careful that none of their students was ever by herself with a gentleman caller. Sarah put her hands to her hot cheeks. She had not just been drinking tea alone with a man in the school parlor! No, she'd been in *bed* with him. At night. Unclothed.

Sarah put a shaking hand on her stomach. Could there be a child growing within her right now?

And why had the man laughed when she'd told him who she was? He had appeared to believe her. He must realize now that she was not a whore.

She took a deep breath and let it out slowly. She would not let her imagination run away with her. There was nothing she could do about it at the moment. She would just tie her stomach into knots fretting.

She wrapped her hair into a bun at the back of her neck and fastened it there with her hairpins. She surveyed the result. Not elegant, but at least she no longer looked like a red haystack. She opened the door.

The man was waiting in the hall, as promised. He looked very elegant and unapproachable with clothes on.

"There you are." He offered her his arm. "Let's go downstairs and brave the dragons."

Sarah stepped closer. Now that he was standing, she saw that he was quite tall. She was used to looking men in the eye, but she came only to this man's shoulder.

"You're not going to introduce her to your aunt, are you, James? I can take her down the backstairs and settle up for you if you haven't had time."

Sarah started. She had not noticed the other person in the hall. It was the red-haired man of last night. She frowned. Why had he put her in his friend's room? She opened her mouth to give him a piece of her mind, but James was already talking.

"We'll sort this all out downstairs, Robbie. I don't relish discussing my business in the hall, nor do we need to go through this more than once."

"But, James, you can't—"

James raised his hand. "Be careful what you say, Robbie. I am most certain you will regret it."

Robbie stared, then shrugged. "As you will. I suppose you know what you're doing. You always do."

Another door opened and a third man stepped into the corridor. He was shorter and broader than the other two, with curly, brown hair. "Morning, James, Robbie, ma'am.

Uh, witnessed the commotion this morning. Shall I take charge of the, um, lady?"

"Good morning, Charles. Do come along." James looked down at Sarah. "Forgive me for not taking the time to make introductions, dear. I assure you, it is better to wait until we have some privacy downstairs."

Sarah nodded. She had no idea what was going on and decided it was better to hold her tongue. She saw Charles shoot Robbie a questioning look. Robbie shrugged.

The little group walked along the hall and down the stairs, stopping before a closed door. "Courage," James whispered, touching her hand.

Sarah and the men stepped into a private sitting room. The tall elderly woman and her shorter companion looked up from their tea. The companion wrinkled her nose, as if she'd happened upon a pigsty.

James smiled down at Sarah. There was a sparkle in his eyes as though he were enjoying some grand joke. He turned to the older women. "Aunt, Lady Amanda, may I present Miss Sarah Hamilton of Philadelphia? Sarah, this is my aunt, Lady Gladys Runyon, and her companion, Lady Amanda Wallen-Smyth."

"Damn!"

Sarah glanced around to see where the expletive had come from. Charles looked bewildered; Robbie looked ill.

Lady Amanda's nostrils flared as if the pig had left the sty and had had the audacity to root around her skirts. "Alvord, I don't care if you import your wh—"

Lady Gladys put a hand out to stop Lady Amanda. "Sarah *Hamilton* did you say?"

"Exactly, Aunt. She is here to visit the Earl of Westbrooke. I believe they are related."

Robbie groaned.

James—Mr. Alvord, Sarah corrected herself—looked positively gleeful when he turned to introduce her to his male friends. "Miss Hamilton, this is Major Charles Draysmith."

Major Draysmith bowed. "My pleasure, Miss Hamilton."

"And this," James said, his grin widening, "is Robert—Robbie—Hamilton. The Earl of Westbrooke."

Sarah gasped. Lord Westbrooke executed a jerky bow.

"You can't be my uncle. You're too young."

Robbie ran his hands through hair that looked so like her father's. "No, sorry about that. I'm your cousin. My father died last year. We've just put off mourning." He smiled weakly.

"So you are David Hamilton's daughter, girl?" Lady Gladys said. Sarah turned back to face her.

"Yes, ma'am."

Lady Gladys nodded. "Now that I look at you, I see the resemblance. Hamiltons always did breed true. And where might your father be? Surely he accompanied you across the Atlantic?"

"My father died in early December."

"I'm sorry, child." Lady Gladys did look sorry. "I always liked your father. He had an intensity about him that was quite compelling. And your mother? Is she deceased also?"

"Yes, ma'am."

"But why did you leave America so shortly after your father's death?" Lady Amanda looked suspiciously at Sarah.

There was no point in hiding her situation, Sarah decided. It would be clear soon enough. It looked doubtful that her cousin could take her in, so she'd need help finding work.

"My father was very active in politics and a respected physician, but he had little interest in practical matters. He gave money away freely and never insisted that his patients pay for his services. I would have had very little to live on had I stayed in Philadelphia. But I couldn't stay— I promised my father I'd come to his brother in England."

Lady Gladys shook her head. "Well, I'm sorry for your loss, Miss Hamilton, but that does not explain what you were doing in my nephew's bed. Certainly that's not how they go on in the colonies?"

Sarah flushed and raised her chin. "I thought it was *my* bed. Mr. Alvord came along later. I was quite as surprised as you to find him there this morning."

"Mr. Alvord? James?"

"Yes, Aunt, we'll sort all that out shortly. What *I* would like to know is why you felt compelled to invade my room?"

Lady Gladys flicked her fingers at him, but Sarah noticed she did have the grace to blush. "You didn't come home last night. I was worried."

"Madam, I am twenty-eight years old. I have risked my life for my country. If I decide not to come home one night, I think that is my own affair!"

"But you never do, James. Not come home that is. You are very responsible. And there *is* the Richard business. Of course I was worried. You might have been seriously hurt."

James looked to the ceiling for inspiration and made a mental note that his aunt knew something about "the Richard business." The Foreign Office could take lessons from his aunt and Lady Amanda. Their spy network was more extensive than either Britain's or France's.

"Did you think to ask the innkeeper how I was?"

"I was worried, James. I didn't think to ask. And

how would he know if something had happened to you in the night?"

"Apparently something *did* happen to him in the night."

James chose to ignore Lady Amanda's muttered comment. "Good God, madam," he said, addressing his aunt, "didn't you even think to knock?"

"I thought you were dying. There was no time to knock." Lady Gladys coughed and glanced away. Her cheeks flushed. "I, um, was quite surprised at the sight I encountered."

"Yes, yes." James didn't want his aunt to go down *that* conversational path.

"You know you will have to do the right thing, don't you?" Lady Gladys gestured towards Robbie. "As head of his family, that idiot there should demand it."

Robbie's hair was now standing at right angles from his head. He squeezed his eyes shut. "James . . ." he began.

"Stubble it, Robbie. I'm more than willing to marry Miss Hamilton." James laughed. "It saves me from the Marble Queen, doesn't it?"

"Marry me!" Sarah could barely get the words out. She felt as if a huge weight had settled on her chest.

"You are most thoroughly compromised, girl," Lady Gladys said. "Half the country saw you stark naked in bed with my nephew."

"But nothing happened!" Sarah frowned. "At least, I hope nothing happened."

Robbie and Charles were suddenly attacked by coughing fits. Lady Gladys and Lady Amanda stared at Sarah as if she had lost her mind.

"What did or didn't happen is immaterial, young lady. I don't pretend to know how things are done in the colonies, but in England when a gentleman compromises a lady—and believe me, there is no doubt that you are compromised—he marries her. James understands that."

"Yes, Aunt."

Sarah turned to Mr. Alvord. "But it was an accident." Even Sarah could hear the panic creeping into her voice.

James smiled reassuringly down at her, then looked at his aunt. "Perhaps it would be a good idea if Miss Hamilton and I spent a few minutes alone to sort this out?"

Lady Gladys snorted. "There's nothing to sort out."

"Still, a few minutes of privacy are in order." James looked back down at Sarah. "Miss Hamilton, will you join me for a short stroll? The Green Man is only a step or two from a rather pleasant little stream. I suggest we go there."

Sarah nodded, though she got the distinct feeling that her concurrence was not required. Mr. Alvord bowed to the assemblage and whisked her out of the room.

"I am sorry for all the confusion," he said when they had finally cleared the noise of the inn. "It's been rather a comedy of errors, has it not?"

"I'm not certain if it is a comedy or a tragedy, Mr. Alvord."

"James."

"But I barely know you. I couldn't possibly call you by your given name."

"Of course you could. I intend to call you Sarah."

Sarah frowned up at him, but he grinned back.

"In any event, 'Mr. Alvord' is incorrect. My family name is Runyon. Alvord is my title."

"Your title?"

"I'm sure your republican soul is not going to like this, Sarah, so I hesitate to inform you that my full name is James William Randolph Runyon, Duke of Alvord,

Marquis of Walthingham, Earl of Southgate, Viscount Balmer, Baron Lexter."

"No!" Sarah stopped walking and gaped up at him.

James shook his head. "It's the truth."

Sarah worked her way back through the long list of titles. "You're a duke!"

"Of Alvord. Yes."

"Does that mean I'm supposed to call you 'my lord'?"

"Technically, you're supposed to address me as 'your grace.' "

"My grace?"

James grinned. "I would love to be your grace."

Sarah thought about that. She shook her head. "I can't do it."

"That's quite all right. I'd much rather you called me James."

"Hmm. Will Mr. Runyon do instead?"

"That would be a little too revolutionary, I'm afraid. It wasn't so long ago that Madame Guillotine was separating our French brethren from their heads. Strip us British peers of our titles and our shoulders twitch."

Sarah looked at James out of the corner of her eye. "You aren't one of those lords who've lost all their money, are you?"

"No, my estate is intact." He raised an eyebrow in query. "Why would you think I was under the hatches?"

"You can't afford a nightshirt."

"A nightshirt?" He snorted. "I'm sure I have a dozen of the things. I just never wear them."

"Why not? My father wore a nightshirt. Do Englishmen not do so?"

"I have no idea what Englishmen as a breed do or don't do. I have not made a survey of it. Might I point out—not that I'm complaining, you understand—that you weren't wearing a nightgown when I made your acquaintance."

Sarah flushed. "That was only because my trunk had an accident in Liverpool—the sailors dumped it overboard when they were unloading. What you see before you are the only clothes I now own."

They had arrived at a pretty little brook shaded by a stand of trees. James led her over to a fallen trunk. Sarah sat; he propped one booted foot on the log and leaned on his knee.

"Why don't you tell me what happened last night," James said. "How did you end up in my room?"

"I didn't know it was your room!"

He smiled. "All right. Tell me how you ended up in that room, then."

Sarah adjusted her skirt. "It's really not so mysterious, but I grant you it shouldn't have happened. I came in on the stage late last night with no maid and no luggage. The innkeeper did not approve of me. He was going to turn me away when your friend—my cousin—came by."

She stared down at her feet. "I knew Robbie was drunk, but I was so tired I didn't ask questions. I was desperate for a room with a bed." She looked back up at James. "I'm not a good sailor. I didn't sleep well on the passage to Liverpool. And since I haven't much money, I took the mail to London and then the stagecoach here without stopping. Last night was the first time in two months that I slept in a bed that didn't move."

James smiled. "Poor girl. When I got to the room, I did try to wake you. When I didn't have success right away, I figured you were exhausted and let you sleep."

Sarah smiled back tentatively. "Does your aunt usually burst in on you like that?"

"No." He shrugged. "She's right, though. I usually am home. I didn't tell her I'd be staying out."

Sarah frowned. "It does seem a little extreme, panicking when you were only gone overnight. It's not as if you are a little boy."

James sighed. "No, but my aunt sometimes forgets that I'm not. She raised me after my mother died when I was eleven. Old habits die hard."

"Yes, I can see that." Sarah shifted on the log. There was no getting around it. She had to ask. "I need to know something."

"Yes?" James grinned. "I hope it has nothing to do with nightshirts?"

"Well, not exactly." She bit her lip. "Don't laugh."

"I'll do my best."

"Your aunt said I was thoroughly compromised."

"Yes, that's very true. I think there is no question of that."

"How thoroughly?"

James chuckled. "Very. I'm afraid you really must marry me."

Sarah swallowed and gripped her hands together. "So I'm with child?"

"What!" James's jaw dropped. Then his eyes lit up, and he slapped his hand over his mouth. His shoulders began to shake.

"You promised you wouldn't laugh!"

He nodded vigorously.

"I know it's silly that I don't know these things, especially since my father was a physician, but I don't. I mean, I have a vague idea. Look." She listed her evidence. "We slept in the same bed, at night. We didn't have any clothes on. You kissed me. Isn't that enough?"

James shook his head no.

"So if I'm not pregnant, how can I be compromised, or at least, *thoroughly* compromised?" Sarah frowned. "Am I still a virgin?"

"You did not lose your virginity to me."

"So if I'm not pregnant and I'm still a virgin, you don't have to marry me, do you?"

James shifted his boot on the log. "It's not that simple."

"Why not?" Sarah crossed her arms over her chest. "Neither of us did anything wrong, so why should we be punished?"

"It's not a matter of *doing* anything wrong, Sarah; it's *appearing* to do something wrong."

"That's ridiculous."

"It may be ridiculous, but that's the way the world— or at least this world—works. And I can't believe society in Philadelphia is so different."

"Well, I wouldn't know. I wasn't a part of Philadelphian society." Sarah smiled. "And since I have no desire to be part of English society, my reputation or lack of it doesn't matter, does it?"

James frowned. "What do you intend to do then, Sarah? From what you told Aunt Gladys, you've cut your ties to America."

Sarah smoothed her skirt over her knees. "Well, yes. I can't go back, that's true. Even if I could find the passage money, I have nowhere to go there, not really."

She thought about the Abington sisters. They would let her continue to drudge for them at the Abington Academy for Young Ladies. She grimaced. She certainly was not braving the Atlantic again for that.

"Frankly, I hadn't considered much beyond just getting here. My father was so insistent that I come. I guess I had hoped the earl could help me. I don't suppose Robbie is married, is he?"

"No."

Sarah sighed. "Then there's no hope there. I can't live with him—even I know that. I will need a job. I have some experience as a teacher. Do you know of a school for girls that could use another instructor? Or a family in need of a governess? I'm better with classical studies than painting and music, but if the child were young enough, I'm sure I could cover those subjects adequately."

James sat down next to her and took her hand. "Sarah, teachers need their reputations more than anyone. I can't think any mother would entrust her daughter's formation to a woman who had secrets in her past—and you now have a secret, a very big secret. You and I know what did—and didn't—happen in that room, but try explaining that to someone who wasn't there. A mother would never get by the words 'bed' and 'naked' and, frankly, 'Duke of Alvord.' No, love, if you are staying in England, you will have to consider your reputation. Would marriage to me really be a punishment?"

Sarah looked into his warm amber eyes with their long, thick lashes. Punishment? Surely he realized that he was every woman's fantasy. She shrugged.

"How can I tell? I don't know you. Maybe you're an inveterate gambler or a wife-beater."

"No to both charges." James smiled. "Well, since I've never had a wife, I can't refute your last accusation with complete certainty, but I've never physically hurt a woman in my life—and I definitely feel no desire to beat you." He took her other hand and tugged gently. She turned to face him.

"Look, Sarah, this arrangement has positives for both of us. You need a home. If you marry me, you'll get that and a ready-made family—Aunt Gladys, who really does have a heart of gold, and my sister Lizzie. Even Lady Amanda. Someday, if we are lucky, we'll have children. And you'll be near your cousin—Robbie lives practically next door."

Sarah flushed. She felt peculiar—warm, breathless, and a little shaky—at the thought of having this man's children. She could not deny that what he offered was appealing. She had had little family herself. Her mother and newborn brother had died together when she was very young. Her father had been so busy with his work and causes, he had let the spinster Abington sisters raise her. It had been a life lacking in love. She felt a wave of longing so strong it took her breath away.

But James didn't love her—nor did she love him, she hastened to remind herself. Why would an English duke want to marry a penniless American?

"What do you get?"

"A wife. I have need of one." He grinned. Sarah noted the way his eyes crinkled at the edges when he smiled. "In fact, I was on my way to London to look for a bride. You've saved me a vast quantity of trouble."

"I can't imagine you would have any trouble finding an English girl to marry. They must be falling all over each other to get to you."

James looked surprised. "I will take that as a compliment. However the London ladies are not pursuing *me*—they are hunting my title and my purse."

"I don't believe that for a second."

He grimaced. "Believe it." He looked down at the water rushing over the rocks. "How about a compromise? We won't get engaged now. As you say, nothing actually happened last night, so there's no rush. You can stay at Alvord with Aunt Gladys and Lady Amanda as chaperones. Then when we take Lizzie up to town in a few weeks, you can help keep track of her. She's seventeen and a bit of a handful. I really don't think Aunt Gladys is up to the task and it sounds as if you have some experience with young girls. You can think of it as your first position, if you like. You'll have some time to get used to me and to the idea of marriage."

"It's not that I don't like you," she hastened to say. "You seem very nice. I just don't know you."

James nodded. "That's completely understandable. There are just two conditions."

"Yes?"

"First, if word gets out about our night at the Green Man, you must marry me. I won't have your reputation shredded. And I won't be the man accused of shredding it."

Sarah thought it unlikely that word would get out. Who would care about Sarah Hamilton? And anyway, the only people who knew about the incident were James's family and friends . . . and the obnoxious innkeeper and footmen.

"I can't imagine that your aunt will spread the story, but those footmen . . . And the innkeeper does not like me at all."

"Don't worry. Jakes won't breathe a word—he knows if he angers me, his inn's days as a profitable establishment are numbered. And he'll see that the footmen keep mum."

"All right, then. And the second condition?"

James grinned and Sarah felt her stomach do an odd little flip.

"Second, I reserve the right to try to persuade you to accept my suit."

"What does that mean?"

"Oh, this and that. Mostly this." He leaned over and covered her lips gently with his.

Sarah no longer heard the gurgling of the brook by her feet or felt the rough bark of the log upon which she sat. Her world shrank down to James and his lips brushing lightly across hers. She was fully awake this time, but still the touch of his mouth on hers did shocking things to her insides.

Only one other male had ever kissed her. The butcher's boy, smelling of sausages and blood, had grabbed her in her father's kitchen. That had been an assault. This was an invitation. But to what? She pulled back, breathless, and looked at James. His eyes had the strange, intent look they'd had earlier, when he had been staring at her . . . at her chest. Sarah flushed.

"I'm not sure this is a good idea, my lord, um, grace."

"James." His voice was low and husky. "I really must insist, love. Your republican lips have too hard a time getting around the lords and the graces."

His eyes focused on those lips. She wet them nervously with her tongue. His gaze sharpened and he started to lean forward again. She stood up abruptly.

"Yes, well, we'll see." She looked at him helplessly. "What were we talking about?"

He grinned. "These," he said, touching her lips lightly with his index finger. He rubbed the rough tip gently across her lower lip. "And the second condition to delaying our engagement—that you'll allow me to court you."

"Do I have a choice?"

His grin widened. "No."

Chapter 3

Sarah tried to ponder her situation as she walked back to the Green Man with James. She had never had a man—the butcher's boy did *not* count—pay her attention, and now she had James, surely the handsomest man she had ever encountered, saying he wanted to *marry* her.

But no, James wasn't just any man. He was a duke—a different species entirely. A British peer who did not hesitate to shed his clothes and climb into bed with any strange woman he came upon. He was obviously very practiced at seduction.

"Damn."

James's muttered exclamation brought Sarah out of her reverie—that and his increased pace. She hurried to keep up with him.

"What is it?"

"My cousin Richard causing trouble."

"Bastard!" A girl with bright red hair and a purplish, swollen eye stood in the inn yard screaming at the black-haired devil from last night's stagecoach. "I did what ye wanted. Ye didn't have to 'it me."

"Molly!" Another girl came running out of the inn. "Molly, are ye all right?"

"Look what 'e did to me, Nan! Look what 'e did to m'face."

Nan hugged Molly and glared at Richard. "Molly's a good girl, sir. Ye shouldn't 'ave 'it her."

"A good girl, is she? Well, she's a very poor whore." Richard grabbed Nan's wrist and pulled her toward him. "Let's see if *you're* worth my money."

"Richard!" James closed the gap between them. "Let the girl go."

"Why? Is she a favorite of yours?" Richard's knuckles whitened and Nan gasped in pain. His cold eyes focused on Sarah, moving slowly from her hair down her bodice to her waist and hips. Her skin prickled everywhere his gaze touched.

He loosened his grip, and Nan collapsed sobbing into Molly's arms.

"Who is your long Meg, James?"

Sarah thought that James would not answer since the silence between them stretched out so long.

"Miss Hamilton, my cousin Richard Runyon." James bit off each word. "Richard, Miss Hamilton of Philadelphia."

"Philadelphia? Going somewhat far afield to find entertainment are you, James?"

"Richard! Miss Hamilton is the Earl of Westbrooke's cousin."

"Really? We shared a coach down from London, did we not, Miss Hamilton? Robbie must love you as little as James does me, if he consigns you to the common stage."

Hatred swirls around this man like flies on a dung heap, Sarah thought. She kept her voice even. "My cousin did not know I was coming."

"Ah, a surprise. I hope Westbrooke likes surprises. And you'll be staying with him, I suppose? Lucky Robbie."

"Sarah will stay at Alvord."

One thin black eyebrow rose. "Oh? How hospitable of you, James, opening your little home to strangers." He executed a short, mocking bow. "Enjoy your stay at Alvord, Miss Hamilton. Perhaps our paths will cross again."

Sarah breathed a sigh of relief the moment Richard was out of sight.

"Oh, yer grace," Nan said, dropping a quick curtsey, "I dunno what we would 'ave done if ye and yer lady 'adn't a'come up when ye did. That Mr. Runyon is the devil hisself."

"I know, Nan." James glanced at the other girl. "How did your friend happen to entangle herself with him? I thought you all knew to avoid him."

Nan nodded. "Aye, that we do. Molly's new to the trade, ye see."

Molly stepped out of Nan's shadow. "My ma's sick, yer grace, and we've got little ones to feed. We needed more money." She looked back at the other girl. "Nan promised me an easy trick."

"Shush up, Molly." Nan threw a harried look at James.

"Well, ye promised, Nan."

"And if ye'd waited like ye was supposed to, ye'd 'ave gotten what I promised."

"How was I to know? Ye said to wait for a lord."

"Runyon ain't no lord, ye booby."

"He looks like a lord."

Nan rolled her eyes. "I *told* ye the lord wanted ye for a *friend,* not hisself."

"Ladies, I believe you can carry on this discussion elsewhere." James turned to the injured girl. "Molly, have a surgeon see to your eye. You may have him send me the bill. And I suggest you consider another line of work. There must be some other way for you to make ends meet."

"Well, I guess there is, only I thought this would be easiest. I's gots some experience in the business, if ye know what I mean. I jist never did the deed professionally."

"Yes, well, I suggest you go put something on that eye."

"Yes, yer grace, I will. Thankee."

Sarah watched Molly and Nan disappear into the inn. "That was the girl Robbie was waiting for."

"It does look that way."

"My hair isn't that red!"

James laughed. "Your hair is beautiful, Sarah." He pushed a loose strand behind her ear. She felt the warmth of his fingers against her cheek. "It is fire and gold. I am very glad Robbie did not encounter Molly last night. I would have sent her on her way the moment I saw her in my bed."

"And then you wouldn't be in your present predicament."

"A predicament, as I told you, I am delighted to be in."

Sarah ignored that comment. "The innkeeper told me the Green Man was respectable, but it looks like it has a thriving trade in exactly what he assumed I was selling."

"Don't be offended. I'm sure old Jakes just wanted to protect the local girls' interests. If you'd hung out your shingle, no one else would have gotten any business."

"That's ridiculous!" Sarah felt her cheeks flame.

"Oh no, love. At first I thought Robbie had imported you from London."

"You thought I came from London in this dress?"

"Well, I must point out that you were not in that dress when I first saw you."

Sarah's cheeks burned in earnest.

"But you could be dressed in a sack—which, if you'll pardon my saying so, you are—and still be beautiful."

His fingers brushed lightly over her face. Sarah found herself turning up to him like a flower to the sun.

"Your hair, your lashes, your lips, and your lovely hazel eyes. You would make a man a fine mistress if you had a mind to—except, of course, you will be making me a fine wife."

His hands cupped her face, while his thumbs stroked her cheeks. Sarah thought he was going to kiss her right there in the inn yard. His face got the intent look she was beginning to recognize. But a coach clattered over the cobblestones and he straightened.

"Let's find Aunt Gladys and Lady Amanda," he said. "I'm sure they are wondering what has become of us."

The ladies were still in the private sitting room when James and Sarah returned. There was no sign of Major Draysmith or Robbie.

"So, is everything settled?" Lady Gladys asked. "You were certainly gone long enough. Are you engaged, James?"

"Not exactly, Aunt. Miss Hamilton has graciously agreed to consider my suit. I'm hopeful that once she becomes more acquainted with me, she'll also agree to our marriage."

Lady Gladys lifted an eyebrow. "How much better acquainted can she be, James?"

"Aunt!" James said repressively.

"So there's no need to hurry the banns along?" Lady Amanda's eyes focused on Sarah's middle as if she could detect an incipient pregnancy. Sarah felt an irrational urge to cover her stomach.

James shook his head. "No. However, Miss Hamilton has agreed to an immediate engagement should gossip of last night's little adventure become public. Since I'm certain that neither my relatives nor my friends will ever breathe a word of these events, I feel confident that we can give her the time she needs to make up her mind. Isn't that right, Aunt? Lady Amanda?"

"Certainly." Lady Gladys smiled. "We have no interest in rushing the nuptials, do we, Amanda?"

"Indeed, no." Lady Amanda was still casting Sarah's abdomen suspicious glances. "If you're sure there is no possibility of an awkward event in nine months' time?"

"Quite sure," James said. Sarah was too mortified to open her mouth.

"That's settled, then." Lady Gladys stood. "Let's go home. I take it Miss Hamilton will stay at Alvord, James? She can't very well go to Westbrooke. Robbie may be her cousin, but he's got only a bachelor household."

"Exactly. I'm sure that I can depend on you and Lady Amanda to be the perfect chaperones."

James escorted the ladies outside to an impressive carriage. Sarah eyed the large, black horse standing nearby.

"You aren't traveling with us?" she asked quietly after James had handed the older ladies into the carriage.

"No. This will give you a chance to become better acquainted with my aunt and Lady Amanda." He raised his voice to address Lady Gladys. "Be nice to Sarah, Aunt."

"Of course we'll be nice to Miss Hamilton, James. We are not animals."

Sarah was not so sure. Studying Lady Amanda's smile as James handed her into the coach, she had an inkling of how the biblical Daniel must have felt entering the lion's den.

"I confess I don't know whom your father married, Miss Hamilton," Lady Gladys said as soon as the coach lurched into motion. "David became the black sheep when he left England. The old earl never spoke of him."

"I didn't really know my mother, either, Lady Gladys."

Sarah had only vague memories of a soft voice and flame-colored hair. "Her name was Susan MacDonald. Her father was a Philadelphian flour merchant."

"A Scottish tradesman." Lady Amanda folded her hands and sniffed.

Sarah did not care for the criticism she detected in Lady Amanda's tone. "He was a very good tradesman. If my father had had a jot of my grandfather's business sense, I'm sure I would not be penniless now."

Lady Gladys smiled. "I'm sure you are right, my dear." She turned to Lady Amanda. "Really, Amanda, Miss Hamilton's connection to trade is not significant. You know that *successful* merchants are always acceptable."

"True. The *ton* overlooks the dirt on their hands for the money in their pockets. And let us not forget, Miss Hamilton *is* an American. Some allowance can be made for her on those grounds."

Sarah straightened her spine. She disliked the criticism of her country even more than the criticism of her family. She opened her mouth to object, but the older ladies had their heads together, completely ignoring her.

"James could marry an actress—not that he would, of course," Lady Gladys said, "and society would accept it."

"Exactly. No one wants to risk losing the Duke of Alvord's favor." Lady Amanda looked Sarah over. Sarah lifted her chin, and the older woman smiled. "She does look a bit like a duchess at the moment. I think she'll do, Gladys."

"I rather think so, too." The women smiled at Sarah; Sarah smiled back cautiously. She had the uncomfortable feeling that she was about to lose control of her life.

"I see you've already put off mourning, my dear," Lady Gladys said.

"Yes. I would have worn black, but there was no

money for a new wardrobe, nor any time to make it. And my father would not have expected it. Why make the world a drearier place, he used to say, by decking yourself out in black?"

Lady Gladys nodded. "Then I hope you won't object to wearing colors and dancing when we take Lizzie up to London?"

"No." Sarah hesitated. "I don't object. I would like to be helpful, but . . ."

"We don't have to put it about when Miss Hamilton's father died," Lady Amanda said. "If anyone is bold enough to ask—as Richard might be—we'll just say they do things differently in the colonies."

"Yes," Lady Gladys agreed. "There may be some raised eyebrows, but it's not as if Sarah is just out of the schoolroom or on the catch for a husband. She'll soon be wearing the Alvord emerald."

Sarah shifted in her seat. "Lady Gladys, I really don't think you should assume your nephew and I are going to get married."

"Of course you'll marry him, girl." Lady Amanda looked at Sarah as if she had two heads. "The man's a duke, wealthy, young, and handsome. What more could you possibly want?"

"I don't know." Sarah shrugged helplessly. "This is all so confusing."

"What's confusing?" Lady Amanda looked at James's aunt. "It seems crystal clear to me, doesn't it to you, Gladys?"

"Yes." Lady Gladys reached over and patted Sarah's hand. "Tell us what the problem is, Miss Hamilton."

The problem, Sarah thought, was that she was a penniless American girl and James a wealthy English duke, but what she blurted out was "I don't dance."

Gladys and Amanda startled as if Sarah had said she didn't eat or breathe.

"You aren't a Methodist, are you?" Lady Gladys asked.

"No. I don't object to dancing, I just never learned how. I've never been to a ball, and I've never had a suitor." Surely now these ladies would see how far removed plain Miss Hamilton was from the glittering world of the Duke of Alvord. "My only friends were the two spinster ladies who lived next door."

"My dear," Lady Gladys said, "how dreadful! It sounds to me as if you've been in mourning your entire life."

"Indeed." Lady Amanda could not have looked more shocked. "No balls, no young men! How very dreary."

Lady Gladys smiled. "Even if you weren't going to marry James—and maybe you aren't," she said as Sarah started to protest, "you deserve some fun in your life, dear. I suggest you take this as an opportunity to live a little. Enjoy yourself. Dress up. Dance. Flirt. I'm confident James can present himself in a credible enough fashion to win your regard."

Sarah looked at the two older women who were watching her so expectantly. For some reason, she did not want to disappoint them—and, if she were completely honest, she didn't want to disappoint herself. The thought of Miss Sarah Hamilton, a lowly teacher at the Abington Academy for Young Ladies and the daughter of a penniless republican, attending such glittering events was dazzling.

"All right."

"Splendid." Both ladies beamed at her. Then Lady Gladys glanced out the window.

"Ah, we're home!"

Sarah leaned forward so she could see where James lived. Her jaw dropped. She was looking at a medieval castle.

"*That's* your home?"

"Yes. The first Duke of Alvord fought with William the Conqueror," Lady Gladys said. "He built the original castle. Subsequent dukes have added on and remodeled the place, filled in part of the moat, extended the grounds and gardens, and built on a terrace in the back. It's very comfortable now, not drafty or damp at all."

The castle was situated on a lake, surrounded by rolling, forested hillsides and meadows. Sarah stared at the gray stone edifice, the crenellated turrets, and the drawbridge. *This* was where James lived? She had taken Richard's words literally when he had said James was opening his "little" home to her.

"Quite an impressive sight, is it not?" Lady Amanda sounded smug. "Alvord Castle has over twenty bedrooms. The grounds cover five-hundred acres."

"Oh, Amanda, stop it." Lady Gladys laughed. "You sound like a penny guidebook."

"I'm sure Sarah has never seen such a stately residence before, Gladys."

"And how kind of you to point it out. Pray, excuse Amanda, Sarah. It must be a touch of the gout that has her out of spirits."

"Gout! You know I do not suffer from gout, Gladys."

The carriage rattled over the drawbridge, under the portcullis, and up a circular drive. It stopped in front of a pair of huge wooden doors. A footman came up to let down the carriage steps. James was right behind him.

"We had a nice visit with your Sarah, James," Lady Gladys said as she allowed James to hand her down the steps.

"Yes," Lady Amanda said, following behind Gladys. "Now if you will just do your part, we can welcome a new bride to Alvord. It's about time you looked to the succession, you know."

"Yes, Lady Amanda," James said meekly. He grinned at Sarah as the other women went inside. "I see you have charmed the ladies. I think they like you."

Sarah wrinkled her nose at him. "*I* think they want to get you married and I'm the likeliest candidate they've seen recently."

James laughed. "Perhaps." He kept her hand as she stepped onto the gravel drive. "Welcome to Alvord, Sarah. I do hope you will feel at home here."

"It's a little overwhelming." That was an understatement. She surveyed the large building before her. Lady Amanda was right. She certainly had never seen anything like this in Philadelphia.

"It is a bit of a barn, but I won't let you get lost in it."

"James!" A girl with James's sun-streaked hair appeared just inside the huge wooden doors. She launched herself at him and wrapped her arms around his waist, hugging him tightly. He hugged her back.

"Lizzie, I was only gone overnight." He shook his head half in amusement, half in exasperation.

"But you are never gone, James. Not without telling us. You are so reliable that we were sure *something* must have happened. A highwayman or . . . or something."

"Lizzie, there are no highwaymen in Kent." He looked at Sarah. "As you can see, I am sadly domesticated. I cannot have a single night of carousing without my womenfolk setting up a hue and cry." He turned the girl to face Sarah. "As I'm sure you've guessed already, this is my scapegrace sister, Lizzie. Lizzie, let me make known to you Miss Sarah Hamilton of Philadelphia."

"How do you do, Lizzie?" Sarah smiled. Lizzie reminded her of many of her older students at the Abington

Academy for Young Ladies. At seventeen, she was on the brink of adulthood. Not yet a woman, but no longer a child, she was a volatile mix of poise and exuberance.

"Welcome, Miss Hamilton. I don't believe I've met someone from the colonies before."

"Lizzie, I think Sarah would prefer that you refer to her homeland as the United States. The colonies won their independence a few years ago, you know," James teased. "At least I hope you know. I'd hate to think I've wasted vast sums of money on your governess."

Lizzie frowned and flushed slightly. "I didn't mean any offense, Miss Hamilton."

"No indeed. And you must call me Sarah. I confess that this is my first journey outside Philadelphia, so perhaps you can help me get adjusted to England. I've already told your brother that I find English titles very confusing."

"And vexing," James put in. Sarah smiled.

"I shall try to conform, no matter how much it goes against the grain, *my grace*."

Lizzie giggled. "It's *your grace*."

"What's your grace?" Sarah asked.

Lizzie laughed harder. "*Who's* 'your grace.' James. He's 'your grace.'"

Sarah felt even more mystified. "Isn't that what I said?"

James laughed. "What my sister is trying to say, Sarah, is that the proper form of address for a duke is 'your grace,' not 'my grace.'"

"Why? Didn't you tell me I could call you 'my grace'?" Sarah thought back over that conversation and blushed. Perhaps that wasn't quite what James had meant. "I don't understand," she said. "I'm supposed to say 'my lord,' aren't I?"

James nodded.

"So why not 'my grace'?"

"You wouldn't address the king as 'my majesty,' Sarah," Lizzie said, "but as 'your majesty.' "

"I address God as 'my God.' Is a king or a duke of higher rank than the Almighty?"

"Some would like to think so," James said, chuckling. He put up a hand as Sarah drew breath to argue. "But, I hasten to add I am not among their number, so you can lower your republican hackles. Now, shall we go in and get you settled?" He took her arm and started walking toward the door.

"Is Sarah staying with us, James? I don't see her bags."

"That's because they are, unfortunately, at the bottom of Liverpool harbor. But yes, she's staying here and going up to London with us for the Season."

Lizzie looked surprised, but was obviously too well-bred to ask more questions. Sarah did not want to go into *all* the details, but she thought some explanation was warranted.

"Your brother is helping me out of a predicament, Lizzie. When my father died in December, he insisted that I come to England. We didn't know that his brother had also died, and that Robbie was the new Lord West-brooke. Since I can't stay with Robbie, your brother has graciously offered to let me stay here."

"He has?" Lizzie grinned, looking even more like her brother. "Well, I'm glad. It will be fun to have you here." She glanced back at James. "You never said what you were doing at the Green Man, James. *Were* you carousing?"

"No, I was not! And even if I was, I wouldn't tell you." He nodded at the very proper, very elderly butler standing just inside the front door. "You weren't worried about me, too, were you, Layton?"

"Of course not, your grace." Layton bowed slightly. He had a thick mane of white hair and a very imposing nose. Sarah thought he looked much more like a duke than James did. "I tried to reassure the ladies, but Lady Gladys will worry."

James shook his head. "I should have given them more reason to worry when I was younger."

"I believe the ladies would say you gave them plenty of reason to worry when you were fighting Napoleon, your grace."

They stepped into a cavernous entrance hall where a short, plump woman waited for them. The brown hair beneath her cap was liberally streaked with gray.

"Ah, Mrs. Stallings, we have a guest. Will you show Miss Hamilton to the blue bedroom?"

"Certainly, your grace. If you will come with me, Miss Hamilton?"

"And I'll help you settle in, shall I?" Lizzie said, linking arms with Sarah.

James frowned. "Sarah might like some time alone, Lizzie."

"I won't be any trouble. You don't mind, do you, Sarah? I'd like to get acquainted."

Sarah looked at the younger girl. Lizzie was smiling hopefully back at her. It was an odd but welcome feeling to have her company sought. None of her students, even those close to her in age, had ever attempted to bridge the gulf between them. She was not sure she would have let them if they had tried. She had been too afraid of losing her authority.

"No, I don't mind."

"Don't be a pest, Lizzie," James called after them as they followed Mrs. Stallings's solid form up the stairs.

Lizzie rolled her eyes. "Really," she whispered to

Sarah, "sometimes James seems to think I'm still ten years old."

Sarah laughed. "I noticed. I envy you. I don't have any brothers or sisters."

"Here we are, Miss Hamilton." Mrs. Stallings opened a door and led the way into a lovely bedroom.

"It's beautiful." There was a note of awe in Sarah's voice.

The room was at least four times the size of her room in Philadelphia. The walls were covered in pale blue fabric, and darker blue swagged curtains and blue-cushioned seats framed the large windows that flooded the space with light. A delicate blue lacquer desk and chair stood off to her left while two upholstered chairs were grouped by the fire. A thick carpet, a geometric pattern of blues and gold, covered most of the floor.

Sarah felt like an imposter. This room was far too grand for her, but then James's servants' rooms were likely more spacious than her small bedroom at home.

"I'll just send Thomas up with your things, miss," Mrs. Stallings said.

"Thank you, Mrs. Stallings, but I'm afraid I haven't got any things." Sarah smiled slightly. "My trunk went overboard in Liverpool. All I have is this sorry dress on my back. But if it wouldn't be too much trouble, I would dearly love a bath."

"You poor thing! I'll have the water sent up directly." Mrs. Stallings surveyed Sarah's dress. "Shall I see if I can freshen your frock while you bathe?"

Sarah grimaced. "I'm afraid it would require a miracle to do anything with this dress."

"Hmm." Lizzie looked Sarah over carefully as Mrs. Stallings left. "You're about my size. There might be something in my closet that you can wear."

"Lizzie, I couldn't borrow one of your gowns."

"Why not? Do you *like* the dress you're wearing?"

Sarah laughed. "No, it's dreadful. It was never stylish, but after having worn it for four days straight now, I truly loathe it."

"I should think so. My green silk should suit. My maid, Betty, can make any alterations that are needed. She's very good with a needle."

Sarah was tempted. She felt so drab, like a weed in a rose garden. Just this once she wanted to be a butterfly, or as close to a butterfly as a tall, red-haired spinster could be. She just wanted to match her surroundings. It had nothing to do with a certain handsome duke.

"Well, if you are sure you can truly spare the dress, I would be delighted to accept."

"Good. And you must know that you can't get by with only one dress—I am *not* counting that object you have on. We'll need to have Mrs. Croft in—she's the village dressmaker."

"Lizzie! I admit I will need some new dresses, but I assure you I can't afford a whole new wardrobe." *I can't even afford one new dress,* Sarah thought unhappily.

Lizzie shrugged. "James will pay for it."

"He will not. That would be terribly inappropriate."

"I don't see why. He has piles of money."

"It's just not done, not in the United States or in England."

"But you need new clothes," Lizzie said reasonably. "*Someone* will have to pay for them."

"Well, it won't be your brother! He is not related to me."

Lizzie grinned. "But Robbie is! He can foot the bill."

The servants arrived then with the tub and water.

"I'll be back when you're done with your bath," Lizzie said, slipping out the door after the footmen.

Sarah looked at the closed door. Then she sighed, shed the despised dress, and climbed into the tub. She sank into the warm water and closed her eyes.

What was she going to do about her clothing? Lizzie was right—she would need some new things. It did not seem right to burden Robbie with the expense. He certainly hadn't asked her to show up almost on his doorstep. And she certainly could not let James buy them for her. The thought was shocking—and strangely seductive. A man bought clothes for his wife, but she could never be his wife. If she had entertained that possibility even for a moment, she was forced to discard it now. She did not know the first thing about managing a place the size of Alvord. Making her mistress here would be ludicrous, as ridiculous as putting the butcher's boy in President Madison's office. It just could not be done.

She rested her head against the back of the tub. Had her father known such wealth? He had been the son of an earl, after all. Yet he had given no sign of having been raised in privilege.

Of course, he had never been terribly interested in things. Ideas, theories, arguments—those were what he coveted. Even people held little interest for him. The first time she could remember her father showing any real concern for her was when he had insisted she come to England. She certainly had never felt from him the warmth that was evident between James and his sister or James and his aunt.

She sighed. She would love to be part of a family like James's. He had offered her that if she married him. Did he know how tempting that was?

She grabbed the soap and scrubbed her arms. A tempting illusion. James did not love her. He was a British duke. He didn't need a wife, he needed a brood mare. A marriage with him would make a family in name only.

She would get a job. She would be fine. She didn't need much. She did not need any broad, strong shoulders in her life. She shook her head to get the picture of those shoulders out of her mind. The Duke of Alvord must be a rake of the worst sort. A thoughtless heartbreaker. After all, she had found him naked in her bed, hadn't she? No, she was definitely better off by herself.

She didn't need to wash her face. For some stupid reason, it was already wet.

Chapter 4

Sarah hung back to let Lizzie enter the drawing room first. Her heart was beating so fast she feared it might leap out of the low neck of her beautiful dress.

She had been struck dumb when she had looked at herself in the mirror upstairs. The woman looking back at her was a stranger. The green dress made her eyes glow. Betty had tamed her hair so that only a few tendrils drifted gracefully around her face. Rather more of her neck and chest was exposed than she was used to, but Lizzie and Betty had both insisted that such was the fashion. Upstairs in her room, Sarah had felt elegant. Now she felt awkward.

"Come on, Sarah. You can't stay out in the hall all evening." Lizzie grabbed her arm and pulled her into the room. "James, I've given Sarah one of my dresses. I think it looks quite good, don't you?"

Sarah thought she might expire on the spot. James's eyes traveled carefully over her dress. She grabbed her skirt to keep her hands from flashing up to cover her bodice. He spent an inordinate amount of time studying that aspect of her attire.

"Beautiful," he said, looking directly into Sarah's eyes and smiling. She smiled back, feeling an odd mixture of relief and tension.

In deference to her limited wardrobe, James had not dressed for dinner. Of course, Sarah thought as she accepted a glass of sherry, the Duke of Alvord could be dressed in rags and still be imposing. Or dressed in nothing. She blushed and glanced at him. The corner of his mouth turned up and his eyes acquired a distinctly knowing gleam.

This will never do, Sarah chastised herself. She raised her chin and willed her voice to remain cool. "You have a beautiful home, your grace."

"Thank you. Did Lady Amanda give you the history lesson when you arrived?"

Lady Amanda sniffed. "Gladys was the one who mentioned that the first Duke of Alvord fought with the Conqueror. She may have neglected to point out, however, that it was his distinguished service at the Battle of Hastings that earned him the duchy."

"No one distinguishes himself in battle, Lady Amanda." James said, a new, harsh note in his voice. "War is an ugly, messy business. I'm certain my illustrious ancestor caused untold suffering to the poor wretches he evicted from these lands."

Lady Amanda frowned. "If I remember correctly, it was not so very long ago that you were anxious to go to war."

"I know better now." James took a large swallow of his sherry.

"But don't you agree that sometimes war is warranted, your grace? To free people from oppression, for example?" Sarah could remember her father and his cronies holding forth about that for hours.

"Yes, surely you can justify curbing that monster Napoleon," Lady Amanda said.

"I rather think Sarah was referring to the American

War of Independence and perhaps our latest contretemps with our former colonies," James replied. "And yes, I suppose some wars are necessary. But war is rarely a simple matter. Political firebrands like to have a clear rallying cry, but most wars include a lot of simple greed, personal and political. It's hard to justify any of that when you watch an 18-year-old boy die in your arms or find a sobbing child alone in the wreckage of her village."

Layton then appeared at the doorway to announce Robbie and Charles.

James smiled, dispelling the bleakness that had tightened his face. "Gentlemen, I was beginning to wonder if you had turned craven." He moved forward to greet the men, bringing Sarah with him.

"I do think Robbie was tempted, James," Major Draysmith said. "Good evening, Miss Hamilton."

"Good evening, Major."

Major Draysmith crossed the room to speak to the other ladies while Robbie took Sarah's hand.

"Cousin." He looked distinctly wary.

"Cousin," Sarah returned tonelessly.

A dark flush covered his cheeks. "My humble apologies about the confusion last night," he murmured. "I was drunk, don't you know. Half-seas over. Never would have made the mistake had I been sober."

"Perhaps you should limit your drinking."

"Uh, right." Robbie looked over at James. "My apologies to you, too, of course."

"We met the lady you were waiting for," James said. "She doesn't look at all like Sarah."

"No, of course not. Didn't think she would. I *said* I wouldn't have made the mistake if I'd been sober. Nan set the thing up. Said her friend wanted to get established in the business. Uh, where did you happen to meet her?"

"In the inn yard," James said. "Apparently she encountered Richard first and decided to take the sure thing. She was regretting her decision. He had blackened her eye."

"Damn. Come to think of it, when I saw him in the common room, he did have a redheaded tart—uh, your pardon, cousin—female with him. They must have ducked into the tap first for a drink before going to the girl's room."

"Do you know many prostitutes?" Sarah asked.

"No, of course not." Robbie ran a finger under his cravat and looked around the room. "It must be time to go into dinner. Where's your butler, Alvord?"

"Here's Layton now. Perhaps you would like to take Aunt Gladys in, Robbie?"

"Happy to." Robbie fled across the room to Lady Gladys. He offered her his right arm and Lady Amanda his left. Major Draysmith escorted Lizzie.

Sarah frowned up at James. "Is Robbie a procurer?" She knew the *ton* was degenerate, but she would never have thought her own cousin might be a panderer.

"Good God, no. You can stop looking so ill. It really was no more than a misunderstanding." James put her hand on his sleeve.

"A *misunderstanding?* I don't see how anyone can have that kind of misunderstanding."

"No, I don't suppose you do." He raised his hand slightly when Sarah opened her mouth to pursue the topic. "No, love. We can discuss this if you want, but later. It truly is not a topic my aunt would welcome at her table."

Sarah sighed. "No, of course not. I beg your pardon."

"Don't beg *my* pardon, Sarah. I hope there will be no

topics we can't discuss—but some things are better said in privacy." This last was whispered near her ear as he seated her. Her breath caught and an odd little shiver ran down her spine.

The dinner went on for what seemed to Sarah a very long time. She limited herself to just a taste of each course, yet still felt uncomfortably full. She couldn't help but think she and her father could have lived for weeks on this one meal.

"Robbie, Charles, you've just come from town," Lady Gladys said. "Tell us, please, who else is bringing out girls this Season?"

Robbie had taken an unfortunate mouthful of wine just as Lady Gladys spoke. He choked and reached quickly for his napkin. "Not much in the petticoat line, ma'am. Can't say I paid much attention."

"Surely you've made note of which mamas to avoid." Lady Amanda, his neighbor at the table, whacked him on the back.

"Ah, my thanks." Robbie shifted so Lady Amanda could not get another swing at him. "Well, I think the Barringtons might have a girl coming out."

Lady Amanda nodded. "No doubt spotted like the last two."

"And the Amesleys."

"Walleyed," Lady Amanda said.

"No, that one came out last Season. This one's the rabbity-looking girl."

"Right. Clarinda or Clarabelle or something." Lady Amanda took a delicate sip of wine. "Of course, the mother's no beauty. I never could understand how she got Billy Amesley to the altar."

"I think it might have had something to do with the fact that the Amesleys' pockets were to let," Lady Gladys said.

"Harriet Drummond was a significant heiress, if you'll remember, Amanda."

"True. The gleam of a well-filled coffer has led many a man into the parson's mousetrap—and as they say, you can't tell a beauty from a beast once the candles are snuffed."

It was James's turn to choke on his wine. "Who says, Lady Amanda?" he asked, a note of laughter in his voice.

"Everyone." Lady Amanda sniffed. "I'm not a member of your mealymouthed generation, James."

"For which I must be grateful."

"I think the Earl of Mardale has a daughter making her bows this year," Major Draysmith offered.

"Mardale—now there was a fine figure of a man," Lady Amanda said. "I'm sure he must have produced attractive offspring."

"Are we embarrassing you, Sarah?" James asked softly as the conversation moved on to rival mantua-makers.

"A little," she admitted. She rubbed her fingers over the soft fabric of her borrowed dress. Now that she had seen—and worn—Lizzie's dress, she knew she could never afford the clothes she would need for a trip to London. She lowered her voice. "Your grace, I've been thinking of my future."

James gave Sarah a slow smile. "I am glad to hear that."

She felt unaccountably flustered. "Yes, well, I think it would be best if I found a situation as a teacher now, instead of going to London."

Unfortunately, there was a lull in the general conversation just then and Sarah's words carried. Lady Gladys put her wineglass down so quickly, she knocked it against her plate. A few drops of wine jumped out onto the tablecloth.

"A situation as a teacher? You aren't going to be a

teacher, Sarah; you're going to be a duchess. If you have such a burning desire to teach, teach your own children. I'm sure James won't waste any time filling his nursery."

Sarah was sure her face was as red as Molly's hair. She was afraid to look at James for fear she'd prove the theory of spontaneous combustion.

"Lady Gladys, it's quite clear that I am not suited for the position of duchess."

"Why not? You're young and female, aren't you? James, do you think Sarah is unsuited to be your duchess?"

"Not at all, Aunt."

Sarah risked a glance at James. His lips turned up into what she could only describe as a smirk.

"I can't say that I've thoroughly investigated all of her credentials of course, but I believe she will suit very well indeed."

"I thought you *had* investigated all her credentials, James," Lady Amanda said. "That's why we're in this situation."

Sarah watched James's smile vanish and his ears turn red.

"Perhaps we should change the subject," he said. "Lizzie, how go the preparations for London?"

Lizzie's mouth was hanging open so wide that her chin just about touched the table. "Did you say you were going to *marry* Sarah, James?"

"I guess we forgot to mention that, didn't we? Nothing has been decided conclusively, but Sarah has agreed to consider my suit."

Lizzie's eyes grew huge. Sarah could tell she was full of questions—the first one, Sarah supposed, was where she and James had met. They had better come up with a plausible story if they didn't want the true tale known.

"We met when I was in America," James was saying.

Sarah turned to look at him. She was very much afraid that she was goggle-eyed. She bit her tongue before she could ask him when he had been in her country. He must have been there once; his family would certainly know if he had not.

"I thought our love was hopeless with an ocean separating us, so I said nothing. I couldn't even bring myself to mention it to Robbie."

Sarah restrained herself from kicking him under the table. He should consider a career writing novels if he could sell that story to anyone. Lizzie looked doubtful; Robbie rolled his eyes.

"Well, James," Lizzie said, "if you're going to marry Sarah, you should give some thought to her clothes. She needs a whole new wardrobe—she doesn't even have a nightdress!"

Sarah knew she would blush if she looked at James, so she studied her plate instead. "Really, your grace, my clothes—or lack of them—is not your concern."

"I'm certainly concerned with your *lack* of clothes, sweetheart. But if you deny me the pleasure of clothing you, certainly you will agree that it *is* Robbie's responsibility as head of your family. We'll just have the bills sent to him, right, Robbie?"

"Yes, of course. Be happy to stand the nonsense."

Sarah looked at Robbie. "I can't impose on you."

"Of course you can. I'm head of your family now, ain't I?"

"But it's such a waste of money."

"It is nothing of the sort." Lady Gladys leaned toward her. "You deserve some fun, Sarah. From what you told me, David was quite remiss in your upbringing. It is just like him to get lost in his causes and never pay attention to the needs of the people around him. And it is certainly Robbie's responsibility to fund a Season for you. His estate can bear the expense, isn't that right, Robbie?"

"Said I'd pay the bills. Not to worry, cousin."

"That's settled then." Lady Gladys smiled and sat back. "We'll have Mrs. Croft up tomorrow. She can make a few necessities now, and we'll get the rest in London."

"There's still one other issue, Gladys," Lady Amanda said. "Sarah doesn't dance. She'll have to learn all the steps before we go to town."

"Very true. Well then, I suggest you gentlemen dispense with your port this evening and join us in the music room immediately. The sooner we get started, the better. We want Sarah to be ready for Almack's."

"What is Almack's?" Sarah asked as she left the room on James's arm.

"What is Almack's?" Lizzie stopped so suddenly, Sarah almost ran into her. "Almack's is . . ." The younger girl was clearly speechless at Sarah's ignorance.

Robbie, Lizzie's escort, laughed. "Almack's is the center of the universe for the *ton's* marriage-minded mamas and their daughters, Sarah. Every Wednesday night during the Season, the girls who can get their hot little hands on a voucher hunt for husbands among the eligible males of the *ton*. To the rest of us mortals, it's a stuffy, boring club."

"It sounds dreadful."

"It *is* dreadful."

"No, truly, Sarah," Lizzie said. "Almack's is wonderful."

"You have never been there," Robbie said. "Once you've eaten the stale cakes, drunk the tasteless punch, and endured the insipid conversation, you'll think differently."

Lizzie frowned up at Robbie. "No, I'm sure you must be wrong."

Robbie rolled his eyes. "Ah, youth."

"You're not exactly a graybeard."

"I don't think I want to go to Almack's," Sarah said quietly to James as Robbie and Lizzie moved ahead.

"No, but we'll have to make an appearance for Lizzie's sake."

Sarah frowned. "Perhaps I won't be able to get these vouchers Robbie says are needed."

"No danger of that with Aunt Gladys as your sponsor. The patronesses would not dare snub the sister and aunt of the Duke of Alvord."

"I'm sure they will snub a penniless American upstart."

"No, they won't. Trust me, sweetheart. I'm an expert in the ways of the *ton*."

"So you think they will accept me?"

James grimaced. "Like they accept everyone—with false smiles and backbiting and the hope that you'll do something really dreadful so they can talk about you until the next scandal presents itself."

Sarah felt the color drain from her face. "That sounds horrible!"

"It *is* horrible. It's why I avoid *ton* parties like the French artillery." James grinned and ran his finger down Sarah's nose. She swatted his hand away. "But now, with you at my side, I find I can bear the agony."

"*You* can bear it! All those awful people will be staring at *me*, the bold American who presumes to insinuate herself into the Duke of Alvord's family."

They entered the music room. It had pale green walls, a beautiful piano—and a very large painting of three buxom women dancing in a meadow. Except for a few wisps of fabric, the women were nude. A muscular man, with a lyre and considerably more clothing, watched the cavorting trio from the shade of a tree.

"*Apollo and the Three Graces*," James said. "My father's acquisition. I never knew the painter's name, but then, I doubt my father purchased it for its artistic merit."

"James, stop admiring the artwork and help Robbie and Charles roll back the rug." Lady Gladys stood by the piano, directing the men's efforts. "And Sarah, come here. Lizzie will show you a few steps. We'll start with a country dance. Will you play for us, Amanda?"

"Well, I certainly am not going to dance. If you plan to attempt the quadrille, Gladys, you will have to take a place and you will still be one couple short."

"I'm sure we'll manage."

Lizzie walked through the steps as the men pushed the carpet aside. Sarah watched Lizzie's feet intently, trying to memorize the patterns. Finally, she shook her head.

"I'm afraid this is hopeless, Lizzie. I'll never remember it all."

"Of course you will!" Lizzie smiled encouragingly. "It will be easier with music and a partner."

"And I suppose I should be that partner," Robbie said, bowing. "If any blood is shed, at least it will be Hamilton blood."

"Not exactly a vote of confidence, Robbie." Major Draysmith bowed to Lizzie, and then looked over at James. "Did you want to join the set?"

"I believe I'll sit this one out," James said, lounging against the piano, "unless you'd like to dance, Aunt?"

"Not likely. You can help me supervise."

"Splendid. I am excellent at supervising."

"I don't doubt—just remember that there are *four* dancers on the floor, James."

"Of course."

Sarah glanced over and saw James wink at her. Then she turned her attention to her feet. She made it through the first pattern without injuring anyone. She smiled, relaxing, and glanced at James again.

"Yipes!" Robbie jumped back, pulling his foot out from under Sarah's. "No, Sarah, step to your *other* left."

Sarah flushed. "I'm sorry. I didn't do any damage, did I?"

"Nothing permanent. However, I think I've done my duty. 'Discretion is the better part of valor,' as the Bard says. I shall pass you off to the gallant Major Draysmith. He was in the Light Dragoons—he's good at getting out of tight places."

Charles took Sarah's hand. "I really don't equate dancing with you to a battle skirmish, Miss Hamilton."

"Perhaps you should," Robbie said as the music started again. "You may sustain more wounds tonight than you did in all your years on the Peninsula."

"Robbie!" Charles turned his head to frown at his friend. "Oww!"

"Oh, I am sorry." Sarah tried to change directions before she put all her weight on Charles's foot, but lost her balance and hopped onto his toe instead. He smiled bravely while he helped her steady herself.

"That will teach you to let your guard down, Charles." Robbie laughed. "Anything broken?"

"Of course not."

"Perhaps we should try the waltz," Lady Gladys suggested.

"A splendid idea." James grinned, stepping away from his post by the piano. "I will partner Sarah this time."

"Think if you keep your hands on her, you'll be able to prevent her from mayhem?" Robbie asked.

Sarah flushed slightly. The idea of waltzing with James was distinctly unsettling.

"I hope you don't expect *me* to play that scandalous music." Lady Amanda got up from the piano.

"I thought your generation wasn't mealymouthed, Lady Amanda," James said.

"We're not, but neither do we engage in lewd, public behavior."

"I don't know about that." Robbie grinned. "Seems to me I've seen Oliver Featherstone waltzing."

"That dirty dish!" Lady Amanda sniffed. "He once rode bare-arsed down Bond Street on a bet."

Robbie shuddered. "Now *that's* a sight I'm thankful I missed. How about you, Lady Gladys? Will you play for us?"

"I don't think so. I was the bane of every music teacher my father hired."

"I believe I can manage to plunk out a respectable waltz." Major Draysmith moved to sit at the piano. Sarah was relieved to see that he wasn't limping. Lady Amanda helped him sort through the music.

"Would you care to waltz then, Lady Gladys?" Robbie asked.

"I *said* I was supervising."

"True." Robbie turned and grinned at Lady Amanda. "How about you, Lady Amanda? Care to try the wicked waltz?"

"I certainly do not! You will have to dance with Lizzie, sir."

"Little Lizzie?" Robbie laughed. "Well, come on then, brat; we shall have to struggle through. Are my toes safe? Have you ever waltzed before?"

"Only with my dancing master."

Sarah watched Lizzie step close to Robbie. There was

an expectant, dreamy expression on her face, quite at odds with Robbie's laughing attitude. It was clear Robbie looked on Lizzie as a younger sister; Sarah doubted that Lizzie had sisterly feelings for Robbie.

"Have you really never been to a ball?" James asked as they waited for Charles to straighten his music.

"Well, I did go to a Christmas dance once at the school where I taught, but I didn't dance."

Sarah remembered it clearly. The Abingtons had bowed to pressure from one of their few wealthy families and had consented to hold the event, much against their better judgment. The sisters would squeeze a penny until it cried, so they were not about to hire extra staff. Sarah had done all the work, cleaning and cooking and listening to the sisters complain about the cost of such a frivolous undertaking. There'd been neither time to sew a ball gown nor any money for fabric, so she'd just worn her best dress, the one she'd worn to every commencement, formal school assembly, and Sunday service since she'd turned sixteen.

"No one asked you to dance?" James sounded shocked. "The men in Philadelphia must all be blind."

Sarah smiled slightly and shook her head. One brave fellow had asked, but surprise had kept her silent too long. Miss Clarissa Abington had sent the young man off with a flea in his ear for his boldness.

"Well, I am not blind," James whispered as Charles played the opening chords of the waltz. "And I very much want to waltz with you, Miss Hamilton."

"Oh," Sarah breathed as James's hand touched her waist. She placed her hand carefully on his shoulder and smiled hesitantly up at him. She saw the faint golden stubble on the strong curve of his jaw; the slight cleft in his chin; and the firm line of his lips, lips that had felt so inviting on hers.

She had been this close to him in that bed at the Green Man. Closer even.

She dropped her eyes and stared at his shoulder.

"No, sweetheart, don't stiffen up." James spoke softly so that only she could hear as he started them moving around the room. "Think of my poor toes!"

A slightly hysterical laugh bubbled up in her chest. "I don't think I can do this."

"Yes, you can. Just relax. Close your eyes and feel the music."

Sarah obediently closed her eyes, but it wasn't the music she was feeling: it was the warmth of his body only inches from hers and the strength of his shoulder under her hand. She was surrounded by him, by his heat and his spicy, male scent, a mix of soap and wine and leather. When she wavered, he pulled her closer and she felt the momentary brush of his leg against her skirts, his chest against her breasts.

His broad, muscled chest with its golden hair, trailing in a thin line down to his navel.

Sarah gasped and opened her eyes. Such wanton thoughts!

James bent his head, his hands urging her even closer to his firm body. His lips were on level with her eyes. If she turned her head, if she leaned ever so slightly toward him, she would feel them on her temple.

She felt his breath against her cheek as he counted.

"One, two, three. One, two, three."

A strange, drenching heat pooled low in her stomach.

"Follow me, love," he whispered, his words stirring the tendrils of hair by her ears. "Come with me."

She did. She forgot about her feet. She forgot the

music room, Robbie and Lizzie, and the others. She gave herself up to James, let her body move with his.

When the music stopped, it took her more than a moment to come back to herself.

"Well, Lady Amanda," she heard Robbie say, "I do believe James and Sarah just showed us why the waltz is such a dangerous dance."

Chapter 5

James closed the heavy account book and leaned back in his chair, stretching the knots out of his neck and shoulders. Everything was in order, as usual. The estate ran itself, with some help from his excellent steward, Walter Birnam. In fact, all of his properties were in good order. None of *his* tenants had been forced to find work in the cities or in the new manufacturing mills. But all that would change if Richard got his hands on the dukedom.

He needed a wife and an heir. A wife now; an heir, God willing, nine months after the vows were said. Ever since he had realized Richard was trying to hasten his journey to the Almighty, the need to secure the succession had weighed on his mind—until Miss Sarah Hamilton had appeared in his bed.

He grinned. The waltz last night had been heaven—but it had been hell keeping his hands where society prescribed. He had wanted to put them on many more interesting places than Sarah's waist and gloved hand. Her breasts, for example. His hands would fit quite nicely over those. God, he'd do almost anything to see them again—even take another pillow to the ear.

He closed his eyes. Mmm, yes. He could stand to get into another pillow fight with Miss Sarah Hamilton. When she'd lifted her hands high to wallop him, he'd seen every inch of her narrow waist and delicate ribs and lovely small breasts with their rosy tips . . . Yes, he would definitely enjoy another pummeling.

He shifted in his chair, savoring the throb of anticipation. Some day—some day soon, he hoped—he would have her back naked in his bed, and they could take up where they had left off at the Green Man. If she were a proper British girl, they'd have set a wedding date already. But she was a prickly, independent American girl who refused to follow British rules.

He would just need to figure out a way to persuade her. He was contemplating a variety of tantalizing methods when Robbie arrived.

"Morning, James. What has you grinning so early in the day?" Robbie dropped down into the chair by James's desk. "Or should I say 'who'?"

James's grin broadened. "You of all men should be happy that I'm content with my fate, since you're to blame for the whole mess. What were you thinking? No, don't answer that. You weren't thinking."

"Not true. It was merely a case of mistaken identity. Nan said she had a friend who was something special. Spun me some tale about the girl having aspirations of going to London. I figured I might help both of you."

"Well, you certainly helped me."

"Sorry about that, though how was I to know? Sarah has red hair—Nan said that's how I would know the girl—and she showed up at the Green Man with no maid or luggage."

"Do you honestly think Sarah looks like a tart?"

"Of course not. I told you, Nan said she was something special. And I was drunk." Robbie's eyes dropped to focus on his boots. "Um, I assume you . . . I mean, she's . . . Well, you did, didn't you?"

"If you are asking if I deflowered your cousin, the answer is no."

Robbie's gaze snapped up to focus on James's face. "You mean she wasn't a virgin? I know she's a colonial and all, so I suppose they might have some different customs, and she is a bit long in the tooth . . ."

"Robbie, for God's sake, stop before I feel compelled to call you out. As far as I know your cousin is a virgin. Things did not progress to the point where I was in a position to ascertain the issue."

"They didn't?" Robbie sounded disappointed. "You were both stark naked, for God's sake!"

James flushed. "Yes. Well, in any event, you should be happy to know that I am quite content to marry Sarah. I confess I am more than relieved not to be offering for Lady Charlotte Wickford."

"I should think so! God, the thought of bedding that iceberg . . . brrr! Sarah has *got* to be better than that. I take it everything is set? You'll be calling the banns before we leave for London?"

James balanced a silver penknife on his index finger, avoiding Robbie's gaze. "Not exactly. Things are still somewhat uncertain; however, do not worry. I will marry your lovely cousin. Now tell me—have you heard any more about Richard's activities in the neighborhood?"

"No. He's lying low. The man does come down to the area on occasion, so his being here may not mean anything. I think he likes to keep an eye on the estate."

"I bet he does."

"Now, James, are you sure you aren't reading too much into events? Accidents do happen, even to war heroes. Murder is a serious charge."

"Do you think Richard is incapable of murder?"

Robbie started to answer, but stopped. Silence stretched between the two men.

"No," Robbie said finally. "I'd like to think Richard couldn't kill, but the man does hate you with a passion bordering on insanity."

"Exactly. Believe me, Robbie, I am not given to flights of fancy. I am convinced that Richard is behind my accidents. If he is not stopped, he *will* be successful. Then he will inherit Alvord and all my other holdings. I cannot let that happen."

"No, I can see that. Besides the fact that death ain't terribly appealing, your cousin Richard is just a damn nasty customer. Your tenants, your servants, Lizzie, Aunt Gladys and Lady Amanda—everyone would suffer if Richard got his hands on the reins."

"I mean to see that he doesn't."

There was a knock at the door, and Sarah looked into the room. "Am I interrupting?"

"Nothing that isn't better interrupted. Please come in," James said. He and Robbie stood. "Were you looking for me or had you heard that your disreputable cousin had come calling?"

"Actually, I was looking for you, your grace, but it's just as well that Robbie is here. Did you know that the dressmaker has arrived?"

"Well, no." James considered Sarah. Her lips were pressed together in a tense, thin line. "Is there a problem?"

"Yes, there's a problem."

"Ah." James threw Robbie a glance. Robbie was eyeing Sarah as though he expected her to explode at any moment. "I trust you will enlighten us as to the nature of the problem?"

"She wants to make me dresses."

"Yes, I imagine she does. She *is* a dressmaker, Sarah."

James watched Sarah grip her skirts so tightly the fabric looked in danger of tearing.

"I *know* she's a dressmaker. Do you know *how many* dresses she wants to make me?"

"Ah, I begin to see the problem. No, I don't. Why don't you tell me?"

"Too many."

Robbie erupted into laughter. Sarah glared at him.

"I don't know what *you're* laughing about. You're the one paying for all this, aren't you?"

Robbie nodded and waved his hand. It was clear he was not going to risk a more coherent reply. Sarah turned back to James.

"Your aunt and Lizzie are in league with this woman. And they say I'll need even more clothes once we get to London. Do Englishwomen spend their entire day changing their clothes?"

"Um, I can't say I've really considered the matter, have you, Robbie?"

"Oh, stop laughing. It's a shocking waste of money! For example, Mrs. Croft wants to make me a riding habit and I don't even ride."

"You don't ride?" Robbie stopped laughing abruptly and gaped at Sarah. She made a face back at him.

"You needn't act as though I'm a freak of some kind. I have two perfectly good legs. Why would I need to sit on some large beast to get around?"

"Are you afraid of horses, Sarah?" James asked.

"No, I don't think so. I've just never had occasion to ride. We lived in the city and walked everywhere."

"Hmm. Well, you'll want to learn to ride," James said.

"I will?" Sarah looked skeptical. "I hope you don't expect me to go chasing over the countryside after some scruffy fox. I won't do it. And I don't care to go jumping over fences either."

"Good God!" Robbie said. James just smiled.

"Simple riding will be fine. I'm not hunting mad myself. I'll give you a lesson or two as soon as your habit is ready. We'll cover the basics now and refine your skills when we come back to Alvord after the Season."

"I hope to have a position by the end of your Season," Sarah said. "I won't be coming back to Alvord."

"No? Well, we'll see."

"You should know that James always gets what he wants," Robbie offered helpfully. "I'm not certain how he does it—sheer pigheadedness most probably."

"Nonsense, Robbie. The trick is to always want what is reasonable."

"If you mean marrying me, your grace, certainly you can see that that is *not* reasonable." Sarah ticked off the reasons on her fingers. "I'm an American; I have no idea how to manage a house this size; I can't dance; I don't ride."

James came around his desk. He grasped Sarah's hand and gently folded down each finger. "You dance very well, Sarah, and we'll work on the riding. Mrs. Stallings has run Alvord for years, even when my mother was alive. I'm sure she'll be happy to continue doing so, under your direction, of course. And while it's true that you are an American, you are also the cousin of the Earl of Westbrooke."

"And that is a great distinction," Robbie said. He gave a short bow. "Well, much as you two will miss me, I'd better be going."

James kept Sarah's hand in his as they walked Robbie to the door. She tugged back slightly, expecting him to release her, but he tightened his grip, linking their fingers.

She was sure the footmen must notice that their employer was holding her hand, but not one so much as blinked. Layton even went so far as to nod and smile at her.

"I was planning on visiting one of my tenants," James said as Robbie rode off. "I'd be happy to have you come along, if Mrs. Croft can spare you."

"She can spare me. My fidgeting was driving her so crazy she was ready to impale me with her needle. Are you sure I'm not too shabby to go visiting?"

James ran his eyes down her body. She felt a faint flush burn her cheeks.

"You'll do. These are old friends. They don't much care about fashion. Go fetch your bonnet."

James was leaning against the gig when Sarah stepped outside.

"You look much too elegant for such a plebeian vehicle, your grace," she said.

"Ah, but I'm just a simple farmer at heart." James handed her into her seat. His eyes laughed up at her. They were almost the same color as his hair, their long lashes tipped in gold. She felt a light tug on her hand and leaned forward. Her eyes settled on his lips. They looked firm and warm. How would they feel today?

She jerked her head back and sat up straight. What was she thinking? They were on the front drive, in full view of the main entrance and hundreds of windows.

James sighed. "I almost had you there, didn't I?"

Sarah shot him her most quelling glance, perfected after years at the Abington Academy for Young Ladies. "Behave yourself, your grace."

He walked around and swung himself up into the driver's seat. "Behaving is not as much fun as misbehaving,

Miss Hamilton. Admit it. Or could it be that you have never misbehaved?"

"Don't be ridiculous." Sarah stared straight ahead over the horse's rump.

"I don't believe you have." James snapped the reins and the horse obligingly ambled into motion. "I shall have to change that."

"And you are a great expert on misbehavior, I don't doubt."

"Not really. I had too many responsibilities to misbehave often, but I'm happy to make up for lost time."

"How old were you when you inherited the title?" Sarah was surprised. From the stories her father and the Abington sisters had told her, she'd assumed the entire aristocracy lived thoughtless lives of endless pleasure.

"Twenty-five. But as firstborn and only son, I was in training from the moment I could toddle around the estate." James snorted. "I wouldn't be surprised if my father quizzed me on planting and precedence while I was still in the arms of my wet nurse. And no, I am not a candidate for pity, if I read aright the look in those big eyes of yours. I will just have to try to kiss you again to see them spark. Today they are green, you know."

"I do not have green eyes."

"You do this morning. They are not a deep green, I grant you. I believe the color depends on your mood or on what you're wearing. I hope you have ordered some gowns in blues and greens."

"I think Mrs. Croft is making up one or two in those colors."

"Splendid," James said. Sarah thought he looked too innocent. "Then I can observe to see if your eyes change color accordingly. Perhaps I shall even write a treatise, *On the Colors of Sarah Hamilton's Eyes*. What do you think?"

"I think you would not sell many copies of such a work, your grace."

"There is one problem," James said thoughtfully.

"*One* problem? I would say there was significantly more than one problem with such a hare-brained notion."

James continued as if Sarah hadn't spoken. "To fully determine the color of your eyes, I should first try to ascertain their hue in isolation, free from any extraneous influence. I know I had the perfect opportunity to begin my investigations at the Green Man, but I confess I found it difficult to make accurate observations while being hit in the head with a pillow."

"Your grace!" Sarah placed her hand on her middle. Her stomach was fluttering in a most unusual fashion. "What *are* you talking about?"

"Eye color, Sarah. Yours, specifically. We need to free your person from all distracting colors, particularly that wretched brown dress, before I can make an accurate determination of their exact hue."

Sarah felt his eyes on her throat, moving down her neck as if he were brushing away the offending brown cloth.

"I suppose we could begin our research now, though I did tell Birnam I would visit this tenant. But let us permit nothing to stand in the way of scientific inquiry. We shall turn the gig around and gallop back to Alvord. My aunt—not to mention Lizzie and Lady Amanda—may be a trifle shocked when we repair to my room, but devoted students of nature must not let public opinion sway their investigations. Unless you wish to shed those offending garments now? We could start outdoors, but it is a trifle chilly and I confess I prefer inside for our first studies. A locked door would prove a definite advantage, I'm certain."

"Your grace!" Sarah could barely form the words, her breathing was so erratic. The thought of entering James's room was beyond scandalous. "Have you lost your mind?"

James laughed. "Not yet, but I confess, I am having a little trouble thinking clearly. The image of your hair against the white of my pillow is quite, um, elevating."

It was early March, yet it could have been the hottest day in August, based on how Sarah felt. Now she understood what the Abingtons had meant by a "warm" conversation. She looked away. Up ahead she saw a cottage with a neat white fence around it.

"I think you will have to drag your mind away from experiments, your grace. We have company."

James sighed. "So I see."

Two boys, about eight years old, hung over the fence, waving enthusiastically.

"Hullo, yer grace! Can I hold Buttercup?"

"Naw, I'm older, Tim, plus ye got to hold her last time."

"Did not!"

"Did too!"

"Buttercup?" Sarah asked.

James laughed. "Lizzie named her. I take it she—the horse, not Lizzie—is partial to buttercups." James stopped the gig and helped Sarah down. "Gentlemen," he said to the squabbling boys, "mind your manners, please."

"Sorry, yer grace."

"Pardon, yer grace."

Sarah looked down at two identical, grubby, young boys.

"Sarah, may I present Thomas and Timothy Pearson?"

James said. "Gentlemen, this is Miss Sarah Hamilton from Philadelphia."

The boys' eyes grew large. Sarah was grateful that Thomas had already lost his front tooth while Timothy had not, otherwise she would have given up all hope of telling them apart.

"Yer from America?" Timothy asked.

"Across the ocean?" Thomas breathed.

"Did ye live with Red Indians?"

"What kind of ship did ye sail on? Charlie Bentworth's cousin's in the navy. He sailed with Nelson."

"Who cares about stupid ships?" Timothy interrupted his brother. "Is it true Indians wear feathers and are very fierce?"

Sarah laughed. "I'm afraid I don't know much about ships," she said to Thomas. "The one I sailed on was big, but it rocked constantly and I was very sick." She smiled at Thomas's disappointed expression and turned to Timothy. "As to the Indians, the men wear feathers when they are dressed for war, I believe, and are very fierce fighters, but in general, I think they are not so very different from you or me."

"Boys, I realize Miss Hamilton is much more interesting than Buttercup, but can one of you take charge of the reins nonetheless?"

Timothy, or maybe it was Thomas—Sarah couldn't see their grins to be sure—took Buttercup. James and Sarah turned toward the cottage. Two little girls came running out, a smaller child following behind them. The girls skidded to a stop in front of James and dropped credible curtseys. Two pairs of large brown eyes turned to Sarah. The baby pushed between their skirts and held her pudgy arms in the air.

"Up!" she demanded.

James laughed and lifted her to sit in his arms.

"This is Ruth." Ruth hid her face in his cravat.

"How old are you, Ruth?" Sarah asked.

Two fat fingers appeared.

"Two years old! What a big girl."

"She's just a baby." Timothy poked Ruth's chubby leg. Thomas had won charge of Buttercup for the moment.

Ruth pulled her face out of James's neck cloth and kicked back at her brother. "Not baby!"

"And this is Miss Maggie and Miss Jane," James said, introducing the other girls.

"Ruth!" A short, comfortably plump woman came out of the cottage, carrying a chubby little boy about eight months old. "Oh, hello, yer grace. I thought I heard the gig."

"Hello, Becky. I've come to have a look at your roof. Is Tom still out in the fields?"

"Aye. He should be home soon fer lunch if ye want to speak to him. Would ye like to come in fer some tea while ye wait?"

The tiny cottage was cluttered, but clean. Sarah squeezed next to James at the worn kitchen table. Ruth sat on his lap. Her tiny fingers traced the patterns on his vest and twisted his buttons while he talked with her mother. He seemed so much at ease, this duke, sitting in a cottage, talking to his tenant's wife. Not at all like the stiff English aristocrats Sarah had imagined. Ruth found his pocket watch and giggled. James's larger hand came up to cover hers. She bounced on his lap and grabbed his hand with both of hers. He laughed and Sarah felt tears burn the corners of her eyes.

A short, stocky man came into the kitchen then with Maggie and Jane. His shirt was rolled up at the sleeves and his hair was wet from where he must have cleaned up at the pump outside.

Ruth twisted on James's lap. "Pa!" She stretched her arms up to her father. James laughed.

"I'm always losing the pretty girls to you, Tom," he said as he handed Ruth over to her father.

"Aye, well, it looks like ye've brought a pretty girl of yer own to visit, yer grace." The man smiled at Sarah and then bent to kiss Becky.

Sarah was able to sit quietly and listen to Tom and James talk about their shared childhood and the scrapes they and Robbie and Charles had gotten into. When Tom finished his meal, he and James went out to have a look at the roof. Sarah helped Becky clean up and get the little ones settled. She was just giving Billy a last pat as he settled down for his nap when James walked in. He came to stand quietly beside her.

"Time to go," he whispered. Sarah felt the warmth of his body next to hers. For a heartbeat she imagined that Billy was their child and that this was their cottage.

Some girls dreamed of weddings and babies, Sarah thought as she let James help her into the gig. Not she. She had never imagined having a family of her own. James slapped the reins and Buttercup ambled forward. She had never imagined having a husband of her own.

The earnest young men who'd joined her father's causes had not appealed to her, nor, she admitted, had she appealed to them. They were too much like her father—single-minded, driven. They took little notice of Dr. Hamilton's spinster daughter. The butcher's boy was the only male who had ever noticed her. She'd been flattered by his attention—until he'd kissed her.

"Let's get out and walk a bit." James pulled the gig to a halt and looped Buttercup's reins over a branch. The fat little horse immediately stuck his nose into a clump of buttercups, sneezed, and began nibbling the tall grass at the base of the tree.

"He doesn't eat the buttercups?" Sarah asked, extending her hand to James.

"Oh, no. They would make him sick—buttercups are poisonous. I imagine he just likes the color." James ignored her hand, gripping her around her waist instead and lifting her easily to the ground. He held her for a moment longer than necessary.

Sarah stared at his cravat, listening to Buttercup's enthusiastic chomping. Somewhere high above her a bird called and another answered. A small animal rustled through the undergrowth.

Was James going to kiss her?

Did she want him to?

They were quite alone. A step or two, and they would be safe even from Buttercup's prying eyes. Sarah suppressed a nervous giggle. She kept her head down and moistened her lips.

James could even begin his research for his silly treatise if he wanted to. Did she want him to?

Of course not! What had gotten into her? The degenerate British air must be corrupting her. That and a degenerate British duke. The image of that particular duke with all his lovely golden skin flashed into her mind and she choked.

"Are you all right?" James put her hand on his arm and turned with her to walk up a short hill.

"I'm fine." She would be finer if she had a fan. She definitely would benefit from a cooling breeze. Thankfully her bonnet hid her reddened cheeks.

They reached a broad clearing that looked out over the surrounding countryside. James leaned back against a tree, putting his hand over hers where it rested on his arm and pulling her close to his side.

Sarah turned to survey the view. "Is all this your land?"

"Yes."

She heard the pride in his voice.

"It's been in your family for generations?"

"Since the Conqueror. For over seven hundred years a Runyon has been at Alvord."

Sarah gazed out at the tidy fields, the fruit trees, the forests, the hills. What would it be like to be part of a family that traced its roots through so many centuries? How far back did the Hamiltons go? She didn't know. Her father had never talked about his family's history. It wasn't the American way. Everything was new in America. Everyone was starting over. She was proud of that spirit, but she could understand why James would want a son to stand here after him.

"Who will inherit if you don't marry?"

"Richard."

She felt his body stiffen. She sighed. "That would be a crime, but I still think marriage to me is not the answer, your grace."

"*James,* Sarah. Please don't talk of marriage, yet call me 'your grace.'"

Sarah heard the plea in his words and responded to it.

"James, I don't have any of the skills you need in a wife. I don't know the first thing about English society. I've grown up on republican tracts. I've only ever lived in a narrow little townhouse. I'm not beautiful or accomplished. Surely there is some English girl who is much more suited to be your wife."

James tugged her to face him. "You *are* beautiful, Sarah, and I don't want an English girl, at least none of the English girls I've yet encountered. They make me feel like a fox running before the hounds. Come to London and you will see. The girls and their mamas don't want me, they want my title and pounds per annum."

"I don't believe that. A girl would have to be blind not to fall in love with you."

James grinned. "Are you blind, then, Sarah? Or does that mean that you've fallen in love with me?"

Sarah flushed. "I hardly know you. And that is beside the point. You need a girl who knows how to go on in your society."

James moved his hands to cup her face, tilting her chin up so he could look directly into her eyes. Somehow he had managed to lose his gloves. She felt the warmth of his palms cradling her jaw, the seductive pressure of his long fingers massaging the sensitive spot just below her ear—the spot his lips had found so disastrously at the Green Man. He was a magician, weaving his spell around her.

"You can learn, sweetheart. I don't intend to spend much time in society. I told you, I really am a farmer at heart." His thumbs smoothed her cheekbones. "Come to London, Sarah, and you'll see how horrible it is. Save me from it, please. I don't want a society girl. I don't want a society marriage, a marriage like my parents had. I want a marriage like Tom and Becky's. Don't you?"

Sarah could not deny it. Suddenly she wanted nothing more than to have a husband and a baby and the love that was so evident in that little cottage.

"Yes, James," she whispered. "Yes, I do."

He bent his head.

He's an English duke, Sarah thought, moistening her lips. *A degenerate, womanizing British peer. A stranger.*

His breath teased over her lips. If she tilted her head just the slightest bit, she could bring her lips to his. She was tempted. Tempted? She was starving for his touch.

But that was too forward. No, it was beyond forward. It was wanton.

She started to pull back, but his hands held her steady. He closed the gap between them, gently tracing her lips with the tip of his tongue and then covering them softly with his.

He didn't feel like a stranger. He felt like home.

That was when the bullet slammed into the tree trunk just above their heads.

Chapter 6

Richard Runyon stood deep in the shade under an oak tree behind the Green Man. "What do you mean, you missed, you bloody idiot?" He struggled to keep his voice low.

"I'm sorry, yer lordship. How was I to know he'd kiss the girl right then?"

"Oh, I don't know. Were they standing close? Did he have his arms around her?"

The man shrugged and shuffled his feet in the dirt. Richard gritted his teeth. God, James would be dead three times over if he could find just one semi-competent accomplice.

"At least tell me what she looked like."

"I'm not sure, yer lordship." The idiot scratched his head. Lice, Richard thought. That would just complete the day if he acquired vermin from this brainless piece of horse dung. "She 'ad on a bonnet. Alvord didn't take it off to kiss 'er."

"Was she tall and thin?"

"Aye, long and skinny. Came up to Alvord's shoulder."

"Damn. Sounds like the Hamilton chit." Richard slammed his hand against the tree trunk. The pain cleared his mind. "Did she struggle?"

"No, yer lordship, not that I could see. 'Course I shot

at 'em right then, so mayhap she would of put up a fuss. I took off as soon as the bullet hit. Yer cousin moves like lightning, ye know."

"Hmm." Richard thought about the possibilities. It was too much to hope that the girl would find James repulsive. No female ever had. And she was staying with James at Alvord. Maybe he didn't have as much time as he thought.

"Uh, yer lordship, about my coins . . ."

"What?" Richard swallowed the anger that surged through him again. He couldn't shout and bring attention to himself. His fingers flexed. He'd dearly love to put his hands around this idiot's throat. "Your coins? Be glad to leave with your life, you stupid . . ."

The man was gone. Richard swallowed again. If only Philip were here. Philip would calm him. But Philip wasn't here; the anger was—wave after wave crashing in his head, his chest, his groin. He would explode soon. He needed release *now*.

He heard a rustle of cloth, the sound of shoes stepping through grass. That girl—Molly—that whore was coming toward the oak. She had called him a bastard. She and her friend had made him look foolish in front of James. He had hated them for that. He had wanted to hurt them, to break that one bitch's wrist. He had backed down then; he would get his satisfaction now.

The girl came closer. Stupid. She was as stupid as all the others. He grabbed her. She started to scream, but his mouth came down hard on hers, cutting off the sound and grinding her lips into her teeth. She struggled, but he was much larger and stronger than she. He thrust her up against the oak's trunk. God, this was better than when he'd taken her in her room. Much better. He was already hard. He managed to loosen his breeches, to raise her skirts. His anger and lust mixed together. He rammed into her, crushing her up against the tree as he pumped his hate into her helpless body.

She got her hands free as he pulled back. She went for his eyes, but his arms were longer than hers. He wrapped his fingers around her neck and squeezed. Her hands flew up, pulling on his hands, but she was not strong enough. Stupid sow, to think she could match his strength. He watched her eyes, the one still purple from where he had hit her before, fill with panic. Watched them bulge, her mouth opening in a silent scream. Watched her face collapse.

He smelled death.

He ejaculated again against her corpse, then let her body slide down the oak trunk to huddle on the ground.

He felt much calmer.

James gazed out the window of his study. Rain ran in sheets down the glass.

"So you think your cousin Richard shot at us?"

"At me. I'm certain he—or rather his accomplice—was aiming only at me."

Sarah moved. He could see her now, reflected in the window. She was wearing one of her new gowns. He wished Mrs. Croft had made the neck lower. That frill of lace trimming the bodice was quite unnecessary. Her lovely throat and lovelier bosom should be displayed to better advantage. He smiled. He would have her—and Lizzie, too, of course—to a London modiste as soon as they got to town. London fashions were definitely more appealing.

"How can you smile?"

He turned and took her hand. "I was admiring your gown. Did you know it makes your eyes blue?"

"My eyes are not blue."

"They are tonight." He bent his head to breathe in her light, sweet scent. "Another section for my treatise."

Sarah pulled her hand free. "You are being absurd, your grace."

"James."

"*Your grace.*" She stepped back, putting the corner of his desk between them. "Didn't you say your aunt and Lady Amanda were to chaperone my stay here? They are somewhat conspicuous in their absence."

"Perhaps they have concluded that since the horse has bolted, there's no need to lock the stable door."

Sarah's eyes shot blue sparks. "The horse has *not* bolted."

"Well, no, but wouldn't she like to?"

James closed the distance between them, lightly imprisoning Sarah's wrists. She pulled back slightly, her cheeks flushed.

"She certainly would not!"

"No? Not even a little?"

"Not the tiniest bit."

"Are you sure?" James pulled Sarah's hands gently forward, drawing them behind his back and bringing her up against his body. "It can get terribly stuffy in a stable." He dipped his head, feathering his lips along her hairline.

"Wouldn't the horse like to poke her nose out the open door?" he whispered. "Feel the breeze? Smell the night air?"

Sarah's eyes had drifted closed, so he detoured to brush his lips over her lids before he traveled across her cheekbone to the sensitive spot beneath her ear. She made a funny little noise in her throat, half mewl, half sigh, and tilted her head so his lips could find the place easily.

He buried his face in her hair.

"Sweetheart." He dropped her wrists so he could put his hands to better use. Perhaps he could do something about that annoying frill around the neck of her bodice. It was most definitely in the way.

"Your grace!" Sarah dodged his hands and returned to her fortified position behind his desk. "Behave yourself."

"Must I?" He looked around his study. "This would be a splendid place to engage in a little misbehavior."

"No."

"You're certain?"

"Very certain. We have more important matters to occupy our minds."

"We do?"

"Today's murder attempt!"

"All the more reason to misbehave. If I have limited time left on this earth, I would love to spend it with you in that comfortable chair by the fire—or even on that nice, thick rug."

"Stop it!" Sarah turned and gripped the edge of his desk. "How can you make light of this?"

James sighed. Apparently Sarah could be as single-minded as a terrier.

"I'm not really making light of it, Sarah. I am doing what I can to protect myself and my family, but it's a little like fencing with shadows. Richard is devious."

Sarah picked up the silver penknife from James's desk, turning it over and over in her hands, running her fingers over the engraved pattern.

"Why do you think it's your cousin who is trying to kill you?"

"Who else can it be?" James shrugged. "I'm no saint,

but I play fair and pay my bills. I take care of my properties; I stay clear of other men's wives and daughters—present company excluded, of course." He paused and leered at her—she waggled the penknife at him.

"None of that, your grace. This is serious. I mean to get a straight answer from you."

"Yes, ma'am. I can see you were an exceptional teacher in your previous employment. Did your students ever have any fun?"

"Very rarely—and certainly not if I had anything to say about the matter. Now answer me."

"No one but Richard has a reason to wish me dead."

"Because he's your heir."

"Yes, but more because he thinks I've stolen the dukedom from him."

Sarah frowned. "How can that be? Aren't your laws of succession quite clear?"

"The laws are clear, it's the facts that are murky. My father and Richard's were identical twins. My father, as the elder by ten minutes, was the heir. Richard believes there was some confusion at the birth—the midwife was not expecting twins—and that the babies were switched. According to him, his father should have inherited when our grandfather died, and so Richard, not I, should be the current duke."

"That's ridiculous—isn't it?"

"Well, perhaps not ridiculous, but certainly unlikely. As far as I know, no one except Richard has ever questioned the matter. His father never did."

Sarah gripped the penknife so tightly, the pattern on the handle dug into her fingers. If she ever needed proof that the English system of inheritance was nonsensical, even dangerous, this was it.

"So how can Richard accuse you of stealing the dukedom when his father never accused your father? That was the rational time to contest the succession."

"True, but Richard isn't rational."

"Your system of primogeniture isn't rational! That's what's at the root of this problem." Sarah pointed the penknife at James. "If England would get rid of all its titles and hereditary falderal, people like your cousin would not spend their lives waiting for someone else to die."

"It's not quite that simple."

Sarah tapped James on the chest. "Richard is a parasite—admit it."

"I admit it. Are you planning to stab me with that?"

"Oh." Sarah looked blankly at the penknife. "No."

"Good." James took the knife and laid it back on his desk. "You will not hear me defending Richard, sweetheart, but I can't believe there are no hangers-on in your own country."

"Well, perhaps there are, but it's not the same at all."

"I don't know about that. You may not call them 'lord,' but I believe you have a number of wealthy men in your country whom someone—a son or other relation—would not mourn if they went prematurely to their heavenly reward, leaving behind their earthly treasures, of course."

"It is still not the same!"

James lifted an eyebrow and opened his mouth to reply, but a scratching at the door interrupted him.

"What is it, Layton?"

"A message, your grace." The butler handed James a folded sheet of paper and withdrew.

James scanned the contents, then crumpled the paper in his fist.

"What is it?"

"Molly, the girl at the Green Man, was just found dead, strangled, outside the inn."

"Richard?"

"I'd bet my life on it." He put the crumpled paper on his desk and pulled her close. His amber eyes were dark, and a deep frown etched a line between his brows. Sarah wanted to smooth it away with her fingers.

"Sarah, it would be much easier to keep you safe if you were my wife and not just my houseguest."

"But wouldn't being your wife put me in more danger, your grace? Now I'm only a poor American nobody. If I married you, I'd be a duchess, wouldn't I? And, I suppose, eventually . . ." Sarah bit her lip and studied James's cravat. "Well, once you have a wife, you could have a son. And a son would definitely upset Richard."

The edge of James's hand pushed gently on her chin. Reluctantly she raised her face. His eyes were no longer dark. They were lit with a most disturbing fire.

"Very true, sweetheart. If I had a wife—if I had you as my wife—I would work most assiduously to produce a son. Morning and night."

"Morning?" Sarah squeaked. Could people do whatever they did to make babies in the daylight?

"Most definitely. Before and after breakfast. Perhaps in the afternoon as well."

Surely *that* could not be possible.

"You are being absurd, your grace."

"James." He ran his thumb lightly over her lips. "You said it very nicely this morning." His eyes traced the path his thumb had just traveled. His voice took on a deep, husky note. "Say it, Sarah. Please. I want to hear my name on your lips."

"This is most inappropriate, your grace." Sarah had

intended to speak forcefully, but it was hard to be sharp when someone was nuzzling one's temples.

"James."

Somehow her fingers had found their way to his chest and were tracing the pattern on his waistcoat. They slipped over the smooth silk, and she remembered with shocking clarity the smooth feel of his naked chest.

"You are a duke, your grace."

"I am a man, sweetheart." His lips teased the corner of her mouth. "Very much a man." They moved to the other corner. "Please. A good American like you should not take note of titles."

His touch was most distracting. Sarah turned her head to meet his lips, but he pulled back.

Wanton. She was acting like a wanton again. She pushed hard on his chest. He loosened his hold on her.

"Come, Sarah. I know you can do it."

"You are ridiculous, your grace."

"James."

"Sir."

"Start with the *J*. It's not a hard sound to make. Try it with me. 'J-j-j.'"

"Oh, for goodness sakes—James! There—will you let me go now?"

"Do I have to?"

"I will call you 'your grace' if you don't."

"You don't play fair." James grinned and leaned forward as if to kiss her, but Sarah slipped out of his arms and fled before she could give in to her wanton wishes.

James poured himself a glass of brandy and sat down by the fire. He sincerely wished that he had Sarah on his lap, but at least he had gotten his name from her lips. He would not let her go back to "your grace" with him.

What was he to do about Richard? He would make inquiries, but he would wager that no one could connect Richard to Molly's death. It was possible that Richard was not involved, but, as he had told Sarah, he wouldn't bet his life on it. He certainly would not bet her life.

Had Richard killed before? There *had* been rumors about that girl at University. He had ignored them, thinking them groundless. Had he been wrong?

How could he keep Sarah safe? She was right. Their marriage would put her at some risk, but she was already at risk now that Richard had connected her with him. If they were married, he would have the right to protect her. He could lock her in her room—in his room. Chain her to his bed.

He smiled, sipping his brandy and imagining all the lovely ways he could keep her busy and out of Richard's reach.

Sarah thought about Richard and the shooting as she walked down to the stable the next morning. She wasn't worried for herself. Richard wasn't stupid. He would realize immediately that the Duke of Alvord could not marry penniless Miss Hamilton from Philadelphia. But what of James? He did not take the danger he was in seriously.

"Sarah!"

She looked up. James was standing by the stable door, the sun lighting his golden hair and the strong planes of his face. Her heart thudded in her chest and her lips spread into a wide smile.

"Hello, James." She saw his grin get even wider.

"Ah, McGee, did you hear my name on Miss Hamilton's lips?"

A short man with gray hair led a horse out of the stable. "Sure, yer grace. I ain't lost me hearing yet!"

Sarah smiled and nodded at McGee. "You are being very silly, your grace."

"No, you can't go back—it must be James from now on, right, McGee?"

Mr. McGee contented himself with rolling his eyes.

James's expression turned serious. "We're going to stay close by the house for this lesson, Sarah. McGee says no one has seen Richard or any strangers about, but there's no need to take unnecessary risks."

Sarah noted that McGee had spat in the dirt at Richard's name. "That's fine with me." She eyed the horse whose reins McGee was holding. "Isn't that a rather large animal, Mr. McGee?" She was not completely successful at hiding the quaver in her voice.

"Here now, miss, no need to worry yerself. Rosebud is as gentle as a lamb."

"Rosebud?" Sarah looked at James. He shrugged.

"Lizzie again," he said. "But McGee is right. Rosebud is very calm. Come here and meet her."

James took the reins from McGee and led the horse a few steps toward Sarah. She carefully put her hand on Rosebud's neck. Even through her glove, she could feel the warmth and the rough texture of the horse's coat. Rosebud shifted and her neck twitched. Sarah whipped her hand back and looked up at James. He was trying very hard not to laugh.

"I promise you, Rosebud is so placid, cannon fire couldn't startle her."

"It'd take a cannon to get that one movin'," McGee muttered.

James raised his eyebrow and Sarah smiled. She turned back to Rosebud and carefully ran her hand down the horse's neck. Rosebud turned and regarded her thoughtfully.

"She does have lovely eyes."

"Let's see how you like the view from the saddle." James put his hands around her waist and lifted her up.

"Ereek!" She stared down at James. He kept his hands around her waist to steady her. She could feel the heat of his palms and each finger and thumb through his gloves and the thick fabric of her riding habit. He wasn't even breathing hard, yet he had just lifted her from the ground, which looked from her new location to be very far away indeed.

She risked a look around. There were an amazing number of stable hands about, presumably to watch her first attempt at sitting on a horse. She cautiously straightened her spine and tested her balance.

"I'm just not accustomed to this, ah, angle on the world," she said.

"Do you like it?"

"I'm not sure."

"Fair enough. I'm going to let go now. Do you think you can keep your seat?"

Sarah was not eager to lose the steadying influence of James's hands, but she couldn't look poor-spirited in front of her audience. "Certainly."

James let go and stepped back. Sarah grabbed the edge of the saddle. James smiled.

"Well done. Here, take the reins. No, don't clutch them; you'll pull poor Rosebud's mouth. Just hold them lightly and get used to the motion while I walk Rosebud down to the practice ring and around it a few times."

Sarah nodded in what she hoped was a confident

manner. James led Rosebud down a gentle incline. At the first step she grabbed the saddle again. *James won't let you fall,* she told herself and released her death grip. She sat up straighter. By the time they had completed two circuits of the training ring, she felt secure in her balance.

"Okay?" James asked.

"Yes. I think I'm ready to try the next step."

"Good!" James nodded to McGee and the groom brought over a huge brown horse. Sarah was glad she wasn't required to sit on it.

"That isn't the horse you had at the inn."

"No, that was Newton. Pythagoras here is in semi-retirement now, but he has excellent manners, don't you, old man?" James patted the horse's neck and Pythagoras nodded as if in agreement. "He's more willing than Newton to move at a sedate pace, and he and Rosebud get along well."

"Pythagoras and Newton?" Sarah watched James swing himself into the saddle. He made it look so easy.

"Right." James picked up his reins and turned to look down at her. "I've always been somewhat keen on mathematics. I got Pythagoras for my fifteenth birthday. Newton I bought myself when I came down from Cambridge. He went with me to the Peninsula."

"Were you there long?"

James looked out over his horse's ears and nudged Pythagoras into motion. Rosebud obligingly followed.

"Long? Not by the calendar, but if you measure time not by days, but by what those days do to you—eons. I was in Spain from the summer of 1811 until the April of 1813, when my father began to fail. I was there for Ciudad Rodrigo, Badajoz, and Salamanca, but I missed Vittoria—and Waterloo, of course."

Sarah saw the muscle in his cheek twitch as he tightened his mouth. Then he shook his head and smiled, turning to look down at her again.

"I actually did go to America after I came down from Cambridge and before I went to Spain. Watch the gate there."

Pythagoras led Rosebud out of the practice ring. Sarah leaned slightly away from the fence and Rosebud obligingly stepped a little farther from the gate so that Sarah's skirt just brushed it.

"That was close."

James laughed. "Rosebud would never intentionally rub you off. She's just a little absentminded."

"She doesn't remember I'm up here?"

"Well, she knows *something* is on her back. Once you figure out how to use the reins, she'll obey you quite nicely."

Sarah leaned over to pat Rosebud's neck. Rosebud shook her head in what Sarah assumed was a friendly fashion, making the bit jingle.

"So you were in America? Did you come to Philadelphia?"

"Unfortunately, no. My father had some investment interests in New York and Boston, so I went there. I had intended to visit your father, but I came back to fight instead. So we almost did meet in the past."

Sarah tried to imagine James in her father's cramped study amid the political pamphlets, medical books, and serious young republicans. He would have stood out like a swan in a duck pond.

"I'm afraid you would have been bored to tears, unless you enjoy arguing politics."

"Did you do nothing for amusement?"

"I kept house and taught school."

"Hmm. So I would not have had to wade through a sea of suitors to gain your attention?"

"No." Sarah glanced over at him. If she saw pity in his eyes, she swore she'd climb down from this beast right now and disappear into her room for a good, long cry.

She didn't see pity. She saw . . . speculation. She raised her chin.

"Are you going to teach me to ride or not?"

James's lips slid into a slow grin. "Yes, love, I'm definitely going to teach you to ride."

When they finally returned to the stable, they had been out for two hours.

"I'm sorry. I didn't mean for the lesson to go on this long."

Sarah waved away James's concern. "Oh, don't worry about me. I'm a good, strong American girl."

He chuckled. "You're going to be a sore American girl tonight. I recommend a hot bath before dinner."

"Thank you, doctor. I shall follow your advice."

James swung out of his saddle and reached up to lift her down.

"Brace yourself on my shoulders."

Sarah nodded, but when her weight came off the horse, her elbows buckled. Her body slid down the length of his.

"Oh!" She felt his hard form from her breasts to her thighs. Heat rushed through her—embarrassment and something else. It was shocking—but she had to cling to him. Her legs had turned to jelly. If she loosened her hold on his shoulders, she'd fall flat in the stable yard dirt.

She looked up helplessly. His eyes had that hot, intent look again.

"Stop it."

"Stop what? You're the one who threw herself at me."

"I did not."

"Hmm." James was not complaining. Sarah's body felt very nice pressed up against his. Very nice indeed. Exhilarating. He moved his hips back slightly so she wouldn't be shocked by just how exhilarated he was and lowered his head to taste her lips.

"James!" she hissed.

"Hmm?" She smelled of horse and outdoors and something else, light and sweet.

"James!" She stiffened and managed to put some space between them. "Everyone is staring at us."

Her eyes were huge between the reddish blond lashes. The hazel had turned from green to gold. Sparks, he thought. Sparks and a touch of panic. The panic reached him. He straightened and looked around. The large number of stable hands present quickly found jobs that needed doing elsewhere.

"Sorry." He grinned. He wasn't sorry at all—or he was sorry that she was embarrassed. Once they were married he intended to kiss her wherever and whenever the urge struck. "But you really shouldn't throw yourself at me like that."

"I didn't!" Sarah looked like an indignant kitten. "My arms gave out, that's all. I was as surprised as you were, I'm sure."

James took his gloves off and tucked a silky strand of red-blond hair back behind the delicate rim of Sarah's ear.

"Surprise was not my main emotion."

Her breath caught and she pulled her head away from his fingers. "Don't look at me like that."

"Like what?"

"Like you want to swallow me whole or something."

James laughed and stepped back, putting Sarah's hand on his arm. "Do I frighten you?"

She considered the question. "No. I'm sure you should, but you don't."

"So how do I make you feel?"

"I don't know." She looked at her hand on his arm. "You make me feel odd. Comfortable, sometimes, but fluttery other times."

"Fluttery?"

Sarah chewed on the edge of her bottom lip. "Nervous, but not unpleasantly so. Excited, maybe, like I'm waiting for something, but I'm not sure what." She looked up and saw James grinning. "You're doing it again."

"Doing what again?"

"Looking at me that way. It is most unsettling."

"Is it?" James put his hand over Sarah's. "Do you know how you make me feel?"

"No." She looked up at him, eyes wide with expectation. "How do I make you feel?"

"Excited, like I'm waiting for something." He leaned closer and leered at her. "But I know what I am waiting for!"

Her eyes blinked once, then she pulled back her hand and swatted his shoulder. She didn't put any muscle into it, so he could tell she wasn't really angry.

"Hey, don't you know you're not allowed to hit a duke?"

"I'm an American. I'll hit any duke I please."

"*That* will endear you to all the old biddies at Almack's." James laughed, picturing Silence Jersey's face should Sarah really slap Devonshire or Rutland or Cumberland. "I shall have to keep a close eye on you when you meet Prinny. Our Regent often deserves a good wallop."

"I'm sure he does. Why do you put up with him?"

"Because he will be king, and unlike you Americans, we English are still attached to our monarchy. Perhaps we fear that if Prinny goes, all the nobles go. I'm not sure I could adjust to being plain Mr. Runyon."

Sarah stopped, pulling James to a stop also. He looked questioningly down at her.

"You would be a wonderful plain Mr. Runyon."

James stared at her. "Sarah." He blinked and looked off toward the house. "Sarah, my love, I do hope you will decide to have me."

"Sarah, James says we're to ride over to Westbrooke today!"

Sarah put aside the book she was reading to smile up at Lizzie. The girl was almost dancing around the library. Her excitement seemed a trifle extreme for something as mundane as a visit to a neighbor. "I can't picture Robbie presiding over a tea tray," she said, laughing.

"Well, he won't really. I mean, I'm sure there will be tea and cakes—Mrs. Mandley, his housekeeper, bakes lovely cakes—but the point is to give you some more riding practice and a chance to see the estate where your father grew up." Lizzie flopped down on the chair next to Sarah's. "Isn't it a good thing Mrs. Croft just finished my new riding habit? It makes me look much more the thing, don't you think? Older and more . . . sophisticated." She managed to sound both confident and anxious simultaneously.

"Oh, definitely. I'm sure, um, James will be quite impressed."

Lizzie stuck out her tongue, and Sarah laughed.

"However, I'm not certain Lady Amanda, if she were

sitting in my chair, would be impressed by your current deportment, miss! I believe she would point out that ladies do not behave with such enthusiasm. They seat themselves with a shade more grace than you just exhibited, and they most assuredly do not stick out their tongues."

"Well, she's not sitting in your chair, and you know I can behave when I want to." Lizzie rose elegantly to her feet and curtseyed. "Miss Hamilton, I trust you have no objection to joining a small excursion this afternoon to Lord Westbrooke's estate?"

Sarah nodded back graciously. "No, Lady Elizabeth, I have no objection at all, that is, if his grace really has approved the plan."

Lizzie dropped her skirts and skip-hopped to the library door. "Of course he has. It was his idea, after Major Draysmith brought word that evil Cousin Richard is safely situated in London."

Later that afternoon, they set out for Westbrooke. Major Draysmith rode ahead with Lizzie while James stayed with Sarah. Her horsemanship had improved greatly from the time he had first lifted her onto Rosebud's back, but she did not feel up to maintaining any pace much faster than a walk.

"I'm sorry to keep you plodding along with me," she said. "You must long to be up with the others."

"No, I don't." James grinned. "I had my gallop early this morning, and I'd much rather be keeping you company than my sister. Charles will see Lizzie comes to no harm. He often took charge of our young recruits on the Peninsula."

Sarah looked ahead to where Lizzie and Charles were riding. They were almost out of sight.

"What will Major Draysmith do now that the fighting is over?"

"I don't know." James frowned. "I'm not sure Charles knows himself."

"Doesn't he have an estate to manage?"

"No. He's the second son—the spare. After he came down from Cambridge, he racketed around London for years, drinking, gambling, whor—" James coughed. " . . .*hard*ly caring what he did. He followed me into the army out of boredom, I think, but it was the best thing he could have done. It gave him a purpose. He was an excellent officer."

Sarah worried her bottom lip with her teeth. She liked Major Draysmith. "And his brother?"

"Knightsdale? What has he to say to the matter?"

"Perhaps he needs an estate manager."

James laughed. "Knightsdale already has an excellent manager, Sarah. Don't worry about Charles. He doesn't need—or want—any help, especially from his brother."

"Why especially from his brother?"

James shrugged. "I don't imagine any man wants to hang on his brother's sleeve, but Knightsdale and Charles don't get along. No bad blood, really, just nothing in common. I'm not sure Charles has slept a night in his ancestral home since he left for Eton. When he's in the neighborhood, he stays with Robbie or me."

"Really?" That struck Sarah as sad. If she were lucky enough to have siblings, she would see that they stayed close. "What about a family of his own then, now that he's free to settle down? Doesn't he want to marry?"

"Not any time soon! He's only thirty, Sarah. Plenty of time for a leg shackle."

Sarah frowned at the space between Rosebud's ears. "You're younger than he is, aren't you?"

"Ah, but I have the burden of passing my title on to

he next generation—a burden I'm so hoping you'll
help me with." James leered down at her. She slapped
Rosebud's reins to encourage the horse to move faster.
Rosebud stopped dead and turned to look reproachfully
back at her.

James laughed and brought Pythagoras up so that his
leg brushed Sarah's skirts. "If you wish to run away
from me, love, you've chosen the wrong steed." He
leaned over, putting his gloved hand over hers on the
reins. "I do hope you don't plan to run away." He started
to bend farther, his eyes on her lips.

"James!" Lizzie's voice sounded surprisingly close.

James straightened quickly. His sister was riding toward them, looking puzzled. Major Draysmith, by her
side, struggled manfully not to laugh.

"Whatever are you doing with Sarah?" Lizzie asked.

James turned an interesting shade of red. Sarah
leaned over to pat Rosebud's neck.

"I believe your brother was giving Miss Hamilton a
few extra riding tips," Major Draysmith said with a
straight face, though his eyes were dancing wickedly.

"Oh." Lizzie looked at James and then at Sarah.
"Well, hurry on, do. At your pace, we'll never get to
Westbrooke."

"It's only over the hill, Lizzie. You and Charles go
ahead. Miss Hamilton is still getting used to riding."

Sarah was not going to risk being alone with James
again, not when she was sure Major Draysmith knew
exactly what James planned to do the moment he and
Lizzie were over the crest of the hill.

"I am sure I can manage a brisker pace." She
touched Rosebud's side with her riding crop. This time
the horse blew a long, gusty breath and obligingly
moved a little faster.

Westbrooke was an immense house of gray stone that looked as if it had once had some thought of being a castle—its huge wooden doors were set between two crenellated towers—but had gotten distracted from that goal over the years. It was now a welter of towers, turrets, chimneys, and bays.

"Don't you get lost in there?" Sarah asked, gaping at the bewildering facade as Robbie greeted them on the broad stone drive. He laughed.

"It's not as confusing as it looks," he said, turning to make a show of kissing Lizzie's hand. Sarah noted the delicate shade of pink that flooded Lizzie's cheeks as Robbie's lips brushed her skin. "Come in and see for yourself."

Robbie led them up the large open staircase. "This is the original section of the house, built in 1610. Subsequent earls added on as they pleased, not much caring if the new style blended in with the old. Ah, here we are."

Sarah faced a long hall hung with the heavy, gilt-framed portraits of two centuries of Hamiltons.

"Here's the first earl." Robbie pointed to a life-sized painting of a man with long reddish brown curls, a spreading white lace collar, and polished armor. Sarah slapped her hand over her mouth, not quite suppressing her startled giggle.

"Very true," James said. "Trim the flowing locks and you have Robbie ready for battle. We looked and looked through the attics, didn't we, Robbie? We never did find that suit of armor."

"We decided it must have belonged to the artist fellow," Robbie said, moving down the line of portraits. He dutifully introduced Sarah to each of her ancestors. He stopped again at a large canvas hung almost at the end of the corridor.

"This was painted by Sir Joshua Reynolds the year before your father left for America. My father used to say they had a terrible time getting David to cooperate."

Sarah could believe it. The older man and woman—her grandparents—as well as the other young man, Robbie's father, were grouped together. They looked relaxed and happy. Her father stood off to the side, stiff and unsmiling. She expected him to take out his pocket watch at any moment and urge the artist to hurry along. It was obvious he thought he had better places to be.

"I believe Sir Joshua captured my father's spirit admirably."

Robbie laughed and turned to the last painting. "My mother was a great admirer of Sir Thomas Lawrence and his more romantic style, so my father commissioned him to do our family picture. I confess I had much sympathy for my Uncle David."

"What do you mean, Robbie?" Lizzie sounded almost outraged. "You look like a very sweet little boy in that painting."

"Well, I hate to disillusion you, Lizzie, but I wasn't. My father bribed me with a pony if I pleased my mother and sat still. It was pure torture, but I wanted that pony very badly."

"I see there's still some blank space on the wall, Robbie." Major Draysmith grinned. "Planning to hang your own family grouping soon?"

Sarah noticed the sudden, keen interest on Lizzie's face.

Robbie threw up his hands as if to ward off evil. "You've confused me with our ducal friend here, Charles. James may be hankering for a leg shackle, but I wish to remain a free man for many years to come."

Sarah opened her mouth to explain once again that

she and James were not going to be married, but she stopped when she saw the shadows in Lizzie's eyes.

James leaned on the terrace balustrade at Alvord and looked down on the moonlit garden. The door behind him opened onto the warmth and light of his library. He breathed deeply, savoring the smell of mud and growth. The early spring wind tugged at his hair as he watched the night clouds scud across the sky.

He loved Alvord. It was in his blood and in his heart. But tomorrow they left for London with its noise and dirt. The *ton* was there with its sharp eyes and sharper tongues. Richard was there. He felt the back of his neck tighten, and he twisted his head to loosen the tension.

They could not stay in the country, much as he would like to. Lizzie needed her Season. So did Sarah. She should have the chance to go to the parties, to dance, and even to be courted by other men before he brought her home and made her his duchess. Before he took her to his bed and filled her with his children.

God, he could hardly wait. He'd have her naked beneath him again, just as she had been at the Green Man, but this time she would not push him away. This time he would finish what he had barely started there.

He took one last look at the moon and the garden. The quiet serenity of the scene would have to last him. Even the gardens in London were noisy, and the moon was too often obscured by fog.

He stretched and then turned back to the library, pulling the door to the garden closed behind him, heading for the stairs and his solitary bed.

Chapter 7

"He's in London." Richard spun the scrap of vellum into the fireplace. The flames caught it and twisted the expensive ink and paper to ash. "He's opening Alvord House for Lizzie's come-out. So gracious of him to invite me to her ball."

"You *are* his cousin." Philip Gadner tightened the belt on his dressing gown and stretched his slippered feet closer to the fire. It was so hard to stay warm these days. He felt the cold and the damp like sharp daggers in his bones. "People would talk if he didn't invite you."

Richard grunted and downed his brandy. "Alvord House should be mine."

"Yes, I know. And it will be yours, Richard. Your plans—"

"Fail at every turn! God Almighty, that son of a bitch has amazing luck. By rights he should have taken a bullet to the brain at Ciudad Rodrigo or Badajoz. At the least he should have come back scarred or crippled, but the bloody bastard waltzes back to England without a scratch."

"Well, yes, that was unfortunate. Who could have known that the French would fail so miserably?" Philip glanced at the bed behind him. He would love to get under the thick quilts. Then he'd be warm, at least for a while. Richard would soon be too drunk to care. That was the way it was these days. There were only occasional flashes of the emotion they had shared when they were younger.

He closed his eyes, shutting out Richard's black scowl. Things would be better when Richard got the dukedom. Then Richard wouldn't need the drink or the women. The rage that infected him would be gone like pus from a lanced boil. He'd be happy.

Philip's lips jerked as the familiar pain flashed through his body. He had believed that story without question when he was seventeen and in love. He had believed it most of the time when he was twenty-five and healthy. But now he was thirty and cold. Why the hell did he stay? He was a decent valet. He could find other work. Someone else would take him on. Not a duke, of course. Maybe not even a peer—he had been with Richard too long. But someone would hire him.

It wasn't the promise of wealth and luxury that kept him with Richard. God, how he wished it were only greed. But no, in spite of all the abuse and neglect, he still cared for the man. His love was a tenacious weed.

"He's got the whore with him."

Philip sighed. "The girl's not a whore, Richard. She's the Earl of Westbrooke's cousin."

"She's got red hair, don't she? Just like that piece at the Green Man."

"That *dead* piece at the Green Man." Philip's long, thin nostrils flared. "You can't leave bodies about the countryside, Richard. It's most untidy."

"Wouldn't have killed the girl if you'd been with me, Philip, I'm sure." Richard poured more brandy and cupped the glass in his hands. "Don't know, though.

God, you should have seen her eyes when she knew it, just when she knew I was going to kill her."

Philip twitched his dressing gown over his boney knees. "You'll not be putting your hands around this girl's neck."

"No?" Richard leaned back in his chair. The fire glinted red in his brandy. "I can't have James getting an heir."

"She's just a houseguest, isn't she? Just Westbrooke's cousin."

"My cousin does not kiss houseguests. He certainly does not kiss them outside on his estate where any passerby can see him."

"Perhaps the bullet reminded James that he should not be planning a future."

"Perhaps." Richard took a swallow of brandy. "Who knows with James? I had better go to this come-out ball and see how he treats her. If he ignores her, I'll ignore her. But if not . . ."

"If not, you'll ignore her, too."

Richard hunched one shoulder and sank deeper into his chair.

Philip felt a stab of panic. "You have to leave her be, Richard. You cannot kill this girl."

"Don't be such an old woman."

"I'm not." Philip struggled not to shout. He knew from long experience that showing his own anger would only fuel Richard's. He swallowed and took a deep breath. "Let's not make any decisions now. Go to the ball and see how he treats her. Then we'll make plans, all right?"

Richard hesitated, then nodded. "All right." He snorted. "I wasn't going to strangle the girl on the dance floor, you know."

"I know." Philip sighed. The storm had blown over for the time being. "I'm for bed now. Are you coming?"

Richard paused and Philip felt a sudden surge of hope. He knew that somewhere deep under the layers of dissatisfaction and anger that the years had piled on, under Richard's obsession with James and the dukedom, the spark of what they had once known still flickered.

"No," Richard said. "I think I'll go out. Night's still young. Don't wait up." ·

"No, I won't wait up."

Philip watched the door close. He heard Richard's footsteps echo down the hall, down the stairs. He heard the front door slam. Richard would be gone all night.

He shed his dressing gown and crawled into the bed that now seemed much too large. He shivered.

It took him a long time to get warm.

"Do you think Richard will be here tonight, Sarah?"

"I would think so, Lizzie. He's been invited." Sarah was thankful she hadn't eaten much at dinner—her stomach was almost as unsettled as it had been on the storm-tossed *Roseanna*. She looked down the sweeping marble stairs to the large foyer. Wiggins, the London butler, stood ready with a small army of footmen. Guests should be arriving at any moment. Where were James and Lady Gladys?

"Richard will be here." Robbie was waiting with them. "He ain't one to pass up a free meal." He frowned. "Do be careful, both of you."

Sarah restrained a slightly hysterical giggle. "It's a little odd having you speak of caution."

"Unjust! I can be quite responsible on occasion. Isn't that right, James?"

Sarah turned, relieved to see James approaching with Lady Gladys on his arm. He was dressed starkly in black and white with a single emerald in the center of his cravat. His height, the dark blond burnish of his hair, and the breadth of his shoulders all caught the eye, but it was the strength in his face, the assurance and unconscious power of the man that held one's attention. Sarah was certain that no other man tonight would look so impressive.

"You look splendid, your grace." Sarah blushed. "As do you, Lady Gladys."

"When one has more than seventy years in her dish, splendid is not usually the first adjective that springs to mind," Lady Gladys said. "But thank you, dear. You look very well yourself, but I'm sure all the bucks will tell you that tonight."

"Indeed," James said, his eyes lit with an unsettling glow. "You will outshine all the other women present, except for Lizzie, of course." He smiled at his sister; she made a face back.

"I wish I could wear an azure gown like Sarah instead of this insipid white."

"You look lovely in white," Sarah said. "Don't you think so, Robbie?"

Robbie grinned and raised his quizzing glass. Lizzie raised her chin. He laughed. "Oh, indeed. The young pups will be stumbling over each other to beg a dance from you."

Sarah was happy to see Lizzie smile and the tense lines around the younger girl's eyes relax. However, none of the tension left Sarah's stomach. "Lady Gladys, your grace, surely it would be more appropriate for me to wait in the ballroom?"

Lizzie's hand shot out and grabbed Sarah's wrist. "You are not deserting me, Sarah. I'm ready to faint with nervousness."

"But Lizzie, I'm no relation to you. Your brother and aunt will be here. You will do wonderfully."

"I don't think you're the only one who is nervous, Lizzie," James said. "Calm down, Sarah. No one will be really vicious in the receiving line—there's not enough time." He grinned at Lady Gladys. "And this torture won't last very long. Aunt gets tired, you know."

Lady Gladys grunted. The elegant white plumes in her purple turban bobbed vigorously as she shook her head. "Balderdash! I don't get tired—you get bored, James. Don't try to deny it."

He grinned. "Well, perhaps I do get a little bored."

Lady Gladys frowned at Sarah. "Take your place in this receiving line, miss. Here, stand next to your cousin. Robbie, I rely on you to protect Sarah from the worst harpies."

Robbie bowed. "My pleasure, Lady Gladys."

"But, Lady Gladys," Sarah said as she took her place, "won't people wonder what I am doing here?"

"Let them wonder. It saves them the trouble of finding other gossip to gnaw on."

There was a banging on the front door and Wiggins moved to answer it. Panic surged into Sarah's throat. "But what am I to say?"

"Just say 'good evening.' If anyone tries to discomfit you, look down your nose at them," Lady Gladys said. "And if you must say something, say I demanded you be here. It's true, after all. Now, stiffen your spine and pin a smile on your lips."

"Yes, ma'am," Sarah said. She whispered to Robbie as the first guests started up the stairs, "Where's Lady Amanda?"

He chuckled. "Probably 'resting' until this blasted receiving line is done with. She's had years to perfect her vanishing act." He turned to greet an elderly woman with a cane and an elaborate, powdered hairstyle reminiscent of the last century. "Lady Leighton," he said, raising his voice, "how good to see you again. Let me make known to you my American cousin, Miss Sarah Hamilton."

Sarah took Lady Leighton's gloved hand. "Good evening."

"Ha!" Lady Leighton peered up at Sarah's face. "I remember your father and your grandfather, missy. It's time you came back from those godforsaken colonies."

Sarah blinked. "Thank you, my lady."

"England, that's where you belong." A light shower of hair powder drifted onto Lady Leighton's bodice as she bobbed her head. "Glad you finally figured that out."

Sarah watched Lady Leighton hobble into the ballroom before her attention was taken by the next person.

In moments, the stairs and entry hall were filled with people. The hum of conversation rose to a roar. Wiggins gave up and left the front door open; the line spilled out onto the square. The shouts of coachmen and the jingle of harnesses mixed with the general hubbub. Sarah smiled and murmured greetings as a steady stream of perfumed, bejeweled ladies and elegant gentlemen streamed past her.

"Enjoying yourself, Miss Hamilton?"

Sarah blinked and actually focused on the face before her. "Major Draysmith!" Her lips stretched into a real smile. "How lovely to see you."

"Will you save me a dance?"

"Of course. I think I've improved enough that you will not have to fear for your toes."

"Ah, now *that's* a relief." He grinned and moved on.

Finally, the river of people slowed to a trickle. "I think

it's safe to desert our positions." James took Lady Gladys's hand. "What do you say, Aunt? Have we done our duty here?"

"Of course. Take Lizzie in and start the dancing."

"I shall be delighted to do so. Come along, Lizzie. That wasn't so bad, was it?"

Lizzie's eyes were shining and her face was flushed with excitement. "There are so many people here."

"Yes, and they are all crowded into the ballroom, waiting for us."

James led Lizzie through the wide double doors and down the few steps to the ballroom floor. Sarah followed with Robbie. She paused on the threshold, pulling Robbie back for a moment.

She had seen the ballroom when they had first arrived in London. Then her feet had echoed in the vast, shadowy expanse and she had shivered a little. Now hundreds of candles flickered from the massive chandeliers. She could barely see the potted trees and banks of hothouse flowers with which the servants had filled the room this morning, there were so many people crowded together. The bright colors of the women's gowns mixed with the white dresses of the young girls and the black of the men's evening attire. She breathed in the smells of candle wax and perfume.

"Oh."

"Impressive, ain't it? James can throw quite a party when he has a mind to—though I suppose Lady Gladys and Lady Amanda had more to say to the matter than James." Robbie stepped forward. "Come on, Sarah. We have to join the dance as soon as James and Lizzie have opened the set." He grinned at her. "I do hope your dancing skills have improved since Alvord. I don't relish bleeding all over this fancy rig—bought it new for the occasion, don't you know."

The sea of people parted to let James and Lizzie walk to the center of the dance floor. Sarah's hand tightened on Robbie's arm as she followed through the crowd. The stares and whispers that marked her progress were unnerving. Robbie's hand came up to cover hers.

"Don't let them get to you," he murmured. "You'll do fine. You're a Hamilton, ain't you?"

Sarah smiled and raised her chin. "Indeed," she whispered back.

"There you go. Sound like a duchess already."

Startled, Sarah looked up at Robbie. "I do not."

"You do. It's in the blood, Sarah. You may be American, but you can't escape your English heritage."

Sarah shook her head, but there was no time to ponder Robbie's words as the orchestra struck the opening note.

Sarah stood by the windows where the air was slightly cooler. She had danced every dance. Her feet were sore and her face felt flushed. She was happy to have a moment's respite. She glanced around to see that no one was watching, then quickly blotted the sweat from her forehead with the tips of her gloves.

James was dancing with a small, blond girl. Sarah frowned as he waltzed by the orchestra. Surely he was holding the girl closer than was proper? And why was she smiling as if they shared an intimate secret? Sarah shifted position to ease the churning in her stomach.

This was the first time she had seen James in his proper milieu. Women fluttered around him like moths around a lantern. And he didn't discourage them. He smiled at every last one.

She was such an idiot. Of course James had been attracted to her at Alvord—he was attracted to anything in skirts. She had just been the only eligible female available for his flirtation. She must not forget he was a duke.

"Ah, Miss Hamilton, isn't it?"

Sarah turned to see two middle-aged matrons smiling at her. Well, their lips were twisted into smiles. Their eyes were calculating. One was short with a sharp, beaky nose. The other was tall and bony.

"Hello." Sarah forced a smile. She would have preferred to ignore these two potential harpies, but politeness and caution won out.

"You don't remember us, do you?" Beaky Nose said.

Sarah shook her head. "I'm sorry. I must have met you in the receiving line, but there were so many people, I confess the faces became a blur."

"Hmmph." The nose twitched upwards a notch. "Well, I am the Duchess of Rothingham." The woman paused and raised her eyebrows. Sarah looked at her blankly.

"*Lady Charlotte Wickford's mother.*"

Sarah smiled politely and watched the other woman's lips thin and her brows dig into a frown. Obviously the duchess was expecting more of a reaction, but Sarah truly had no idea who Miss Wickford was. She looked over at the duchess's companion. The poor woman's jaw had dropped to her slippers.

"This is Lady Huffington." The words barely made it through the duchess's stiff lips.

Sarah nodded. "Hello."

Lady Huffington, still obviously dazed, closed her mouth. She nodded back.

The duchess's prominent nostrils flared. "We understand you are staying with his grace, the Duke of Alvord?"

"Yes."

"You are a special friend of the family?"

Sarah wondered what gave this woman the right to stage an inquisition. Doubtless she thought her rank permitted such rudeness.

"No, not at all. I didn't even know the duke existed until a little over a month ago."

"Indeed?" The duchess's voice was a mix of incredulity and ice.

"Oh, yes." Sarah tried to open her eyes wide and look brainless. "I was so lucky the duke and his family took me in. You see, my father was the Earl of Westbrooke's brother—I mean, the current earl's uncle. When he insisted I come to England, he didn't know his brother had died. Of course, I couldn't live in my cousin's bachelor household. If the duke and his aunt hadn't offered me a place in their home, I don't know what I would have done." Sarah paused for breath and smiled. "I'm so happy to be able to help the family a little in exchange for their generosity. I've some experience with young girls, so I'm keeping an eye on his grace's sister during her come-out."

"Ah." The duchess's lips creased up at the corners. "So you are a companion for dear Lizzie. How nice." She turned to Lady Huffington, ignoring Sarah as if she were suddenly invisible. Sarah smiled slightly. For some reason the duchess had seen her as a threat. But servants weren't threats and, as a companion, Sarah was just an overdressed servant.

Until the music stopped. James appeared with his dance partner in tow. The girl's head barely reached Sarah's shoulders. She had delicate features and a cool, serene manner. She looked like an expensive porcelain doll.

"Sarah, I see you've met the duchess and Lady Huff-

ington. This is the duchess's daughter, Lady Charlotte.
Charlotte, Miss Sarah Hamilton from Philadelphia."

Sarah smiled. The corners of Lady Charlotte's lips
twitched up as if she'd had a moment of indigestion.

"A pleasure," Lady Charlotte said and yawned, covering her tiny mouth with her tiny hand. Her eyes never
rose above Sarah's bodice. The duchess could have
taken lessons on haughtiness from her daughter.

The orchestra played the opening strains of a waltz.

"May I have this dance, Miss Hamilton?"

The temperature in their little patch of ballroom plum-
meted. Sarah let James lead her out onto the dance floor.

"Am I wrong, or did the ladies suddenly seem a trifle chilly?" James murmured in Sarah's ear.

"Glacial." She tried to suppress the frisson she felt
when his hand settled on her waist. She was just another
dancing partner, she reminded herself. "I think you may
have committed a tactical error, your grace," she said as
he swung her into the movements of the dance.

"*James,* Sarah. If you whisper it in my ear, no one
will hear how bold you are."

James whispered this in *her* ear. Her breathing became a trifle irregular.

"Stop it."

"You say that much too frequently, sweetheart. Do not
let it become a habit, for those are certainly *not* the
words I will wish to hear when I've gotten you back in
my bed. Practice saying 'yes' or 'oh, yes' or just 'oh'—
with the proper intonation, of course. Short and breathy,
perhaps, or long and drawn out like a moan."

"James!"

"See, I knew I could get you to say my name." James
chuckled in her ear. "But why do you think I've com-

mitted a tactical error? I thought I had executed a flaw-
less retreat."

"I had just persuaded the duchess and her friend that I
was a complete nonentity, far below their notice, and then
you raise me back into their sights by dancing with me."

"Oh." James glanced back at the women. "They *are*
staring at us," he reported, "and they don't look particularly happy." He grinned. "Of course, they never look
particularly happy."

Sarah felt a spurt of pleasure that James had lumped
the porcelain doll in with the older women. She
squelched that feeling, too, reminding herself that he
would probably criticize her to the next London beauty
with whom he danced.

"What about you?" he asked. "Are you enjoying
yourself? You seem to be dancing every set."

"Major Draysmith and Robbie have been very good
about seeing that I have partners."

"I doubt that they have had to work too hard. I've had
more than a few men ask me who you are."

"Really?" Sarah caught her breath as James swung
her through an especially exhilarating turn.

"Really."

They danced a moment in silence. Sarah felt the be-
ginnings of the familiar languor that infected her
whenever she was too close to James. She searched
frantically for a distraction. "Is Richard here yet?"

"I don't think so." James looked over the crowd. His
gaze stopped at the doorway. Sarah felt his body tense,
then he pulled her closer. "He's here."

"Is he looking at us?"

James nodded. "Can't you feel his evil gaze?" His
lips flattened into a thin line. "God, I wish he'd leave
me alone."

"Ignore him." She hated to see the bleak look on his face.

"I wish I could." James looked down at her. "I don't want anything to happen to you, Sarah."

"Nothing is going to happen to me. Stop worrying."

"I can't." The last note faded into silence. James kept his hands on her a moment longer. "Be careful, sweetheart. Don't let Richard get you alone."

"I won't."

"Be sure you don't." He led her over to where his aunt and Lady Amanda were standing.

"Saw Richard, did you?" Lady Amanda said. She nodded at a young girl standing nearby. "Don't want him to think you live in Sarah's pocket. Go ask the Warrington chit to dance."

James glanced over at the girl. "The Warrington chit's out of the schoolroom already?"

"This is her third Season, James."

"Right." He walked over to the girl.

As soon as James left, a short balding man with a prominent stomach approached the ladies. "Lady Gladys and Lady Amanda, how delightful to see you again." The man bowed, emitting a definite creak.

"Ah, Symington, it's you." Lady Gladys sounded distinctly unenthusiastic. Sarah could not blame her. The man looked as interesting as leftover mutton. "Have you been well?"

"As well as can be expected after such a damp winter. Damp, chilly spring, too." Mr. Symington shivered. "Terrible weather. But at least the gout's not bothering me at the moment." He coughed, clearing his throat. "You heard my Lucinda passed on?"

"Yes, we did, didn't we, Amanda? So sorry for your loss."

Mr. Symington nodded dolefully. "Lucinda was a good wife." He heaved a great sigh testifying to his loss . . . and his lunch of liver and onions. "But it's been a year now— a man gets lonely. Thought I'd toddle up to town and look over this year's beauties." He looked pointedly at Sarah. "Might I trouble you to recommend me as a suitable partner for this young lady, Lady Gladys?"

Lady Gladys frowned as if she might deny his request. "Sarah, this is Mr. Symington," she said finally. "Sir, Miss Hamilton is the Earl of Westbrooke's cousin from America."

"America, heh?" Mr. Symington's ample eyebrows shot up as though they might fill the vacant spot on his head. "Place is full of savages, ain't it?"

"No—" Sarah began, but Mr. Symington interrupted.

"Would you care to dance?" He took her arm before she could reply. She looked back at the older women as she followed him onto the dance floor. Lady Gladys smiled slightly and shrugged.

Sarah and Mr. Symington took their places in the set.

"Say, you do know how to dance, don't you?" he asked, suddenly looking alarmed. The couples on either side of them stared, and one of the women giggled.

"Yes, I do." Sarah promised herself a few false steps aimed at Mr. Symington's toes.

The music began. Mr. Symington's waistcoat looked in danger of popping its buttons. As the dance progressed, it was clear the gentleman had also partaken liberally of garlic at his most recent meal—the odor became stronger as the beads of perspiration collected on his bald head and rolled down his bulbous nose. His labored breathing fanned Sarah's décolletage. It was a most unpleasant sensation. At least he had no air left for speaking.

At the conclusion of the set, Mr. Symington looked near collapse. Sarah did not want to spend any more time with him, but neither did she want him expiring in James's ballroom.

"Would you like a glass of lemonade?"

"Ah, ah, thank, ah, you," Mr. Symington panted. "I'll just—oh!" Suddenly his breathing was shallow and fast. His eyes fixed on a point over Sarah's right shoulder. She reached to grab his arm, thinking he was going to faint.

"Ah, the charming Miss Hamilton." Richard's voice was unmistakable. "And 'Simple' Symington."

Sarah turned to face James's cousin. She glanced back at Mr. Symington. Another man might take Richard to task for his blatant rudeness, but Mr. Symington just fiddled with his watch fobs.

"Mr. Runyon, uh, a pleasure, uh, I'm sure. Um, of course you've met Miss Hamilton. She is, ah, staying with your cousin."

"I know."

Mr. Symington ran a finger under his cravat. It was clear to Sarah that the man desperately wanted to be elsewhere.

"We were just going to get some lemonade," she said.

"An excellent idea. Run off to James's refreshment room, Symington. I'll keep Miss Hamilton here. No need to drag her along, is there?"

"No, no need at all." Mr. Symington's head bobbed like a cork in a flooding river. "That would be splendid, I'm sure. I'll just be going then." He left without a backward glance.

Mr. Symington, Sarah noted, had no aspirations to chivalry.

The orchestra chose that moment to begin another waltz. "My dance, Miss Hamilton."

Sarah stiffened. Once again she was going to be a reluctant dance partner, but this time she felt a spurt of fear in place of boredom. She had to go with Richard— she couldn't cause a scene—but she would not go easily. She slowed her steps, causing him to pause.

"Well, I'll grant this of old James. He seems to have found a filly with some spunk," Richard said as he hauled her into his arms.

"I beg your pardon?" Sarah tried to step back, but Richard's hands were made of iron. Her breasts brushed against the front of his chest. She knew he was holding her much too close. Already the conversations around them had stopped. More than one furtive glance was sent their way.

"Don't play the fool with me," Richard hissed. "I know James wants you."

"Mr. Runyon, not that it is any of your business, but I assure you the duke and I are merely acquaintances. I was in need of a place to stay that provided female companionship and he graciously extended his hospitality. In return I am helping a little with his sister's come-out. I fail to see how any of this could possibly concern you."

"I saw you dancing with him."

"I've danced with many men tonight." Sarah struggled to keep her voice level as a mixture of anger and fear surged through her.

"You don't understand, Miss Hamilton. I saw James. I know my cousin. He wants to get under your skirts."

"Mr. Runyon!" Sarah would have left him on the dance floor then, scene or no scene, but she couldn't. His grip on her was unbreakable.

"Just remember," he said, his voice low and menacing, "your continued good health depends on James's bachelorhood."

"Mr. Runyon," Sarah gasped, praying he would loosen his hold soon, "I have no matrimonial designs on your cousin."

"I hope not. I cannot have James getting a brat on you." He dragged her past the orchestra in silence, his brow furrowed. Sarah hoped he had finished all he had to say. She was not so lucky.

"Even if your marriage would not be a great inconvenience to me—and a definite threat to you," Richard bared his teeth in what Sarah assumed he meant for a smile, "I'd hate for your American heart to be broken."

Sarah felt a hysterical giggle threaten to escape her throat. Richard cared about her heart? If it broke, he'd be eager to count the pieces.

"Do not doubt me, Miss Hamilton. If you are foolish enough to marry my cousin, your heart *will* be broken." He jerked her through a turn and she had to grab his shoulder to keep from tripping. "You are new to our ways, so I shall enlighten you."

"I'm quite certain that is not necessary."

"I'm quite certain that it is, Miss Hamilton. If you had grown up among us, you would know all this without anyone saying a word. You would know James's reputation."

"His reputation?"

"Oh, it is not so terrible—for a duke. We lesser mortals . . ." Richard shrugged. "Well, society is somewhat less understanding, shall we say?"

"I believe you have said enough."

Richard laughed. "I don't think so. You know James is a member of the *ton,* Miss Hamilton, but do you realize that *ton* marriages are simply business deals? The man supplies his name and fortune; the woman produces an heir. Love—or, to call it truthfully, sexual satisfaction—happens elsewhere."

"Mr. Runyon, please! I'm sure you should not be saying such things."

Richard ignored Sarah's words. "You women must wait until you've presented your husband with his squalling ticket to the next generation. We men don't have to wait. We can sleep where we will, when we will. Why, on his wedding night, the Earl of Northhaven bedded his young wife at ten, his mistress at eleven, and Lord Avery's wife at midnight—and then toddled off to Madame Bernard's exclusive whorehouse."

"That's disgusting! I don't believe you."

"Believe me, Miss Hamilton. It is hardly remarked upon, it is so common. Keep your eyes and ears open at any *ton* gathering and you will soon learn I speak the truth. So, if you are expecting to find love in James's marriage bed, you will be sadly disappointed. And satisfaction? Perhaps you *will* find that—if you are braver than most virgins."

Sarah shook her head and pulled back. Richard's grip tightened again. There was no escaping him.

"Do you know my cousin's nickname, Miss Hamilton?"

"No, and I don't want to know it." What Sarah wanted was for the dance to end.

"If I don't tell you, someone else will. People love to gossip, and a duke's sexual exploits are so interesting."

Sarah looked Richard in the eye. "Mr. Runyon, I must ask you to stop this immediately. Your conversation is highly inappropriate."

She might have saved her breath.

"James is called 'Monk,' my dear. A joke, of course. James is not exactly a candidate for holy orders."

* * *

"I believe this is my dance, Miss Hamilton?"

Sarah looked up at Major Draysmith. He frowned.

"You look a little pale. Would you prefer to sit out this set? I would be happy to accompany you to the refreshment room."

"Yes, please." Leaving the ballroom sounded very appealing. She was trying to maintain her composure, but she was certain all the gossips in the room had made note of her dance with Richard and were studying her reaction.

The room James had set aside for food was much cooler. The only other couple there left when Sarah and the major entered. Sarah sank gratefully into a chair as the major went to get their drinks.

She should not have been surprised by Richard's words. He had just confirmed what her father and the Abington sisters had always told her about the British *ton*. Certainly James had shown her his polished powers of seduction.

But she was surprised. Shocked.

She was an idiot.

She watched Major Draysmith cross the room. He was a handsome man. His military bearing emphasized the breadth of his shoulders, and his light blue eyes with their dark rims were striking. Her stomach should have been fluttering with excitement. When he handed her the lemonade and his gloved fingers brushed hers, she felt only the pleasant anticipation of a cool drink.

She was definitely an idiot.

"Your pardon, Miss Hamilton, but I couldn't help noticing you with Runyon. Did that blackguard say anything to overset you?"

She shrugged slightly. "My short acquaintance with Mr. Runyon has led me to expect him to be unpleasant.

He did mention some nickname his grace had acquired as though it were significant."

"Yes?" Charles looked baffled for a moment. "Oh, you mean 'Monk.' Runyon stuck James with that label at university. No one calls him by it anymore—at least not to his face."

"I see." Sarah carefully placed her lemonade on the table. Suddenly it was impossible to swallow even a mouthful.

"Forgive me, Miss Hamilton, but you shouldn't let such a little thing upset you."

"No, of course not. And please, call me Sarah." She stared down at her drink. Her unhappiness was her own fault. She had let the weeks at Alvord lull her into thinking of James as an American with an odd accent. Stupid. She had met the man in bed, after all. Naked. He obviously wasn't bashful about shedding his clothes with strangers.

How many of the women in the ballroom tonight had welcomed the Duke of Alvord into their beds?

"Then you must call me Charles. And you shouldn't let Runyon upset you," Charles was saying. "He's vermin that the *ton* has chosen not to rid itself of, unfortunately. When you marry James, Runyon will be shown the door as he should be. Until then, avoid the man. I do."

"I intend to avoid him." She sighed. "And please, don't think that I will be marrying his grace."

Charles's face assumed an interesting blankness. "I see."

Sarah laughed. "You don't intend to argue with me, do you?"

Charles grinned. "No, ma'am. We soldiers learn early which battles are not worth the blood."

Sarah tried to take a sip of lemonade. She could get

a little down now. "Tell me, Charles, why do the English insist on this ridiculous system of primogeniture? It sets brother against brother—cousin against cousin—does it not?"

"Now, Sarah, don't judge us by Runyon's conduct! I'm a second son and I don't hate my brother. I don't envy him his title at all. If anything, I pity him."

"Pity him? Why?"

"Because his life's not his own." Charles leaned forward, propping his elbows on the table. "He's the Marquis of Knightsdale. That's his title, but it might as well be his name. He's never been just Paul Draysmith. He was born Earl of Northfield and became Knightsdale while still at Eton. He seems content enough with his lot, fortunately. The land is in his blood. But he's never had a choice, don't you see?"

"Yes." Sarah did see. James also had the land in his blood. And he also had no choice. He had to protect Alvord. He had to marry, even if it meant marrying a redheaded American. But that didn't mean that he needed to limit himself to his wife's bed.

"I think I have a better life," Charles was saying. "I have the freedom to follow my own path. I joined the army. I could go to America tomorrow, if I wanted, as your father did. No, I sincerely hope my brother has a long life and many sons. I have absolutely no desire to ever step into his shoes."

Charles finished his lemonade and looked at his glass. "I must have been daft to take this stuff. Champagne's what we need. What do you say?"

"That I've never had champagne?"

Charles laughed. "Then I'd better let James introduce you to it. He wouldn't take kindly to my getting his betrothed tipsy."

"I am not his betrothed!"

"Right." Charles leaned back. "You really should consider it, though. You'd be getting a comfortable position and doing James a favor at the same time. He needs to marry soon because of Richard. That night at the Green Man, he was on the verge of asking Charlotte Wickford to marry him. He certainly deserves better than *that* life sentence."

"Oh." Now Sarah understood why the Duchess of Rothingham had sought her out.

"Ah, this is where you've gotten to."

Sarah's heart lurched at the sound of James's voice. She looked up and smiled before she could stop herself.

"Just giving Sarah a respite from the ballroom, James," Charles said. "Did you know that she's never had champagne?"

James lifted an eyebrow. "And have you been giving her some?"

"Not I. I leave that to you."

James nodded. "Would you like to try some champagne, Sarah?"

"Yes, please."

She looked down at her hands as James went to get the drinks.

"Are you all right?" Charles asked. "You look pale again."

"No, I'm fine." As fine, she thought, as a woman could be who suddenly realizes that she might be in love with a rake. James returned and handed her a glass. She took a quick sip. The bubbles tickled her nose.

"Did you need a rest from dancing, Sarah?" James asked. "Don't tell me your feet are tired."

"They are, actually. It's nice to sit for a while."

Sarah took another sip and watched James from the

corner of her eye. His dark blond hair glowed in the candlelight, and the clean, strong angle of his jaw stood out against the snowy white of his cravat. He was so handsome. Sinfully handsome. Of course women wanted him. She wanted him. She swallowed another mouthful of champagne. The bubbles tickled her throat as well as her nose.

"I think Runyon was causing trouble," Charles said.

"Was he?" James looked intently at Sarah. She ducked her head and put the champagne glass to her lips again. "What did he do, Sarah?"

"Nothing, really. I think he was trying to frighten me. I told him you and I were just acquaintances, but he didn't believe me." She took another sip of champagne.

Charles snorted. "Of course he didn't believe you— the two of you just about set the ballroom on fire with that waltz."

"Damn!" James sounded both angry and frustrated.

Had he kissed Charlotte Wickford, Sarah wondered. He must have, if he had considered becoming engaged to her. She took a larger swallow of champagne. The bubbles were definitely nice.

"Can't say I like him getting near Sarah," Charles said.

"*You* can't like it?" James's voice rose. He lowered it. "God, I *hate* it, but I can't order the man out of London, much as I'd like to. At least he's gone now. I saw him leave just before I came in here."

Sarah let the men's words wash over her as she watched the champagne bubbles stream up from the bottom of her glass. She raised it to her lips again.

"I think that is probably enough, sweetheart," James said, taking the glass away. "Let's go dance, shall we?"

Sarah felt as if her head were floating above her shoulders. She smiled at Charles. "If you'll excuse us?"

"Ma'am, James was my commanding officer. Of *course* I'll excuse you."

"Wise, Charles. Very wise." James put his hand under Sarah's arm and helped her to her feet. She swayed slightly and leaned into him. "No more champagne."

"Why not?"

"Because you're tipsy, sweetheart."

As they entered the ballroom, the orchestra was starting another waltz. Sarah smiled. She much preferred the waltz to all the other dances—especially if she was going to be dancing with James. He took her into his arms and she closed her eyes, savoring the music. She felt light and graceful, surrounded by James's strength. There was nowhere else she would rather be. She decided Richard's words were unimportant.

"Am I putting you to sleep, Sarah?"

"No." She looked up at him, still under the spell of his closeness. The right corner of his mouth twitched up.

"Keep looking at me like that, my love, and the *ton* will never recover from the scandal I may feel compelled to enact."

Every inch of Sarah's skin burst into fiery bloom. Her body began to throb in a most embarrassing place and her knees were suddenly wobbly. She was afraid she was going to melt into him.

"James!" she said, weakly.

He laughed. "We are probably scandalizing society enough just dancing together. I suggest a mental diversion. Perhaps you should recite the *Declaration of Independence*."

Sarah's mind went blank. All she could do was stare at James's lips. She knew that was a very improper, even stupid thing to do, but she had lost all control of her muscles.

"I don't think so."

"Hmm. Well I have to admit I am exceedingly pleased to have reduced you to such a mindless state, sweetheart, but we do need to change the subject. My inexpressibles are getting much too expressive."

"What?"

"Never mind. What exactly did my unpleasant cousin say to you during your dance?"

Sarah missed a step. James steadied her, pulling her a little closer than proper. Her breasts brushed against his chest. She felt the contact all the way to her toes. "Nothing," she whispered. "Nothing at all."

"I think that's quite enough." Robbie plucked the champagne glass out of Sarah's fingers.

"You should talk." Sarah had to concentrate to get each word past her uncooperative lips. She knew she wasn't completely tethered to reality. She liked the feeling. She watched James dance by with a tall, buxom brunette.

"Exactly. An excess of spirits led to your current predicament."

"*Your* excess, not mine." Sarah would have argued further, but she couldn't focus on the issue long enough to marshal her fuzzy thoughts. She watched the brunette smile up at James. Had he been in her bed yet?

"Does James know you've been sampling his champagne so freely?"

Sarah shrugged. "He doesn't care."

"Oh, I think he cares very much. Come on, this is the last dance. I'll haul you around the floor in the hopes that you'll sober up."

"I'm not drunk."

Robbie smiled. "Not quite, perhaps. I'll bet you have a headache in the morning, though."

"Are you going to dance or lecture me?"

"Dance, I think. Come on."

Sarah stepped on Robbie's toes twice. She lost her balance through one of the turns, but Robbie kept her upright. As the music ended, he led her over to James. The brunette had already been deposited with her chaperone.

"You want me to lean Sarah in the corner somewhere?" James examined her. She glowered back at him.

"A little too much champagne?"

"No," she said.

"Yes," Robbie said.

"Come along." James took her arm. "It's time to say good night to our guests. If you stand still and don't talk too much, you'll be fine."

Robbie was the last to leave. After the door closed behind him, Lizzie skipped over and hugged James.

"That was wonderful!" She spun across the entry hall, her dress whirling out in a frothy billow. "I danced every dance! I'm so excited, I'll never be able to sleep."

"Then I guess we'll just have to turn away all the young bucks who come visiting in the morning," Lady Amanda said as she started up the stairs. "We'll say you're indisposed."

Lizzie stopped in mid-spin. "Oh, no! Don't do that!"

Lady Gladys chuckled. "Off to bed with you then, if you don't want to look hagged for all your admirers." She took Lizzie's arm, but paused on the first step to glance over her shoulder. "Coming, Sarah?"

James took Sarah's hand. "I'm afraid I'm going to detain Sarah just a few more minutes. We have some things to discuss."

Lady Gladys rolled her eyes. "You don't fool me, boy. I was young once, you know, hard as that may be to believe. Just don't get too lost in your 'discussion.' I'm all for your early wedding, but I don't want the guests counting the months till your heir is born."

James chuckled. "Aunt! Please be a little more discreet. Poor Sarah and Lizzie are as red as pomegranates."

"Balderdash. Come along, Lizzie. We'll leave these two lovebirds alone."

Lizzie winked at Sarah and helped Lady Gladys up the steps. Sarah watched them until she felt James tug on her hand. She went with him into his study. She knew it was not a good idea, but her brain was no longer in charge of her actions. Something else was guiding her now, some need she didn't understand. Her good sense was just a spectator.

James closed the door quietly behind them. Sarah's awareness of him, of his body with its planes and angles, muscles and strength, hit her in the throat. Her eyes traced the line of his jaw against the soft whiteness of his cravat, stopping at the defined curve of his lips. She wanted to touch those lips, to feel them on her skin. She was breathless, expectant.

He led her over to his big chair. The room was shadowy, lit only by the banked fire. He sat down and tugged her gently onto his lap. She sank into the strength of his thighs, the wall of his chest, the warmth of his arms.

"Mmm, you taste good." James's words rumbled past her ear as his lips, soft as worn velvet, grazed over her earlobe, down her jaw, to the pulse fluttering at the base of her throat. "I thought I would go mad whenever I saw you dancing with another man tonight. When I found you in the refreshment room with Charles, I felt battle rage, and Charles is one of my closest friends."

His tongue flicked over the seam of her lips. She inhaled in surprise, and he came into her, filling her. She was overwhelmed by the intimacy of the action, transfixed by the rough sweetness of his tongue, the tangy smell of his skin, the latent power of his body. Her head fell back against his shoulder. She pulsed with a dark, wet heat that pooled between her legs. His hand cupped her breast and she moaned. She ached there, too. She shifted in his lap, trying to get closer. His thumb rubbed lightly over her nipple.

It was the faintest touch, but the shock of it flashed through her body, clearing the champagne fog from her mind. She stiffened and struggled, pushing against his chest. His arms loosened immediately and she sat up, gasping and shivering.

James had had his *tongue* in her mouth and his hands on parts of her body even she barely touched. And the throbbing down there . . . Sarah shook her head, but the thought and the feeling didn't leave. God in heaven. James was definitely turning her into a wanton. Was this how he started with all his women? Made them so mindless they would do whatever he wanted? Or was this just how the *ton* behaved—all those beautiful, sophisticated *worldly* women. Well, Sarah wasn't worldly. She was just a provincial, naive American.

"Sarah?"

"Richard said the *ton* calls you 'Monk.'"

"Did he?" There was no inflection in James's voice, but his body told the truth of it. His hands dropped away from her. She was still sitting in his lap, but she might as well have been sitting in the straightest, most formal chair.

She didn't need to ask, but she did anyway. "Is it

true?" The words were shrill, defensive. Just like the foolish little virgin she was.

"Yes," he said. "It's true."

Chapter 8

James heard the door close behind Sarah. He should have risen when she had, but his manners had abandoned him. Truthfully, he couldn't move. The pain of Sarah's rejection was paralyzing.

He stared into the fire. What had he done wrong? He could have sworn Sarah had responded to him. He had felt her sweet bottom squirm against his heat, had heard her little moans of pleasure. Had he misunderstood? Had he been so caught up in his own passion that he had misinterpreted her reactions?

When she had first pulled away, he'd thought he had frightened her, that he had gone too fast. But then she had thrown that bloody nickname in his teeth.

He rubbed his eyes with the heels of his hands. God, desire still pounded through his body, making it hard to think. He took a deep, shuddering breath.

What the *hell* had he done wrong? In an instant she had gone from hot and pliant to cold and stiff. Her beautiful lips, swollen from his kisses, had twisted in disgust. He had felt like a clumsy boy again.

He leaned his head back and closed his eyes. The bloody nickname went back to Cambridge and Richard, of course. Richard had spread it throughout the school once he'd gotten wind of James's disastrous trip to the Dancing Piper.

It was an ugly memory. On James's sixteenth birthday his father had paid him a rare visit.

"Sixteen! Time you learned to be a man, son."

"I thought I was learning to be a man, Father." James had actually been happy to see the duke. He missed Alvord; he missed Aunt Gladys and Lizzie, who was then only five years old. "How are things at Alvord?"

"Well I'm sure. They'd send word if anything was amiss. Haven't been at Alvord for a while, you know. Came out from London. More to do there."

James had stared at his father. At sixteen, he couldn't imagine anything better than being at Alvord.

"Now, James, I've got quite a treat planned for you." His father had looked everywhere but at him. "You aren't still a virgin, are you? Haven't tumbled one of the maids at Alvord? That yaller-haired girl—Meg's her name. Or is it Mary? She's quite accommodating, as I remember. Had a piece of her, lad?"

James had felt his ears burn. He'd swallowed, his mouth as dry as dust.

"No, heh? Well, that's why I came, James. Hell, by the time I was sixteen, I must have laid at least a half-dozen girls. I'm giving you a birthday present, lad. We're off to the Dancing Piper."

James had heard Richard and the other boys talk about the Dancing Piper. Nerves twisted his gut. "I don't think I can go, Father. I have to finish my Cicero."

"Put those damn books down. There's more to life than books, boy. It's past time you learned that."

James had to admit, as he matched his steps to the duke's, that excitement twisted alongside the dread in his stomach. He *was* sixteen. He noticed women. He'd been dreaming of them for a while, but his fantasies always turned vague at the most interesting parts. Perhaps now he would be able to fill in some details.

He had walked past the Dancing Piper many times, detouring to view the building that held such mysteries. The outside was not impressive. It looked like any other tavern or small inn. The sign needed a fresh coat of paint and one of the windows was cracked, but James was willing to reserve judgment.

"Place's grown a bit shabby," his father muttered. He pushed open the front door.

The first thing that struck James was the smell—the stink of stale ale and stale bodies. The common room was dark; the ceiling, low. Smoke from the candles and the fireplace made the air thick. James felt the walls close in on him and his stomach twisted again. He took a deep breath. A mistake. He started coughing. His father whacked him on the back.

"Yer grace, what a surprise!"

James found himself staring down at the largest breasts he had ever seen. He straightened quickly. The breasts belonged to an otherwise small woman. In the murky light, her hair looked blond. Squinting, James saw the lines she had tried to cover with paint around her mouth and eyes. He was appalled to see her link her arm through his father's and lean those large breasts against his father's side.

"To what do we owe the honor of yer presence?"

James watched his father preen under this female's attention.

"I've brought my son for a little polishing, Dolly. Well, more than a little. He's got no damn experience at all."

Dolly turned her small, calculating eyes to James. "A fine, strapping lad like this and never been with a woman?" Dolly did not bother to keep her voice down. James saw a pair of older boys he knew sniggering.

"He spends all his time with his nose buried in his books." His father shook his head. "Hard to believe he's my son."

Dolly laughed. "True. If he didn't look so much like ye at that age—and if his mother wasn't that cold piece ye married—I'd have my doubts. Well, don't worry, love, we'll take care of him. Can't guarantee that he'll be the expert his papa is, but at least he'll know his way around a bed when this night is over."

"I'm not asking for miracles. Whom do you have in mind?"

Dolly scratched her ear. James was very much afraid that he saw some movement in her elaborate hairstyle. Not lice, too. He desperately wanted to be back in his room with his Cicero.

"Fanny. She's had years of experience with young cubs. They can be very, um, frustrating, ye know." Dolly checked the timepiece pinned inside her minimal bodice. "She should be finished with her customer soon. Roland never takes very long. Ah, here she is now."

James looked up at the couple coming down the stairs. His eyes slid past the balding, paunchy man—and then swung back. He truly was afraid he would puke right there in front of everyone. The maligned Roland was Mr. Richardson, his Greek don.

"Fanny!" Dolly called out. James slumped down and tried to back into a darker shadow. Fortunately it appeared that Richardson was exceedingly drunk. "Fanny, come here."

Fanny bestowed a farewell pat on Richardson's rump and slouched over to them. Her eyes immediately fastened on the duke. She was a businesswoman, first and foremost, James surmised. She knew who had the deepest pockets. When Dolly indicated that James was her chosen customer, she shrugged and turned her attention to him. He felt her eyes assess his face, his shoulders, his hips and his groin. He felt naked. His palms began to sweat. His stomach twisted sharply, and he swallowed bile.

Fanny smiled. James's eyes fastened on her painted lips and rotting teeth.

"Come on, then, dukeling. Fanny will teach ye what ye need to know."

James looked at his father, sure his eyes rolled like a panicked horse's, but his father was too busy staring down Dolly's dress.

"Go along, son. Dolly will keep me entertained, won't you, m'dear?"

Dolly took his father's hand and put it on one of her breasts. "Very entertained," she purred.

Fanny grabbed James's arm and started pulling him up the stairs. "Don't be bashful. Fanny gots just what ye need."

James felt that what Fanny very much needed was a good scrubbing. She smelled of garlic and onions, sweat and Richardson.

Her room was small. The bed took up the main area—the sheets were still rumpled from her work with Richardson. James averted his eyes. A mistake. The walls were decorated with pornographic prints.

"Like the pictures, do ye?"

James turned his eyes back to Fanny. She had made short work of ridding herself of her dress.

She was the first woman James had seen naked. She was probably in her mid-to-late thirties, old enough to be his mother. Her sizable breasts drooped onto her ample stomach. She scratched the matted thatch at the apex of her legs. His face began to sweat and he looked for the chamber pot. *Please, let it be empty,* he thought. He had hopes. That was one scent he had not yet detected in the room. He sidled towards the bed. The chamber pot should be near it.

"Eager, are ye?" Fanny walked toward him. James increased his pace. She laughed. "Ye cubs are all the same. Eager to bed, eager to come. Fanny'll teach ye how to slow down."

James thought he saw the pot under the bed. He was almost within reach. He swallowed. If he breathed through his mouth, he wouldn't smell anything. Maybe his stomach would settle.

"I'll help ye with yer breeches." Fanny stepped close in front of him. James watched a large louse navigate an oily brown strand of hair that had fallen over her forehead. She grabbed his crotch and leered up at him.

"How's that?"

It was too much. The smells of unwashed hair, sweat, sex, and rotting teeth were strong enough for James to taste. He made a dive for the chamber pot. His last coherent thought was a prayer of thanksgiving that it was empty. Then he concentrated on emptying his stomach.

James sat up in his chair, shaking his head to dispel the memory. From the distance of all these years, the scene was almost funny. Fanny had been extremely put out to have a man puking in her room, apparently as a result of her charms. She stormed out to find Dolly and complain. Dolly was entertaining the duke and neither she nor James's father had been pleased to be interrupted. His father had stalked into Fanny's room, tucking his shirt in as he came. He had grabbed James by the collar and hauled him down the stairs, out into the blessedly fresh air.

He got up to pour himself some brandy. That evening had been a disaster. Wickam and Landers, the boys who'd seen him, had spread the tale. By the next morning—if not before—Richard had known every detail and had publicly christened him "Monk."

He watched the brandy tumble into his glass.

But that did not explain why he had become a monk in truth. Why had he lived up to Richard's stupid nickname? He couldn't really say. He certainly thought about sex enough. But Dolly and Fanny had given him a bad taste for brothels, and he didn't much like the notion of using another man's wife. Plenty of maids and serving wenches had offered to warm his sheets, but taking them seemed wrong, too. He was a duke, a peer. How could he use girls with so little freedom for his personal satisfaction? His duty was to protect his people, not prey on them. And merely because a girl did not live on Alvord land, did that make her any less worthy of his protection?

Truthfully, until he'd seen Sarah in his bed, he had not been seriously tempted.

But Sarah—he wanted her like a starving man wanted food.

He studied the brandy in his glass and added a touch more. He took a sip and held it on his tongue. Nothing could warm the chill he felt at Sarah's leaving.

This proposed marriage had become more than a rational arrangement. Somehow the dreamy boy he'd been before his trip to the Dancing Piper had been resurrected. That idiot who had believed in love and goodness, honesty and faithfulness was now haunting his body. His heart, which until this moment had done an adequate job of keeping him alive, ached for an intangible pipe dream. For Sarah. For her love.

His fingers convulsed around the stem of the brandy snifter. He thought about throwing it into the fire, about how the glass would shatter and the brandy would make the flames flare. But he would still have this infernal ache.

Carefully, he put the glass down on his desk and went upstairs to bed.

"He wants her."

Philip Gadner stuck his finger between the pages of Byron's *Childe Harold's Pilgrimage* to mark his place. He leaned back in the leather chair and looked up at Richard.

"Why do you say so? Did he drool down her décolletage?"

"Didn't he just?" Richard reached for the brandy decanter. "If he hadn't been in the bloody ballroom, he'd have had her skirts over her head." He threw the glassful of brandy down his throat. "*Ball*room—ha! That's exactly what old James wanted—room to ball his American whore."

"James?" Philip frowned. He could not imagine James losing control of himself. "What exactly did he do?"

"He danced with the whore!" Richard hurled his glass at the fireplace. It exploded against the stone.

"How many times?" If James had been so lost to propriety that he had singled this girl out, then perhaps Richard was right and the situation was indeed serious.

"Once." Richard shrugged. "He may have danced with her again. I didn't stay to see."

"Once!" Philip felt his own anger surge. "For God's sake, Richard, he only danced with the girl once?"

"Once was enough, damn it." Richard threw himself

into the chair opposite Philip. "I know James, Philip. You know that I do. God, I've watched him and studied him my whole bloody life. I saw his face when he danced with her. I've never seen him look that way. I tell you, he wants her."

"Wanting doesn't necessarily mean marriage." Philip was thinking quickly. He needed to come up with a plan before Richard did something stupid. "Why not wait and see if he loses interest?"

"He won't lose interest." Richard drummed his fingers on the chair arm. "Not in time. He wants her in his bed, and he'll have her there if I don't do something soon."

"But maybe she doesn't want him. She *is* an American, and Americans hate titles, don't they? Maybe she doesn't want to marry a duke."

Richard reached for the brandy decanter again, but his hand seemed steadier. He poured two glasses this time and offered one to Philip.

"I danced with her. She claims she is not interested in James, but I don't believe her." Richard took a long swallow of brandy. "Something's holding her back, but it's not lack of interest. I looked at her, too, when she and James were dancing. She wants him. I'd swear it." He studied the firelight in his brandy glass and smiled. "I may have sown a seed of discontent, however. I told her that James was a rake."

"James?"

Richard laughed. "You know that's one explanation of James's nickname that circulates through society."

"Yes. So you've already dealt with the problem."

"No." Richard shook his head. "No, I don't think so. Not definitively. Women are so fickle. They drift with the wind and the wind of James's desire is going to blow this American into his bed. No, I still think I had better kill the girl."

Philip leaned forward. "Richard, I promise you if you kill Miss Hamilton, the authorities will not look the other way as they did with the whore at the Green Man. This is London and the girl is the Earl of Westbrooke's cousin, besides being a friend of the Duke of Alvord— and of Lady Gladys and Lady Amanda Wallen-Smyth."

"I can handle the situation."

"No, you can't. There has to be another way."

"I can kill James instead."

"No. We've been through that before." Philip swallowed a large mouthful of brandy. He'd been arguing with Richard against his assassination efforts for months. The man seemed incapable of comprehending the simple fact that, should James die under suspicious circumstances, the authorities would look to Richard as the natural suspect. Who else would benefit from James's untimely death?

Each time Richard had hired some new accomplice to attempt the deed, Philip had had nightmares. He did not want to see Richard dancing from the end of a rope, nor did he want to join him on the gallows.

"There must be another way to manage this problem."

Suddenly, Richard grinned. "I could rape the girl. Make it look like she wanted it. James would never take my leavings."

Philip sat up, his brandy forgotten. He believed— prayed—Richard had more sense than to kill Sarah Hamilton. Rape, however, was a different issue. It would take just a few moments in a darkened garden to accomplish that task.

"No, Richard, don't do it. James would kill you."

"James? My little cousin, James?"

"Your little war hero cousin James, lauded in the dispatches for the number of Frogs he sent to their Maker."

"You worry too much, Philip."

"You don't worry enough." Philip's mind raced. "If you want to do this, we need to find someone to do it for you."

"I'm done with using incompetent fools."

"Yes, but I've heard Dunlap is in town."

"The New York whore trader?"

"The same. He's competent and ruthless and you have him by the balls."

"True." Richard swirled his brandy around his tongue. "Still it would be very pleasant to plow a female James fancied."

Philip leaned over and put his hand on Richard's forearm. He couldn't keep a note of panic from creeping into his voice.

"Please, Richard. Dunlap will get the job done at no risk to you."

Richard stilled, staring at Philip's hand on his arm. Philip was afraid Richard would shrug him off. It would hurt, but he had been hurt so much in the last few years, what did another wound matter?

Instead Richard's other hand came up to rest on Philip's.

"You really worry about me?" There was a note of vulnerability in his voice that Philip hadn't heard in a long time. He turned his hand over to grip Richard's.

"I do."

Richard kept his head lowered, staring at their clasped hands. "After all I've done to you?"

Philip squeezed Richard's hand. "Yes," he said. "I love you."

Richard looked up. His face was strained, his eyes bleak. "Show me, Philip. Please."

It was the invitation that Philip had been waiting months—years—to hear. "Of course."

"Richard Runyon's here to see ye."

"Shit!" William Dunlap leaned back from his ledger books, pushing his chestnut hair out of his eyes. "What the hell does he want?"

"Damned if I know." Belle LaRue, the madam of this particular establishment and Dunlap's occasional mistress, frowned. "He's not a regular here, I can tell ye that. Came once and mauled Gilly pretty bad. Had to have the surgeon see to her."

"That doesn't surprise me." The Rutting Stallion, being on the Thames, was one of Dunlap's rougher whorehouses, but Runyon could be meaner than any seaman or docker. Dunlap sighed and stood. "I'd better see him. The sooner I find out what he wants, the sooner we'll be rid of him. Where'd you stow him?"

"In the red parlor. Figured ye didn't want anyone else to see him."

"Exactly right, love." Dunlap put an arm around Belle's ample waist and took a kiss. He liked his women big, with wide fleshy hips, lovely soft bellies and thighs, and tits a man could lose himself in. His boys he liked young and skinny. Contrast, he thought as he opened the door to the red parlor, was the spice of life.

And Runyon was the rot. Dunlap had dealt with some pretty awful characters in his line of work, but Runyon was one of the worst. He took a moment to observe him.

Runyon stood by the window, peering out between the heavy red drapes. The weak morning light did not soften the sharp angles of his nose and cheekbones, nor warm his cold blue eyes. Runyon always had a whiff of madness about him, but Dunlap sensed he was closer to the brink since last he'd had the unpleasant occasion to be in his presence.

"Runyon," Dunlap said cautiously, "what brings you to the Rutting Stallion so early? The girls won't be ready to entertain for a few hours."

Runyon let the curtain fall. "I'm not here for the girls, Dunlap. I'm here to see you. I have a little job that needs your special skills."

"Oh?" The room was too damn dark. Dunlap wanted to see Runyon's every move. He walked to the near window and pulled the drapes wide. The chances that a denizen of this neighborhood would be up so early were minimal, and most would know that there'd be nothing interesting to gain from peeping into this room's windows.

"I have a girl I need you to seduce as publicly as possible."

"A girl? Why don't you do it yourself? I'd say you were quite capable."

"Capable? Oh, yes. More than capable. But there are" — Runyon paused and smiled slightly—"complications."

"Complications?" Dunlap felt the pit of his stomach drop, though he kept his face expressionless. He'd had years of dealing with scum. A man didn't build a small empire in the flesh trade if he didn't know how to hold his cards close to his chest. "What kind of complications?"

"Nothing you need be concerned about."

Those were the worst kind. "What's the girl's name?"

"Sarah Hamilton. She's an American, like yourself."

"So? And why exactly does she need seducing?"

Runyon examined the nails on his right hand. "My cousin James has a slight interest in her. I wish to scotch it before it becomes a problem."

"Your cousin James, as in the Duke of Alvord?"

"Yes."

Shit, Dunlap thought, this was bad. Not only was Alvord physically imposing, he had vast financial and political power. He had friends, even some who lived on the shadowy side of London. Dunlap did not want to make an enemy of the Duke of Alvord. He had not lived to the ripe old age of thirty-five by antagonizing powerful men. If Alvord cared about this girl, he would make inquires. Dunlap kept his business interests as discreet as he could, but he was no damn magician.

Well, he hoped the duke's interest in this girl was indeed slight, because he couldn't flat refuse Runyon. Runyon knew too much about that unfortunate mistake in Paris with the Earl of Lugington's son.

"How am I supposed to meet this American?"

"Come to the Easthaven ball tonight."

Dunlap snorted. "The Earl of Easthaven's a regular at one of my houses, true, but I'm not on his guest list, I assure you."

Runyon shrugged. "I didn't think you were. I'll get you an invitation—and an introduction to Miss Hamilton. Just be sure you show up."

"And if I'm successful and Miss Hamilton is ruined in grand style? Do you really think Alvord will die of a broken heart?"

Runyon smiled, a chilling pull of lips and teeth. "Death comes to all men."

"Sometimes with help," Dunlap said, hoping Runyon didn't expect him to do that chore, too.

Runyon's grin widened. "Sometimes with help," he agreed.

* * *

"I shall have to make you known to Miss Hamilton, Mr. Dunlap. She's from the colonies, too."

"That would be delightful." Dunlap smiled faintly at his dancing partner, Lady Charlotte Wickford. Runyon had introduced him to this pocket harpy the moment he'd crossed Easthaven's threshold. She had looked him over carefully. He was used to women assessing him, but usually they were looking for their own use. Not Lady Charlotte. Her eyes were as cold as Runyon's. He would bet a night's profits that she also wanted to separate Miss Hamilton from the duke.

It was a huge joke that he was here waltzing with the *ton*. Most of the men in the room had visited at least one of his whorehouses. Some were avid patrons. Yet not one of them knew who he was. He knew them, however. He chose his madams carefully. They were shrewd businesswomen and excellent spies. Knowledge was power, and Dunlap loved power, even more than money and certainly more than sex.

The music drew to a close and Lady Charlotte dragged him off the dance floor. She had spotted her quarry. They were bearing down on a tall, thin, redheaded girl, half hidden by a small forest of potted palms. Dunlap sighed. He'd known this chore would not be enjoyable. Well, it wouldn't be the first time he'd humped an unappealing female. For a few years while he was growing his fortune, he'd had a side business servicing wealthy, bored wives. He'd screwed everything from young matrons, barely wed, to wrinkled matriarchs. He would get this job done, too.

Sarah hovered by a small patch of palms, waiting for young Mr. Belham to bring her a glass of lemonade. The ballroom at the Earl of Easthaven's house was hot and crowded. She had again danced every dance, but instead of feeling exhilarated, she felt sweaty and out of sorts.

She had barely spoken to James since she'd left him in his study the night of Lizzie's come-out. That was just as well, she reminded herself frequently, but she still felt a distinct hollowness in her middle. She saw him just a few yards away and faded farther into the palms. Mr. Belham might have difficulty locating her, but she'd rather risk that than James snubbing her.

"Think Alvord will offer for the American?"

Sarah froze, then turned her head slowly. A palm frond brushed along her cheek. Her retreat into the greenery had brought her within a foot of a small group of society bucks. If she moved away now, they might well notice her. She would prefer to avoid that embarrassment.

"That's what the odds favor at White's." The man snickered. "Hard to see why the Monk would want to bed that skinny mare."

The other men laughed. "Certainly ain't much to pillow the ride."

"Must like 'em that way. The Wickford chit doesn't have much meat on her bones, either."

"Come on, Nigel! The American has to be warmer than the Marble Queen."

"Hear she ain't warm in the pockets, though. Hasn't got a feather to fly with."

"Alvord's got enough of the ready—don't need a wife to add to his coffers. They're already overflowing."

"True." The first man dropped his voice. "Maybe she's got other, less obvious charms. Suppose she's learned some bed games from those Red Indians? Savages, don't you know. Still part animal, some say."

There was complete silence for a moment. Sarah feared her concealing palms would combust from the heat of her cheeks.

"Do you suppose he'll share? Once he gets his heir, of course," one man whispered.

"Don't know. I'd get in line for her—especially after the Monk teaches her all the tricks he likes. Man must have tried almost everything."

"Heard he had three whores at once—and they weren't skinny bitches, either."

"Three? How was there room in the bed?"

"The whores were the Monk's bed."

"Ah, the Monk's hard cot."

"Ain't the cot that was hard."

"Miss Hamilton."

Sarah jumped. She turned quickly to find Lady Charlotte Wickford looking at her through the palm fronds.

"Uh, hello, Lady Charlotte." Sarah stepped out of the greenery. She was still distracted by the conversation she had just overhead. She hadn't understood everything the men had said, but she'd understood enough.

Lady Charlotte twitched her lips in what passed for her smile. "How fortunate that I saw you hiding in the foliage, Miss Hamilton. Let me introduce Mr. William Dunlap to you. He is a fellow countryman."

"Oh." Sarah looked at the tall man standing next to Lady Charlotte. He was the most beautiful male she had ever seen. He had thick chestnut hair, dark brown eyes, and finely sculptured features. A small scar by the right corner of his mouth and the slightest bump in his otherwise classically straight nose kept his face from being perfect.

"How do you do?"

He took her hand and lifted her fingers to his lips.

"Very well, now. It is so pleasant to meet another American. Would you care to dance, Miss Hamilton?"

Sarah felt unaccountably flustered. There was something almost predatorily male about this man.

"Well, I am waiting for Mr. Belham."

"Here's your lemonade, Miss Hamilton."

Mr. Belham had returned. He was not the most handsome of London bucks in the best of circumstances, but compared to Mr. Dunlap, he was actually grotesque. He looked as though he had been pulled into this world by his nose, with his forehead and chin left to catch up. They had not yet done so. Sarah suspected he was buzzing around her in the hopes of meeting James.

"Mr. Belham," Lady Charlotte said, "how nice to see you. I'll take that lemonade, if you don't mind. Miss Hamilton was just going to dance with Mr. Dunlap."

Mr. Belham's eyes widened and his small chin flapped harmlessly under his prominent nose. The orchestra struck the opening notes of a waltz.

"You go ahead, Miss Hamilton. Mr. Belham and I will have a comfortable coze, won't we, sir?"

Apparently the thought of a comfortable anything with Lady Charlotte Wickford struck poor Mr. Belham dumb. Still, he managed to nod.

Sarah looked back doubtfully as Mr. Dunlap led her onto the dance floor.

"I suspect Lady Charlotte, like many of her friends, doesn't realize that there is a difference between Boston and Baltimore. So, where are you really from, Miss Hamilton?"

Sarah laughed. "Philadelphia. And yourself?"

"New York, but I have been to Philadelphia."

"Alas, you are more well traveled than I. I had never left my city until I boarded the ship for Liverpool."

Mr. Dunlap was an accomplished dancer and an entertaining conversationalist. Sarah enjoyed their set. She hadn't realized how homesick she was for the familiar tones of an American accent. It was a relief to discuss politics with someone who, like she, did not believe in monarchy or primogeniture. Still, there was something about Mr. Dunlap that made her uneasy. He was pleasant, educated, and witty, but she couldn't shake the feeling that his performance was a well-polished act, that his handsome face and cultivated manner were a façade behind which something very different lurked.

She laughed, shaking off her fantasies. If it was a façade, it was a very striking one. Other women were eyeing him and sending Sarah nasty looks. She might as well enjoy their envy until the music stopped.

James was staring, too. She caught his gaze as Mr. Dunlap expertly swung her through a graceful turn. Was he jealous? Good. He had been ignoring her so assiduously, she had wondered if she had turned invisible. She was tired of being the little American charity case.

When the music ended, James appeared by her side.

"Hello, Sarah. Introduce me to your partner?"

There wasn't much else she could do. "James, this is Mr. William Dunlap of New York. Mr. Dunlap, his grace, the Duke of Alvord."

James nodded curtly. "Dunlap. If you'll excuse us, I believe this is my dance?"

Sarah believed nothing of the kind, but she wasn't going to wrestle with James. His gloved hand had already imprisoned hers. She smiled brightly.

"Thank you for a very pleasant dance, Mr. Dunlap. I hope we will see each other again."

* * *

Shit. Dunlap watched Alvord dance with Sarah Hamilton. He hadn't needed an introduction; he knew the duke by sight. Alvord had never visited one of his establishments, but a savvy businessman always knew where the deepest pockets lay.

He also knew where the deepest pitfalls lay, and he was teetering on the edge of one now. He'd known Runyon was lying when he'd said Alvord had a "slight" interest in the Hamilton girl. Slight! Alvord's breeches were bulging with his interest. Dunlap would have been a corpse rotting in a New York alley long ago if he had not learned to tell when a man had staked a sexual claim to a woman. Separating Miss Hamilton from the duke was going to be a very dangerous undertaking indeed.

James breathed in Sarah's sweet scent and his body grew even harder. His gloved hands touched only her gloved hand and the small of her back, but he remembered the soft, heavy warmth of her body in his lap and the gentle curve of her breast in his hand. He remembered the feel of her throat under his lips, the fiery silkiness of her hair brushing his face.

He needed to taste her. She had been so cold to him since Lizzie's come-out. It had been hell. And then to see that Dunlap fellow with his hands on her. God, he couldn't think of the man without an overwhelming urge to rearrange his pretty face.

He had Sarah through the doors and down the steps into a darkened section of the garden before he consciously made the decision to leave the ballroom.

She wasn't struggling. That was a good sign.

He waltzed them in slow circles to the faint strains of music floating from the open windows. The dense foliage managed to muffle the din of the city and shelter them from the worst of the soot and stench. He could almost imagine he was back at Alvord.

Sarah shivered and he urged her closer to his warmth. Warmth? He was more than warm at the moment—and his temperature was definitely rising. His legs tangled in her skirts as his lips found her temple.

"I've missed you, sweetheart." His voice was slightly husky to his own ears.

"Hmm?"

He looked down. Her eyes were closed, her lips curved in a slight smile.

Should he talk to her about that blasted nickname? He didn't understand why it upset her. Why would she care that he had never slept with a woman? Given her reaction when she'd found him in bed with her at the Green Man, she was not partial to rakes. He'd certainly never been called a lecher before—nor been beaten by a naked woman with a pillow. He grinned. Now *that* was an experience he wouldn't mind repeating, with a more satisfying ending. If Sarah wanted him to have some experience, he'd be more than willing to get it with her. Beginning now perhaps.

He had better things to do with his mouth than talk.

Sarah was happy. She was exactly where she wanted to be—in James's arms. Here in the darkened garden, away from the *ton's* prying eyes, she could pretend she was in Philadelphia and James was a nice, solid American.

The air was slightly chill. She shivered, and James's broad hand on her waist urged her closer. She went willingly. She felt sheltered by his large, firm body. Safe. Cherished.

An illusion. He was a rake. He had admitted it, acknowledging without excuse that stupid nickname. Certainly Nigel and the other young bucks by the palm fronds had no doubts concerning James's amatory exploits.

She felt his lips on her skin and heard his voice, deep and husky. She breathed in his scent.

If only he were an American and they were in Philadelphia. He would take her out walking on Sunday afternoons. They would stroll along Chestnut Street or perhaps along the river. He would be polite and proper. He would most assuredly not waltz her into someone's darkened garden and kiss her eyelids in such a disturbing fashion. He would not brush his lips along her jaw, nor lick the spot under her ear, nor suck lightly on the skin there. And surely his hands would stay where they belonged, not wandering to her bottom or tantalizingly close to her breast.

Her body would not ache in this most improper manner if James were a proper American.

He wrapped his arms around her and she felt his hard length from her breasts to her knees. She was forced to put her own arms around his neck or puddle to the ground in a boneless mass.

She moaned, and his tongue slipped past her lips as it had that night in his study, but this time it was not shock that pulsed through her body. It was something else, something hot and hungry. Her head fell back against his shoulder and she opened her mouth wider, letting his silky-rough tongue stroke deep into her, everywhere he wished. Everywhere she wished.

He freed her mouth and she panted into his cravat.

Promenading with a proper, polite American suddenly did not seem so appealing.

James tried to clear the lust from his mind. It appeared Sarah was not going to stop him, so he had better stop himself. He wanted her—God, did he want her!—but not here in Easthaven's garden where any idiot of the *ton* might stumble upon them.

"You'd better go back inside, sweetheart. Alone."

"What?" Sarah blinked up at him, clearly not yet returned from the wonderful, hot place they had been together. At least he hoped they had been there together.

"Go back inside, Sarah." He straightened and held her away from him, looking her over as best he could in the dim light. Fortunately he had halted his explorations before he'd gotten to rearranging her hairstyle or dress. She would do—barely. "I'll stay out here for a while."

"Why?"

Because even if her clothing passed muster, his breeches would proclaim to all exactly what they had been doing in Easthaven's delightfully dark garden.

"Because people might wonder what we had been doing if we came in together, love."

"Oh." If there had been enough light, James was sure he would have seen bright red spots on Sarah's cheeks.

"Slip in the side door, Sarah. It will take you directly to the ladies' retiring room."

"Yes, all right."

He watched her hurry down the path to the door he had pointed to, and then he leaned back against a handy tree trunk. God, he ached. More than just the most obvious part of his anatomy throbbed in frustration. His mind, his heart, maybe even his soul wanted Sarah. If tonight's performance was any indication, she wanted him, too. But would she let herself acknowledge her desires? Would she marry him?

He didn't know.

"Sarah, we were just looking for you."

Sarah stopped inside the garden door. Lady Gladys and Lady Amanda stood in the hall between her and the retiring room.

"Where have you been?" Lady Gladys frowned. "We saw James dance you out the door ages ago. I can't imagine what he was thinking."

"I can." Lady Amanda's eyes had focused on Sarah's neck. "Time to call for John Coachman, wouldn't you say, Gladys?"

"Why? Oh!" Lady Gladys also studied Sarah's neck. "Oh, dear me, yes. We'll get our cloaks immediately."

Sarah glanced in a mirror as she hurried after the ladies. A small red mark glowed brightly on her white throat where James's lips had been such a short time earlier.

Chapter 9

"Lady Gladys, may I have a moment of your time? I wish to discuss my future."

Lady Gladys and Lady Amanda put down their teacups. Sarah had never been in Lady Gladys's sitting room before. It was a pleasant, sunny place, but she was too nervous to pay much attention to decor.

Lady Gladys eyed the high-necked gown Sarah had chosen to wear that morning. It was stylish—and it hid the reddish mark on her throat.

"Seems to me you and James spent some time last evening discussing that topic. I would say the issue was decided."

Sarah wiped her palms on her skirt. It was precisely last night's "discussion" that had prompted her to seek out James's aunt this morning. Any more encounters of that nature and she'd be giving London ladies lessons in wantonness.

"Indeed, miss." Lady Amanda chuckled. "You've got poor James thinking with what's in his breeches rather than what's under his hat. He's usually not so indiscreet. Keeps his amorous interests to the bedchamber."

"Amanda is right, Sarah. James has never singled a young lady out for such marked attention before. Society is taking notice."

"The Duchess of Rothingham certainly is. Has that great beak of hers quite out of joint. Never enjoyed a sight more in my life, I tell you."

"Amanda!"

"Well, it's true. Admit it, Gladys. You're as delighted as I am to see Suzie Bentley in a dither. Why she thought she could foist her brat off on James is more than I can fathom."

Lady Gladys nodded. "She always had rocks for brains. It's no surprise she gave birth to the Marble Queen."

"She was insufferable as a girl, and marrying Rothingham just made her worse."

Sarah tried to bring the conversation back to her problem. "If society is taking notice, Lady Gladys, then so is Mr. Runyon. He does not want his grace to marry."

"Richard doesn't want his grace to live, Sarah, but that doesn't mean James will climb into a grave for him. Don't worry about Richard. James will take care of him."

"But do you think the duke really wishes to marry?"

"Oh, pish!" Lady Amanda flicked her fingers at Sarah. "What man *does* want to marry? I'm sure they'd all like to flit from woman to woman, like a bee in a garden. And James has certainly made it clear that he'd like to sip the nectar of *your* flower, girl. Knows the only way to do that is to marry you."

"But his reputation . . ."

"What reputation? Oh, you mean that ridiculous Monk business."

Lady Gladys turned to stare at Lady Amanda. "What ridiculous Monk business?"

"You know, Gladys. The silly rumors that have James cavorting with half the ladies of the *ton* and all the whores of London."

Lady Gladys snorted. "Are those stories still making the rounds?"

"They get more outrageous each Season."

Sarah felt a rush of relief. "So they aren't true?"

"Oh, I'm sure some of them are, dear." Lady Gladys shrugged. "James *is* twenty-eight."

Lady Amanda nodded. "You must just take them with a grain of salt, Sarah. Why one of the tales has James sailing down the Thames with half a dozen barques of frailty. Have you ever heard anything so ridiculous? I'm sure there couldn't have been more than two or three of the fashionable impure aboard." She paused, tapping her finger to her lips. "Well, three or four. James *is* quite exceptional."

"Quite."

Sarah blinked. Lady Gladys sounded rather proud of James's alleged sexual prowess.

"But James knows what's due his position, Sarah." Lady Gladys smiled. "Don't worry. He'll do his duty and be discreet about his other activities. You won't have cause for embarrassment."

"If you will just decide to let the boy *do* his duty," Lady Amanda said. "Say yes, Sarah, and put him out of his misery. Episodes such as last evening's precipitous trip to the garden delight the gossips, but generally only make men frustrated and out of sorts."

Lady Gladys frowned. "Yes, Sarah, if you don't intend to have James, then you should not be teasing him by disappearing into the shrubbery with him."

"You do intend to have him, don't you, miss?"

Sarah looked back helplessly at the two older ladies. Her feelings were a roiling mass of confusion.

"I don't know."

***

James was just stepping out of his study when Lady Amanda accosted him.

"I don't mean to tell you how to conduct your love affairs, boy, but dragging a virgin into the bushes is not one of your most inspired notions."

"I beg your pardon?"

"Oh, don't poker up, James. You scandalized all the old biddies at the Easthaven do, which would have been fine if you'd gotten a 'yes' out of the girl, but you didn't. Spooked her, more like. Best keep your distance till you can keep your pants buttoned."

"Lady Amanda! You go too far."

"You're the one who went too far. If you're going to kiss the girl, don't leave a mark—or at least not where everyone can see it. Haven't you wondered why Sarah is wearing only her high-necked dresses?"

"You are in for a treat this evening, Miss Hamilton." Mr. Symington tugged on his waistcoat. A futile exercise. It rode back up over his paunch the moment his fingers left the fabric. "Mr. Edmund Kean is reprising his role as Shylock in *The Merchant of Venice*." He leaned closer and patted Sarah's hand. "That's a play by Shakespeare, you know—a very famous English playwright. Dead now, unfortunately."

Sarah gritted her teeth and tucked her hand under the folds of her skirts, out of Mr. Symington's reach. She did wish that he were not so fond of onions. Talking to him was enough of an ordeal without the added trial of breathing in the odor of his last meal.

"Shakespeare's fame *has* spread across the Atlantic, Mr. Symington."

"Really?" Mr. Symington smoothed his three strands

of hair over his pink scalp. "Glad to hear some culture has reached the savages."

Sarah inclined her head and imagined the pleasant thwacking sound her fan would make if she broke it over Mr. Symington's bald pate. She glanced at Lady Gladys for help, but she was talking to Lord Crossland, the elderly peer who had escorted them this evening. Lady Amanda was determinedly studying the other side of the theater. Both ladies were too wily to be trapped into tedious conversation with Simple Symington. Lizzie, sitting next to Lady Amanda, caught Sarah's eye and winked, but made no move to rescue her. Sarah swallowed a sigh and turned back to her companion.

"Kean brought the house to its feet in '14 with his performance," he was saying. He coughed modestly into his hand. "Wasn't there myself. Couldn't come to town. Had to stay in the country with my poor wife."

Poor wife, indeed, Sarah thought. She probably died of boredom, happy to be free finally of her husband's droning voice. She pinched herself for her uncharitable thought, but she feared that many more moments of Mr. Symington's pompous prattle would put her in her own grave.

She looked around the theater. She did feel a bit of a savage tonight. She had never been to a play before. She had heard her students talk of attending Philadelphia's Walnut Street Theater, and she had dreamed of going there herself one day, but she had always known that was a vain hope. Her father and the Abington sisters had no time for such frivolous pursuits.

The grandeur of the room was overwhelming, as was the sound of so many people talking. A noisy broth of people bubbled in the pit, while rows of boxes filled with elegantly attired chattering ladies and gentlemen rose to the ceiling. It seemed that no one but herself was quiet. She tried to keep one ear tuned to Mr. Symington's remarks as she admired the women in their colorful dresses, jewels, and plumes and the men in their black coats and white cravats.

Her eyes froze on one man in a box directly across from her. James, who had been too busy to escort his family to the play, was sitting between Lady Charlotte Wickford and the Duchess of Rothingham. As Sarah watched, James said something, his head close to Lady Charlotte's. Lady Charlotte laughed and tapped his arm playfully with her fan.

Sarah heard a sharp snapping noise. She looked down into her lap. Her own fan was in two pieces.

James's arm stung where Lady Charlotte had hit it. That was the twelfth time she had punctuated a comment with her fan. Why she thought that action was endearing was beyond him. He would have moved farther away from her, but he was trapped by the duchess on his other side. Outflanked by the enemy—an embarrassing tactical defeat for a former officer.

At least he had a good view of his own box and Sarah. He would never tire of looking at her. Tonight she was wearing a dark blue gown cut low over her bosom. He let his eyes linger where his hands itched to go—over her beautiful reddish hair, caught up to show the lovely angle of her jaw and the seductive curve of her neck, over her delicate shoulders and her creamy white skin, down to the dark line of her dress where it skimmed the tops of her small, perfect breasts.

He wanted to be over there, sitting in the chair that Symington occupied. He wanted it so much he ached.

Everywhere. He shifted position to take some of the pressure off his desire. That was why he had to stay away. Much as he had hated to hear Lady Amanda's words, he had to agree they held a modicum of truth. It had been a colossally stupid thing to do, taking Sarah out into Easthaven's garden. He might just as well have made love to her on the ballroom floor under the *ton's* avid eyes.

A strangely appealing thought. The ballroom floor, that was, not the spectators. Making love to Sarah in any location would be heaven. He found himself spending much of his day imagining the act in detail. And his nights . . . well, he was not sleeping much.

Charlotte said something and he murmured a noncommittal reply. He spared her hand a glance. It hadn't moved. If she hit him one more time with her bloody fan, he swore he would grab it and hand it back to her in pieces.

He chuckled inwardly, watching Sarah struggle to be polite to Simple Symington. Symington had foisted himself on her just moments after she'd stepped through the box's door. He must have been lurking by the theater entrance, waiting for her to arrive. Poor girl. It was clear the man wanted a new wife and had selected her as a feasible candidate. What a crashing bore. Sarah would have to be a bedlamite to accept an offer from him.

James saw her smile and look over her shoulder. Someone new had entered the box. A tall, athletic-looking man with thick chestnut hair. William Dunlap.

Bloody hell. James felt no desire to chuckle now. He watched Dunlap skillfully maneuver Symington into giving him his seat. Then he sprawled in the chair, barely within the bounds of propriety, his long legs bumping into Sarah's skirts. Somehow, his arm came to rest on the back of her chair. James's eyes narrowed as he watched one of

Dunlap's long fingers brush the warm, smooth skin of Sarah's shoulder. She flushed, shifting forward in her seat. Dunlap laughed and withdrew his arm. James clenched his fists. God, if he weren't on the other side of the damn theater, he'd grab the American by his elegant cravat and toss him into the pit.

The play began, but James was far more interested in what was going on across the theater than in any of the action on stage. Dunlap was certainly more of a threat to his interests than Symington. He had the advantage of being American, as well as being damn good-looking. Still, there was something off about the fellow, something dangerous. Did Sarah feel it, too, or did she just see Dunlap's pretty face?

He should warn her to take care. She was new to Society, and she had led a very sheltered life. He was certain she had never dealt with a man of Dunlap's stamp.

James shifted his attention to the stage. Shylock was brandishing a butcher knife, passionately demanding his pound of flesh. James eyed the long, sharp blade. He'd like a pound of Dunlap's flesh—and he knew just what part of Dunlap's anatomy he would excise. The man had best keep his hands to himself if he didn't want to be singing in a higher key.

He would see if he could take Sarah aside for a moment tonight, after they had all returned. It was his duty, really. A few moments in his study. A girl could easily be led astray by a polished rake like Dunlap.

* * *

"Sarah, a moment if you will."

Sarah stopped with her foot on the first stair. James was standing in the doorway to his study. She certainly was not going into that room alone with him again.

"James." Lady Gladys stopped also. "Did you enjoy the play?"

"It was tolerable. I need to speak with Sarah for a moment, Aunt."

"Sarah's been keeping very late hours." Lady Gladys turned to her. "It's been a long day. Do you wish to stay up?"

"No." Sarah definitely did not want to stay up with James, especially after he had spent the evening with Charlotte Wickford. "I really am very tired."

Lady Gladys linked arms with her. "Then perhaps we'll see you in the morning, James."

James leaned against a stone column at Lady Wainwright's ball and stared at Sarah dancing with Dunlap. He frowned. It had been a hell of a week. He had not been able to get Sarah alone to talk to her. For some blasted reason, his aunt and Lady Amanda had become exemplary chaperones.

Well, perhaps he knew the blasted reason, but they wanted him to marry her, didn't they? How was he going to persuade her if they weren't going to give him any time alone with her?

He really had been very persuasive at the Easthaven ball. A few more minutes and he would have persuaded her out of her gown.

"Oh, your grace, how delightful to see you! I don't believe we've had a moment together since that night at the Drury Lane theater."

James looked down and tried to smile. "Hello, Lady Charlotte."

"I see you are watching Miss Hamilton and Mr. Dunlap. Don't they make a lovely couple?"

James grunted. Lady Charlotte apparently took this for assent.

"I introduced them, you know. They are both from the colonies. It seemed a perfect match."

James had never wanted to do physical violence to a woman before, but the thought of twisting Charlotte's smug little smile off her face was quite appealing.

"You introduced them?"

"Yes, indeed."

"I confess I don't know much about Dunlap. What can you tell me of his background? Since Miss Hamilton is staying under my roof, I feel some responsibility for her, you understand."

Lady Charlotte shrugged. "Well, I can't tell you much, really. Your cousin, Mr. Runyon, might know something. It was he who introduced Mr. Dunlap to me."

Alarms clamored in James's head as his body surged away from the wall. He took a deep breath. "I see. Perhaps I will have a word with Richard."

James did not find Richard, but he did see Sarah returning from the ladies' retiring room. He grabbed her hand, pulled her into a deserted room, and closed the door.

"James! What's the matter?" Sarah looked around the small sitting room. "Are you mad? If we are found in here, you'll have to marry me."

James wasn't listening. He put his hands on her shoulders and pulled her close. He breathed in her sweet scent. God, he wanted to . . .

He dropped his hands and stepped back.

"Stay away from Dunlap."

Sarah blinked, and her brows drew together. "I beg your pardon?"

"Stay away from Dunlap."

"He's the most beautiful man in that ballroom, and he is interested in me. Why should I stay away from him?"

"He's not interested in you, Sarah."

Sarah's cheekbones suddenly seemed tighter, and her eyes narrowed. "Oh, he's not, is he? I'm not attractive enough to hold his attention, I presume?"

"No!" James tried to shake the lust from his brain and think clearly. This conversation was going all wrong.

"You think I could only be of interest to the Belhams and Symingtons of your world, the scavengers who pick through the dregs of the Marriage Mart?"

"Sarah—"

"Mr. Dunlap is very charming and I will dance with him if I want to. Don't try to stop me, your grace."

"God!" James had had enough. His hands shot out almost by themselves. He grabbed Sarah's shoulders and pulled her hard against his body. His mouth came down to stop her acid words. His tongue flashed in on her gasp of shock and plundered her sweetness. He felt her sag against him and his hands slid down her back to cradle her bottom. He brought her closer against the part of him that ached so badly for her.

"God." He let her mouth go free as his lips traveled down over her soft skin to nuzzle her ear. "God, Sarah."

She stiffened and shoved hard against his chest.

"Stop mauling me." There were tears in her eyes. "Leave me alone."

His hands dropped to his sides, and she rushed out of the room.

***

Damn! James stood where he was, trying to rein in his emotions. That was as impossible as controlling a high-strung, unbroken thoroughbred. The moment he wrestled his breathing under control, another memory of Sarah—how she felt, how she tasted—would send his blood pounding wildly again.

He had to get away. Outside. If he didn't leave immediately, he was going to explode and he wasn't sure what form that explosion would take.

He nodded to acquaintances and put off friends as he wound his way to the front door and freedom. The *ton* might have its tongues wagging over his precipitous exit, but it couldn't be helped. As long as no one attributed his turmoil to Sarah, he didn't care. The blades and biddies could speculate all they wanted, with his blessing.

He snatched his hat and walking stick from a footman, and the poor fellow almost leapt out of his skin to open the door for him. James didn't even try to nod at the man. Best take himself out into the night where he belonged, where he could dissipate his feelings without harming anyone. He strode down the pavement, eager to put as much space between himself and Lady Wainwright's townhouse as possible.

But he couldn't put space between himself and his thoughts.

God, what was he to do if Sarah formed a *tendre* for Dunlap? He couldn't let her marry the man. He couldn't let her marry any man other than himself. If he did—the thought opened a black pit deep in his soul.

He slashed at an innocent fence with his walking stick. The clang of the contact was lost in the creak of waiting carriages, the jingle of harnesses, and the drone of coachmen's conversations, but a stray dog heard and darted into an alley.

James picked up his pace. He needed to get control of himself. He was a man, a soldier, not some sensitive Tulip to wallow in a morass of emotion.

He turned a corner, careless of his direction.

He should be the one to marry Sarah. He was the one who had compromised her. His honor demanded marriage.

He wished some misguided denizen of the dark would decide he was an easy mark and invite him into a fight. It would be a relief to release some of his tension through his fists.

He was not so lucky. The streets were uncommonly quiet.

At least he could investigate Dunlap. He should have done that the moment the man had stepped over Easthaven's threshold. He had the resources, the connections to discover anything he needed to know. Hell, if Dunlap had a freckle on his ass, his men would find it. Tomorrow morning he'd have a long overdue word with Walter Parks.

After she left James, Sarah fled back to the retiring room. Thankfully, it was empty.

She pressed her gloved hands to her flushed cheeks. She didn't know herself anymore. How could she have said such terrible things to James? Anger had never loosened her tongue in the past. But then she had never felt such a bewildering torrent of emotion in the past.

And why had James kissed her right after she had ranted at him like a fishwife? She dropped her head into her hands, covering her eyes. It had been more an assault than a kiss—and how her treacherous body had craved it! She could still feel the mark of his fingers and palms on her bottom, the rough invasion of his tongue in her mouth. Her knees wobbled and she sat down abruptly.

Mr. Dunlap certainly never made her feel this way.

"Miss Hamilton. Sarah." Major Draysmith bowed. "May I have the next dance?"

"Of course, Charles." Sarah smiled. She had not seen James or Mr. Dunlap since she'd returned to the ballroom. She was relieved. Her nerves could not have survived a dance with either man. But Charles would not try her precarious emotional calm.

She was mistaken.

"Sarah," Charles said as he led her onto the dance floor, "where is James?"

She stumbled and Charles caught her arm to steady her.

"I don't know. He was here just a short time ago."

Had he rushed off to maul some other female? Sarah was certain any number of society women would welcome James's attentions. Mrs. Thorton was missing tonight—had James left the ball for her bed? Or was he in Lady Cresten's room? Her scantily clad figure was also missing this evening.

"Have you settled on a date yet?"

"A date?"

"For your wedding."

"Charles, you know a duke can't marry an American."

"Why not? James has offered, hasn't he?"

"Well, yes."

"So what's the problem? He doesn't care about rank. Is it you who does? You won't have him because he is titled?"

"No." Sarah swallowed. Just the mention of James

made her flushed and achy. Her emotions were so disordered, she was afraid she would burst into tears in the middle of the ballroom. "Please, Charles, can we just dance?"

"All right, but Robbie and I mean to get to the bottom of this. If you won't tell us the problem, we'll ask James."

"Don't do that!"

Charles gazed down at her. "Why not? Sarah, I'd give my life for James. I want to see him happy."

Does no one want to see me happy? Sarah swallowed the words. They were childish but true.

She was alone. She must not forget that. Lizzie and Lady Gladys were James's family, not hers. Lady Amanda, Charles—even Robbie—cared first for James. They knew him.

She was the stranger—to them and to their ways. She was American, not British. She wanted love and fidelity, not rank and wealth.

But what was love? She hadn't spent much time pondering that question in the past. Something pure and selfless? Or the hot, breathless neediness that consumed her whenever James touched her?

She and Charles finished their dance in silence. She barely noticed when he bowed and departed, she was so lost in her thoughts.

Could she be happy with James? No, it was impossible. He was a duke; she was a republican. He was a libertine; she was not . . . yet. But if she kept company with him much longer . . . She closed her eyes in embarrassment—and saw the image of James's lovely naked chest.

"You are looking a little lonely, Miss Hamilton."

"Mr. Runyon." Sarah preferred her isolation to *his* company.

Richard held out his hand. "Come."

"I'm a little tired. I believe I'll just stay here, but thank you anyway."

Richard kept his hand extended. Sarah heard the chaperones start to whisper. She looked over. They were staring at her with bright eyes, like feral dogs scenting blood.

"Very well."

"Wise choice, Miss Hamilton. You don't want those harpies eavesdropping on our conversation," Richard said as the music began.

"No?"

"No." He looked around the dance floor. "I don't see Cousin James."

"He was here a little while ago. I'm sure he's sorry he missed you."

"I doubt it." He jerked her through a turn. She narrowly managed to avoid bumping the couple next to them. "I assume you've taken my warning to heart, Miss Hamilton."

"Excuse me?"

"About James's single state. Surely you remember? I thought that was the reason James was not sniffing around your skirts."

Sarah stared back into Richard's cold eyes. "I see your manners have not improved, Mr. Runyon."

His lips moved upwards in a parody of a smile. "My manners are the least of your concerns, Miss Hamilton. You just be sure to keep your legs together around my cousin."

Sarah knew she was gaping. Fortunately, her feet moved to the music automatically.

"You *have* stayed out of his bed, haven't you?" He

studied her face. "You still have the look of a virgin. Am I right?"

"Mr. Runyon!"

"Must be. You couldn't fake that shocked expression. Take a breath, Miss Hamilton, and listen carefully. It is definitely in your best interests to stay a virgin, at least where my cousin is concerned. Trying to become a duchess would be a very *grave* mistake."

At that, Richard dropped his hands and walked off the dance floor, stranding Sarah in the middle of the ballroom. The other couples, the sharp-eyed young girls and their foppish partners, swirled around her. She heard their sniggering and whispering, felt their gloating eyes. The hundreds of candles flickering throughout the room in the chandeliers and wall sconces could well have been the fires of hell.

She wondered if she would ever waken from this nightmare.

Robbie and Charles found James at White's the next week.

"Gentlemen," James said, putting down his newspaper, "to what do I owe the pleasure of your company?"

"It ain't a pleasure, Alvord." Robbie took the chair across from him. "Damn, you look like *hell*."

"Thank you, Robbie. Always complimentary. Do you have some observations of a personal nature to make also, Charles?"

Charles dropped down into the seat next to Robbie. "He's right. You *do* look like hell."

James bowed his head in acknowledgment. "I shall take due note of my declining physical state." He picked up his newspaper. "Don't let me keep you from your engagements."

"That's exactly it, James," Charles said. "Why isn't there an engagement?"

"I beg your pardon?" James looked at them over the edge of his paper.

"Now don't go all ducal on us, James," Robbie said. "Charles is right. I thought you were getting engaged to my cousin. Honor requires it, don't you know."

"I will not discuss Miss Hamilton."

"You damn well will discuss her or I'll be meeting you at dawn."

"Robbie," Charles said, "lower your voice. I don't think we need to make your cousin's troubles the talk of White's any more than they already are."

"Damnation." Robbie looked around. The other men in the room were studiously reading their newspapers, ears cocked in their direction. He lowered his voice. "Look, Alvord, while you've been making yourself scarce, the damn *ton* has been tearing Sarah apart. Your bloody cousin left her in the middle of the dance floor at Wainwright's last week, and even that American— Dunlap—ain't around much anymore."

"Robbie." James shut his eyes.

"What's wrong, James?" Charles said. "All of what Robbie says is true. I thought you cared for Sarah."

James took a deep breath and let it out slowly. "Gentlemen, you have delivered your message."

Robbie gaped at James. "That's all you have to say?"

"That's all I *can* say."

"You're not going to tell us what is going on?"

"No."

"Well, dammit, James, at least promise to see her.

Come to the Palmerson do tonight. Sarah will be there. See for yourself."

"Robbie . . ."

"No, I'm not going to let you out of it. Charles and I will find you and drag you there if need be, right, Charles?"

Charles nodded. "We have to know that you've seen her for yourself, James. If you still want to go on as you have once you've seen her, well . . ." Charles spread his hands. "I can't believe you could be so cold, but at least I'll feel like we did our best to bring you to your senses."

"Do we have your word that you'll be there?" Robbie asked.

James sat still, then nodded once. "It will not make any difference, but I will come."

"Good. Come on then, Charles, let's get out of here."

James did not watch Robbie and Charles leave. Instead he took the note he had received after the Wainwright ball out of his pocket. He opened it, but he didn't need to read it. He had memorized the words:

> *Miss Hamilton says she is still a virgin. Since her continued good health depends on her maintaining that state, you would be best advised to avoid her.*

The note wasn't signed, but James recognized Richard's writing.

Damn. He'd thought Richard was a danger only to him, but if he were threatening Sarah . . .

Had Richard murdered Molly, the girl at the Green Man? And that girl back at University, the one they had fished out of the River Cam, her neck broken—had he killed her, also? James had discounted the rumors then. Perhaps he had been wrong to do so.

And Dunlap—who the hell was he? He was obviously connected to Richard in some way, but he was proving to be an extremely elusive fellow. Parks had not been able to gather any definite information on him yet.

He felt so bloody powerless. He'd put men to trailing Richard. He'd sent Parks and his associates out to scour the seedier sections of London. He'd hired a couple of Bow Street Runners to keep an eye on Sarah.

And now he'd follow this damn note's dictates until he had a clearer view of Richard's plans.

He didn't want to stay away from Sarah. He didn't want to let her out of his sight—not ever. He wanted to guard her day and night. Especially at night. In bed. He'd cover her sweet body with his. To keep her safe, of course.

He crossed his legs and turned to the financial page, making certain the newspaper covered his lap. God, to be sitting in the middle of White's on St. James's Street, probably as far from any female as possible in London, and *still* grow hard thinking of Sarah.

He made himself focus on the solid numbers. He would go to Palmerson's tonight. He had given his word. If he didn't go on his own, Robbie would find him and drag him there anyway. And truly he was starved for a glimpse of Sarah. Maybe he would see a way to bring an end to this agony.

"Lady Gladys, I really don't feel up to going to the Marquis of Palmerson's tonight," Sarah said. "I have a headache."

"A headache?" Lady Gladys put down her sewing and frowned.

"Balderdash." Lady Amanda pointed her needle at Sarah. "Stiffen your spine, girl. Don't let a bunch of old fools keep you from going about."

Sarah sighed. "Lady Amanda, I have stiffened my spine till I think it will shatter. I wish you and Lady Gladys would just concentrate on finding me some employment. I'm sure I could be a companion, if not a teacher."

"I thought I had already found you some employment, Sarah, as companion to my nephew."

"And I thought your nephew was not such a cod's head." Lady Amanda clipped a knot. "When I told him to be more circumspect, I didn't mean for him to vanish."

"You spoke to his grace?"

"After the incident in Easthaven's garden, I did."

"Oh, no." Sarah closed her eyes.

"I'm not certain that was the best idea, Amanda."

"Someone had to speak to the boy. He was making micefeet of things."

Sarah sat quietly next to Lady Amanda in the carriage on the way to Lord Palmerson's townhouse.

"Should be quite a crush." Robbie's voice was a trifle too hearty. "I'm sure *everyone* is going to be there."

"I suppose you mean James will make an appearance?" Lady Gladys sounded skeptical.

"Said he would, didn't he, Charles?"

"Yes. He promised he would come."

"Did he say why he's been avoiding us?" Lizzie asked.

"Well, no, can't say that he did." Robbie coughed. Sarah felt his eyes on her. "Something important, I'm sure. You know how James is."

"Not anymore, I don't," Lady Gladys said.

Sarah wanted to seep into the carriage cushions.

Lady Amanda leaned over and patted her hand. "Don't worry, dear," she whispered. "Everything will work out for the best."

Sarah appreciated Lady Amanda's gesture, but she didn't take much comfort from her words. Her only solace was that soon the ladies would have to give up their plans to marry her off to James.

"Miss Hamilton, so glad you could come." Lady Palmerson made a show of looking behind Sarah in the receiving line. Robbie was greeting her husband. "And the Duke of Alvord? Is he out of town?"

"I don't believe so." Sarah kept her voice level.

"No? So odd—he had become such a regular at the Season's entertainments, we had come to expect him." Lady Palmerson's faded blue eyes sharpened. "He is rather conspicuously absent, is he not?" She might as well have licked her chops, she was salivating so over the juicy morsel of gossip she sniffed in James's absence.

"I believe he may look in tonight," Robbie said, disengaging his hand from Lord Palmerson's flaccid grasp.

"Really? How delightful. I will look forward to seeing him."

And to seeing what a stir his presence will cause, Sarah thought as she entered the ballroom on Robbie's arm.

She danced the opening set with Robbie. She felt she did a good job of ignoring the sideways glances, the muffled giggles, and the whispers and murmurings. She kept smiling, even though her stomach was knotted into a hard ball.

She sat out the next two sets. The Duchess of Rothingham condescended to keep her company for the last of those.

"I don't see the duke here tonight."

Sarah tried not to sigh. Or to scream. "I don't believe he has arrived yet."

"Oh, is he coming then?"

"I really can't say. My cousin, Westbrooke, says so."

The duchess adjusted the ruffle on the low neck of her dress. "I thought you were staying at Alvord House."

Sarah gritted her teeth. "I am."

"And you don't see the duke to speak to? How odd."

"He's very busy. I'm really here to keep his sister, Lady Elizabeth, company."

"Oh." The duchess smiled. "I see."

"My dance, I believe?"

Sarah had never been so delighted to see Charles. She turned to the duchess and forced a smile to her lips. "Excuse me, please."

The duchess inclined her head.

Sarah danced twice with Charles and once more with Robbie before Mr. Symington presented himself. As he steered her clumsily around the perimeter of the dance floor, she scanned the ballroom. James still had not arrived. She swallowed her disappointment. She *knew* she should not have listened to Robbie when he'd said James would come. More, she should not have allowed herself to hope James would take her in his arms and waltz her past the nasty little gossips of the *ton*.

The music ended. Sarah smiled at Mr. Symington, but he was looking over her shoulder at someone entering the ballroom.

The couples around her began to murmur, their eyes darting from her to the new arrival. The tide of whispering rushed outward to the farthest corners of the room.

Sarah closed her eyes briefly, swallowed, and then turned. The entire room held its breath.

She looked directly into James's eyes. She might have seen a flash of warmth there, but it was gone before she could be certain.

He turned away, inclining his head to Lady Palmerson. "I'm sorry I'm so late."

"Quite all right, your grace," Lady Palmerson said, shooting Sarah a look of wicked glee. "We're happy you could come at all."

Simple Symington stared, goggle-eyed, at James's retreating back.

"Please excuse me." Sarah kept her head up and walked slowly over to where the chaperones were sitting. She felt every eye on her, heard the murmuring *ton* relish her humiliation. Well, she would refuse to look humiliated. She lowered herself into a chair. Her eyes were on the dance floor, but all she saw was James's face.

She felt a gentle hand on her knee. She glanced to her right, but Lady Amanda was already moving away. She watched her cross the room and stop to whisper something in Mrs. Fallwell's ear. Mrs. Fallwell's head came up like a startled deer's. Her glance darted to Sarah, then she turned and said something to Lady Amanda. Lady Amanda smiled and shrugged.

Robbie came to collect his second dance. "I'm so sorry, Sarah," he said quietly as he bowed over her hand. "I asked James to come tonight. I never thought he'd treat you this way."

"It's all right, Robbie." Sarah did not want to talk about James. She did not have that firm a grip on her composure, and she knew everyone was watching her to see when she would break. She did not want to give them that satisfaction.

"I'll call him out, I swear, and put a bullet through him." Robbie grimaced. "If I can. The blood—blasted man's a crack shot."

"Don't, Robbie." Sarah was touched that her cousin cared about her enough to confront his friend. It made her feel less alone. "You know I always said I couldn't marry James."

"Well, I don't see why you can't. It would be the best thing for both of you."

Mercifully, from Sarah's perspective, the music began and she and Robbie were separated by the patterns of the dance.

Afterwards, Robbie returned her to her seat. The women near her moved, whispering and throwing her sidelong glances. If she had felt shunned before, she now felt like a true pariah.

She watched James dance with Charlotte Wickford. They made a lovely couple, if one were fond of statuary. Lady Charlotte might be a good match for James in rank and background, but a marriage between them would be a disaster. James's face held none of the warmth and humor she remembered from their weeks at Alvord.

She sighed. It was time for Mr. Symington to claim his second dance. She saw him approaching and tried to smile. Then Lord Stevenson, the biggest prig she had ever met, stopped his progress. She was not disappointed. Every moment Mr. Symington was delayed was one less moment of his boring monologue.

Lord Stevenson kept talking. Mr. Symington looked over. He said something to Lord Stevenson and the other man nodded. Then Mr. Symington shook his head and turned away.

How odd. Sarah was relieved not to have to listen to him go on about his children and grandchildren, but he had never missed a dance before. Perhaps an emergency had occurred. But no, he didn't leave the ball. He asked Mrs. Lombard to partner him.

Sarah sat alone through three more sets. Finally, she decided she had earned a retreat to the ladies' retiring room. She had no trouble making her way around the crowded dance floor. The knots of people parted like the Red Sea to let her pass. She sighed with relief when she stepped into the hall and out of the *ton's* view. She hoped the retiring room would be deserted.

She was not in luck. Just as she was about to enter, she heard the distinctive nasal tones of Lady Felicity Brookton, possibly her least favorite of the girls making their come-outs. Sarah drew back, hoping Lady Felicity would leave soon.

"She was stark naked!"

"Really?" Sarah couldn't place the second voice. It was breathless with a horrified excitement. "And Alvord?"

"Naked, too." Lady Felicity dropped her voice. "They were in bed together."

"No!"

"I'd like to see Alvord naked," said a third voice.

"Julia!" There was a great deal of giggling.

"Well, I would. Those shoulders! Those legs!"

"You shouldn't be thinking about such things!" said the second voice. Then all three girls went back into a fit of giggles.

"I can't believe she has the audacity to show herself among polite company." That was Lady Felicity again. "Lady Gladys must not know."

"I hear they do things differently in the colonies," Julia said.

"What, they allow their whores into society?" Lady

Felicity laughed. "Well, I suppose the men might like that, but you'd think the women would protest. I certainly would."

The girls—Lady Felicity, Miss Julia Fairchild, and Lady Rosalyn Mannerly—came out of the retiring room and saw Sarah. Their jaws dropped in unison so that they looked like three beached fish. Sarah would have found the spectacle funny, had she not misplaced her sense of humor. Then Lady Felicity snapped her teeth shut, put her nose in the air, and pulled her skirts back so they would not touch Sarah as she walked past. The other girls followed.

Sarah barely saw them. She was struggling to get a breath. Her head spun. She braced herself with one hand on the wall.

The story of the Green Man was out. All those people in the ballroom were talking about her and James, speculating about them, imagining they knew everything that had gone on between them.

Suddenly, the retiring room was not far enough away. She needed to get outside. A group of men blocked the front door, so she darted into the ballroom. People stepped out of her way, but this time she didn't notice. Her sole focus was the door to the garden and freedom. She had to get out of the suffocating heat and smell of the *ton,* out of the bright light and into the anonymous darkness.

Chapter 10

Dunlap had had a rough week. Unpleasantness was crowding him from every direction. He had been slipping out doorways and around corners, avoiding Runyon and Alvord. Runyon wanted Miss Hamilton raped immediately, and the bloody evidence of the deed displayed on the door to Almack's. Alvord wanted Dunlap's balls strung from the Tower. His spies had been sniffing much too close to Dunlap's carefully guarded business interests.

He would have avoided the Palmerson affair altogether if he could have. Unfortunately, Runyon had gotten wind of the fact that he had not attended the last few *ton* events. He had sent him a pointed note, threatening to give his name and direction to the Earl of Lugington immediately. Lugington was not a gentle, understanding man. Dunlap did not want to be buried in English soil.

He heard the rumor that Miss Hamilton and the Duke of Alvord had been cavorting naked at some inn the moment he stepped through the door. He was skeptical. He could have sworn the girl was a virgin—that innocent look was too hard to fake. He should know, he'd tried to train countless whores to mimic it.

But he also knew how these swells operated. True or not, the rumor had ruined the girl, so Alvord would marry her. Dunlap had just run out of time. Runyon would get his wish. Whether Miss Hamilton was or was not a virgin now, she definitely would not be one by the end of the evening. Alvord would have to postpone his nuptials at least three or four months if he wanted to be certain that his heir was his own, and not a cuckoo sown by an American whoremonger.

A lot could happen in three or four months. The world was a dangerous place.

Dunlap saw Sarah hurry down the hall and dart into the ballroom. He followed her. He watched her go out into the gardens, then he slipped outside himself.

James saw Sarah rush past. She had the look of a sol-dier emerging from a death-drenched battle. He nodded at Colonel Pendergrast, no longer listening to him. He had to follow her, but he couldn't be obvious about it. He looked over the heads of the crowd and spotted Robbie.

"Excuse me, Colonel. I see someone I must speak to. So sorry." James detached himself from the old jaw-me-dead and tried to work his way through the crush. Normally his size and rank caused people to step aside, but now he felt as if he were swimming through quicksand.

He noticed other oddities. All conversation stopped as he approached and resumed as soon as he moved away. Gaggles of young ladies blushed and giggled when he looked at them. Mrs. Sparks, a widow notorious for her accommodating morals, winked and pulled her bodice lower when she caught his eye. Damn. Something was very wrong.

"Alvord!"

James cringed. He recognized Featherstone's gravelly,

rough whisper. The man had been a dirty dish even at Aunt Gladys's come-out.

"Featherstone," he said, swallowing his impatience.

"Jolly good joke, old chap."

"Indeed?" James's tone could have frozen hell, but Featherstone was not very perceptive.

"Foisting your whore on society! Heard you even got the gal vouchers for Almack's—that's one for the record books. Bet old Silence Jersey is beside herself." Featherstone wheezed in what James took to be laughter. "But since it looks like you're finished with her, I'll be happy to take her off your hands. Won't be squiring her to respectable balls and such, of course. Ain't quite the thing, don't you know. Surprised Gladys and Amanda put up with it, unless you had them fooled, too?"

James felt an overwhelming urge to grab Featherstone's scrawny neck and wring it like those of the chickens he'd dispatched many times for supper on the Peninsula. He flexed his fingers. Some of his feelings must have shown on his face, because Featherstone stepped back.

"No offense meant, old man," Featherstone gabbled. "Thought you was done with her, that's all. If you're not, well, then, there's no more to be said, is there?"

"Featherstone," James began, but stopped when he felt a hand on his shoulder. He turned to see Robbie.

"James, you'll have to kill this fellow later. I need to talk to you."

"Yes, right, don't want to detain you." Featherstone's hands fluttered about his cravat like elderly sparrows. James ignored him. He pulled Robbie toward the doors to the garden.

"What the hell is going on?" James kept his voice low. It was clear that everyone within earshot was listening. "I saw Sarah leave the ballroom a few minutes ago. We need to find her."

"Damn right we do."

James and Robbie stepped out onto the terrace.

"The story of the Green Man is out, James."

"Damn!" James looked around, but the terrace was deserted. "Where the *bloody hell* is Sarah?"

Robbie put a hand on James's arm. "I'll go look for her."

James shook him off. "No, we'll both go. Do you know if Dunlap is here?"

"The American? I think I saw him a moment ago. Why?"

"He's my charming cousin's accomplice. Come on. We have to find Sarah quickly." James took the steps down into the garden two at a time.

Sarah barely saw the garden. She ran down the paths through the darkness, away from the lights, away from the eyes, away from the sniggering. Her thoughts were as thick and tangled as the greenery.

How had the story of the Green Man gotten out after all this time? Had someone recognized her? Why had he—or she—waited until now to speak? She was already firmly on the fringes of society. Why would anyone want to push her beyond the pale?

Was this Richard's work? But he must know that the story would force James to marry her. That was the last thing Richard wanted.

It was certainly the last thing James wanted. Sarah thrust aside a low-hanging branch. It should be the last thing she wanted, too, but disgust at the thought of tying herself to a rake was not one of the feelings churning in her stomach. Where was her self-respect? Gone, apparently.

She stopped near a large tree at the far corner of Palmerson's garden. She put her hand on the solid trunk and drew in a deep breath. She had to think, but her mind refused to function. She kept hearing those tittering young girls, kept seeing the disdain on their silly little faces. They were only seventeen, pampered and protected by their rich, influential papas. What did they know about anything? Why should she care what they thought?

It wasn't what they thought—it was what the entire ballroom thought. Sarah moaned, laying her head against the tree trunk. How was she ever going to find the courage to go back into that house?

"Ah, Miss Hamilton. So nice of you to pick the farthest, darkest section of this lovely garden."

Sarah's head shot up. Standing just three feet from her was William Dunlap. He looked . . . different. The beautiful face now held a threat. Her heart slammed into her throat. She took a deep breath and dug her fingers into the rough bark. She could not faint. She had to be alert.

"Mr. Dunlap." She was happy to note that her voice was steady. "I'm sorry, but I prefer to be alone at the moment."

Dunlap sighed. "I'm afraid, Miss Hamilton, that your preferences no longer matter."

"What . . . what do you mean?" Sarah stood up straight and balanced forward a little on her toes. The only path of escape was past Dunlap and he could stop her just by lifting a hand.

He came closer. Sarah kept herself from backing up. She didn't want to be caught against the tree trunk.

"There is something about this whole situation that doesn't ring true. I don't know what it is, but I trust my instincts." Dunlap shook his head and shrugged. "Well, it doesn't matter. I can't take chances. My associate insists on certainty, I'm afraid."

He reached out and grabbed Sarah's shoulders. His fingers dug into her skin. She could smell the wine on his breath, but he was cold sober.

"I regret that circumstances require me to rape you, Miss Hamilton." His right hand hooked her bodice and jerked down. There was a sound of cloth ripping and the cold night air hit her skin. He took one of her breasts in his hand and squeezed. Sarah felt tears sting her eyes.

"I really don't care for skinny girls. Their sharp bones dig into me like the lumps in a cheap whorehouse mattress. I'll just have you against this tree, shall I?"

Sarah screamed. Her knee flew up and connected with the soft tissue between his legs. His hands left her and he grabbed his groin.

"You bitch!" He had more curses, but Sarah didn't wait around to hear them. She picked up her skirts and ran.

James was frantic. Palmerson had the largest, darkest bloody garden in London. There was no sign of Sarah.

"Robbie, you go that way. I'll go this way. Yell if you find her."

"Won't that attract some attention, James?"

"I don't care if you wake the dead in Westminster Abbey, Robbie. I want to bloody know if you find Sarah."

"Right."

The men split up. James strode down one dark path and then another. At least he didn't flush any lovers from the bushes—everyone was too damn entertained inside, shredding Sarah's character. Blast it, where *was* Sarah? He felt like he'd been searching for hours. *Think,* he told himself. *Keep calm. She's only been out here a few minutes.*

He wished he didn't know how much damage a man could do to a girl in just a few minutes.

Then he heard the scream. He started running before the sound had faded. *Just let me not miss her,* he thought. The garden was so bloody dark.

He saw a figure running toward him. A woman, hair down around her shoulders, white skin, torn dress—and then she was in his arms and he was holding her tight. She struggled.

"Shhh, Sarah. It's James. You're safe now."

"Thank God," she whispered and buried her face in his shirt.

"James!" Robbie came running up. "Did you hear—" he broke off when he saw Sarah. "Is she all right?"

"I think so. She came running from that direction." James pointed with his chin. "My guess is it's Dunlap. I need to go after him." He bent his head. "Sarah, Robbie is here now. Stay with him, will you?"

Sarah shook her head and buried deeper into his shirt. Her arms snaked around his back and locked together. It would have taken some force to detach her. James didn't want to hurt her, but he couldn't let Dunlap get away. He looked at Robbie.

"I'll go. If that bastard has hurt her, I'll kill him."

"No, Robbie, I will kill him. But first we have to catch him."

"Right. I'll be back."

Robbie ran off. James bent his head to whisper in Sarah's ear. "Sarah, love, you need to let go of me. I'm not going anywhere. I just need to get my coat off so I can cover you with it. Your dress is badly torn, sweetheart."

Sarah gulped and nodded. She loosened her death

grip, but still stood very close. He shrugged out of his coat and put it around her shoulders. The front of her dress was down to her waist, her pale breasts and darker nipples completely exposed.

It was too dark for James to see how badly hurt she was. He didn't want to question her and shatter the fragile hold she had on her emotions. That would have to wait until they got home.

"Put your arms in the sleeves, love, and I'll button the coat up so you're covered."

She obeyed automatically.

Robbie came back then. "The bastard got away. He was just going over the wall when I got there."

"We'll find him later." James put his arm around Sarah, pulling her close again. "I don't suppose Palmerson's garden is the best place to deal with the situation, anyway."

"No, it's not." Robbie nodded to Sarah. "Is she all right?"

"I think so, but she obviously can't go back into the ballroom. Could you tell John Coachman to wait for us at the corner? I'll take Sarah out the back gate and down the alley."

"I'll tell him."

"Don't tell the others though. I'm sure enough people will notice that Sarah and I are both gone, but it might help if the ladies stay and act as if nothing untoward has occurred. You'll see them safely home later?"

"Of course." Robbie glanced worriedly at Sarah. "Do you think that bloody bastard did more than tear her dress?" he asked under his breath. Sarah didn't indicate that she had heard him.

"I don't know, but I will find out. Don't worry. I'll take care of her."

James guided Sarah to the back gate. The moon lit a path down the center of the alley. She still hadn't spoken, but he wasn't worried. She was using all her energy to hold herself together.

John Coachman was waiting for them on the street. James handed Sarah up and then climbed in after her. She sat stiffly on the edge of her seat. He didn't try to touch her but sat quietly watching her, waiting for the coach to make the short journey to Alvord House.

Wiggins met them at the door.

"Bring some warm water, cloths, and salve," James told the butler.

"Yes, your grace."

James hurried Sarah into his darkened study and settled her in his big upholstered chair. Then he went to the cabinet to get the brandy. He poured two glasses and brought one to her. Pulling up a footstool, he sat in front of her.

"Drink this, Sarah." He wrapped her hands around the glass. "It will help."

"Here are the items you requested, your grace," Wiggins said from the doorway.

James kept his eyes on Sarah. "Thank you, Wiggins. Put them on the desk, will you?"

Wiggins paused. "Do you require any help, your grace? I'm sure Mrs. Wiggins would be happy to assist Miss Hamilton."

James frowned. Sarah still had not taken a sip of her brandy. "No, Wiggins, we are fine. Just close the door behind you when you leave."

James waited until he heard the quiet click of the door shutting.

"Drink some brandy, Sarah."

She put the glass to her lips and took a sip. She sputtered and choked, but her eyes had more life to them.

"One more sip, sweetheart, and then we need to talk."

Sarah swallowed another mouthful before James took

her glass and gently pulled off her gloves. He held her hands in his. Her fingers felt like ice.

"Sarah, I'm sorry to have to ask you, but I need to know. You mustn't be afraid to tell me." James forced down the fury that rose in him as he looked at Sarah's face. If Dunlap were in the room now, he would be dead. But Sarah had had enough violence tonight. She did not need to hear anger in his voice. He spoke quietly. "Did Dunlap rape you?"

"No!" She shook her head frantically. "He, he grabbed me. He t-tore my dress." She closed her eyes. "He t-touched me." Her chin started to tremble. She opened her eyes again. She looked lost, like a child in the grip of a nightmare.

James gathered her close. Her arms went around his neck; her face buried into his cravat. He lifted her up, sat down in the chair and settled her on his lap. Her whole body was shivering. He wrapped one arm tightly around her waist and cupped the back of her head with his other hand, holding her face to his chest, resting his lips on her hair.

Sarah sought warmth. She was so cold. She was shivering inside and out. Her teeth chattered and her stomach clenched and jumped. She could not get warm. She felt as if even her fingernails were cold and tight.

James sat with her as he had the night of Lizzie's come-out ball, but this time he just held her. At first she was frantic for him, for the strength and safety he promised. She buried her face in the soft warmth of his shirt. His heat surrounded her. His chest pillowed her cheek, his arm supported her back, his breath stirred her hair. She would have climbed inside of him if she could have.

She was tired of being alone. She was tired of trying to be strong. She pressed her cheek tighter against James's chest and listened to the steady, calming beat of his heart. She breathed in the warm, familiar scent of him and felt his hand moving over her scalp and down to her neck, slowly stroking her hair. His voice rumbled under her cheek. She didn't try to understand the words. She just wanted to *be* with him, not to think or to feel, but just to know that he was there, close around her, making her safe. Slowly the fear drained out of her and James's warmth seeped in. Her muscles relaxed.

"Tell me what happened, sweetheart."

She shook her head. She didn't want to remember the ugliness. Putting it into words might make it real again.

"Tell me, Sarah. Trust me, it will be better to get it all out. Then the hurt won't fester." His big hand wove through her hair, his fingers rubbing the base of her skull. "You've been in a battle, love, just like in war, and the men who talked most about the battles they were in, about the horrors they'd seen, were the ones who got free of the violence."

Sarah shuddered. "He was so much stronger than I," she whispered, feeling the helplessness again.

James's hands tightened on her. He too was stronger than she was, but his strength was reassuring, not frightening.

"I knew I had to get away or he would do something terrible. He was going to push me up against a tree. I would have been trapped. I couldn't have moved him."

James's hand kept up its gentle stroking. "But he didn't trap you. You got away. How did you do it, love?"

"I kneed him."

Sarah could feel James smile against her hair.

"Good girl. Who taught you that trick?"

"My father. He said if I ever was caught by a sailor on the wharves, I should drive my knee up between his legs as hard as I could and the man would let me go. It worked."

James chuckled. "Believe me, sweetheart, it will always work."

"At first, I didn't think I could do it, but then I had a flash of panic and my leg moved without my thinking."

"Good for you. Robbie and I heard you scream, but it might still have taken us a few minutes to find you." James's hand paused in her hair. "Why were you in the garden, Sarah?"

Sarah turned her face into his chest again. Her words were muffled in his shirt. He felt her lips move, felt the warmth of her breath through the fine linen on his chest.

"Everyone knows about the Green Man, James."

"I see." He resumed his rhythmic stroking of her hair. She was stiff with tension again. "You know what that means, don't you?"

Sarah hunched one shoulder and kept her face in his chest. He smoothed her hair off her forehead.

"It means, sweetheart, that now we have to marry. I will send the notice out tonight so it makes the morning papers."

"No."

"Yes." James tried not to let the pain he felt at her refusal show in his voice. Her feelings and his were immaterial now. "It will silence the gossip, Sarah. I've already had one old roué ask me if I were done with you. If the announcement of our engagement doesn't appear tomorrow, all the rakes and riffraff will think they are free to proposition you."

Sarah shuddered. "All right." Her voice was small and toneless.

James frowned. An engagement would stop the gossip, but it would enrage Richard. Once the notice appeared in the papers, there was no way James could honorably call off the wedding. The deed was as good as done. His—and Sarah's—lives were about to get exceedingly more dangerous.

Anger and frustration surged through him and his grip on Sarah tightened reflexively. She whimpered, and he loosened his hold.

"Did Dunlap hurt you? I can't do much about bruises, but I have this salve that should help with any cuts."

"I think his ring scratched me when he tore my dress."

Sarah's face was still buried in his chest, but James could not remember seeing any marks there. The scratch must be hidden under his jacket. Perhaps Dunlap's ring had caught her on the neck or upper arm.

"Do you want me to have a look?"

She sat completely still for a moment; then her head nodded slightly.

"Yes," she whispered. She sat back a little in his arms and started to undo his jacket. Her hands shook too much for her to manage the buttons. James gently brushed her fingers aside and took over, moving slowly so she could stop him if she wanted. When he finally had the buttons all undone, he folded back the coat.

A long, angry red scratch ran from her collarbone to the tip of her left breast. James reached for the cloths Wiggins had brought. He dipped one in the water and gently stroked it down the scratch.

"Does that hurt?" Even he could tell that his voice was huskier than usual. Sarah shook her head. Her eyes were huge in the firelight. He put the cloth down and dipped his index finger in the salve. Slowly he rubbed thick ointment into Sarah's soft skin, from collarbone down to the tip of her breast. In the light he could see that a bruise was beginning to form. He skimmed his thumb over the spot.

"He hurt you here, too."

"He grabbed me." Sarah's voice was barely above a whisper. "He said I was skinny. He said he was going to take me against a tree so my sharp bones wouldn't dig into him."

James looked into Sarah's eyes and saw the question there. He held her injured breast gently in his palm. He felt the sweet weight, the gentle give of flesh so different from his own.

"You are beautiful, Sarah. I would love nothing more than to have you beneath me, but on a large, soft bed."

"Other women have more . . . bigger . . . don't you want . . ."

"I want you, Sarah. Only you."

James let his fingers carefully explore the treasure in his hand—the rounded underside, the smooth slope tapering to the darker circle at the tip, the hard little nipple at the center. He heard Sarah draw in a breath when he touched her there. He let his thumb rub back and forth, and the little nub got harder and stiffer. Like a part of his anatomy, he thought, smiling.

Sarah's breath came in little gasps and she squirmed on his lap. Heat flooded him. He wanted to see how this small part of her tasted. He wanted to put his tongue where his thumb was, to flick that hard little nub with moisture. To take her into his mouth.

He did not hear the click of the study door opening, but he heard the sharp, indrawn breath, the one that had not come from Sarah.

"It looks like we can finally set a wedding date," Aunt Gladys said.

Chapter 11

The announcement that James William Randolph Runyon, Duke of Alvord, was to marry Miss Sarah Marie Hamilton of Philadelphia appeared in the morning paper. Betty delivered it with Sarah's chocolate.

"We're all that happy, miss," Betty said, setting the tray on the table by Sarah's bed. "I'll tell ye, we've been right worried, but all's well that ends well, I always says."

"Umm." Sarah stared down at the paper. She had slept like the dead, too exhausted by the emotional storm she had weathered to have nightmares. In fact, the events of the previous night now seemed like a bizarre dream. The horror of Dunlap's roughness and the heat of James's gentleness were equally unreal.

She took a sip of chocolate, running her fingers over the words of the announcement. How would she feel if this were a normal engagement? Excited? Wildly happy? But it wasn't a normal engagement. She hadn't been asked; she'd been told. No, not even told. Propelled by forces outside her control, like a ship before a gale. And if she were honest, there was a different kind of gale within her propelling her toward this marriage, sweeping all rational thought away before a storm of feeling whenever James touched her.

She closed her eyes and leaned her head back against

her pillow. He had had his hand on her naked breast. Her whole body flushed in an agony of embarrassment. The heat that surged through her pooled low in her stomach, throbbing in the strange, new way that was becoming all too familiar. She didn't know herself anymore. She must be ill. A brain fever, perhaps. She certainly felt feverish.

Thank God James's aunt had blocked Lady Amanda and Lizzie from seeing into the study.

She put her cup down and closed the paper.

How did James feel? He had said he wanted only her. Did he mean it, or was that something he told all women? She supposed it could be true—at any one moment he might want only the woman he was with. If he was with only one woman, Sarah thought, remembering the gossip of Nigel and his cronies at the Easthaven ball.

"Sarah!" Lizzie burst into the room. "I saw the paper! Why didn't you tell me you and James were getting engaged?"

"Good morning, Lizzie," Sarah said weakly.

"You sly thing! Here we were, worried that you and James had had a falling-out, and you two go and get engaged." Lizzie flopped down on the foot of Sarah's bed. "What happened last night?"

"Which part of last night?"

"All of it! When did he propose? How did he propose? Tell me everything."

"Certainly you heard the rumors in the ballroom?" Only the dead could have missed them, Sarah thought.

"Well, yes, I heard them. It's amazing how quickly a story can get out of hand. Did you know that people were saying you and James were *naked* and in *bed* together?"

Sarah blushed furiously. "Yes."

"So that was why James proposed?" Lizzie sounded

very disappointed. "Well, at least he gave you the Runyon engagement ring, didn't he?"

"Well, no. Things happened rather quickly."

"Oh." Lizzie flipped over on her back and stared up at the ceiling. "Who do you think spread the story?"

"Richard saw me with James at the Green Man. Maybe he was the one."

Lizzie shook her head. "That doesn't make much sense. Richard doesn't want you to marry James, but he must know that James would be honor-bound to marry you if word got out that he had ruined you."

"He *didn't* ruin me!"

Lizzie turned her head to look up at Sarah. "It doesn't matter what he did, Sarah. The story has ruined you—or would ruin you, if James weren't marrying you. But he is so, voila," Lizzie snapped her fingers, "you aren't ruined."

"Wonderful. I feel *so* much better."

"So, Walter," James said, "tell us what you have discovered about William Dunlap."

James gave his full attention to the little man on the other side of his desk. Walter Parks had been an excellent soldier and now he was an excellent shadow. He had grown up poor in Tothill Fields and had learned early on how to be unobtrusive. James wished he could say it was sheer brilliance on his part that he had recognized the man's special talents when Parks had been hauled before him for stealing from a fellow soldier, but it was luck. He'd had no stomach for a thrashing and so had assigned Parks to make restitution by acting as the wronged soldier's servant for a week. The two soldiers had ended up friends and James had won Parks's loyalty.

"William Dunlap," Parks said. "A businessman, yer

grace. His birth is murky, don't ye know, but I gathers he was spawned in a New York brothel. Howsoever that might be, he got into the flesh trade early, first as a worker, if ye will, and then as an owner."

"A worker, Walter? I don't suppose you mean he helped with the upkeep of the place, do you?"

"Naw. Ye know there's men who likes boys. Ye seen enuff of that in the army, right? But Dunlap was a smart lad and saw how the thing should be run. Now he's got whorehouses in New York and Lunnon and other places."

"An enterprising man, Mr. Dunlap," Robbie said. He was lounging by the mantle, his hands stuffed deep in his pockets.

"That's right, m'lord. Only, he got into a spot of trouble a year or so ago. Details ain't quite clear, but Chuckie Phelps, the Earl of Lugington's heir, ended up dead in Dunlap's Paris house. Had his pants down around his ankles and Dunlap's drawers around his neck."

Robbie straightened. "Good God, man, how could they tell?"

" 'Bout the drawers?" Parks shrugged. "Guess lots of coves has seen Dunlap with 'em on or off, whichever. They're rather special—red silk, with his initials embroidered all over. WAD—middle name's Anthony."

"Bloody hell. And this vermin was dancing with my cousin? How did he get through the friggin' doorways of half the *ton?*"

"Richard probably got him the first invitation. He *is* quite an attractive adornment to a gathering—from the purely physical point of view." James nodded and stood up. "Thank you, Walter. You've been invaluable, as always." He took a generous purse from his desk drawer and offered it to the man.

"Huh, yer grace. Ye know I'd do anything ye asked fer nothing."

"Yes, Walter, I do know that, but this is business, too, and you have to eat, right? Take it, please, and continue to keep your eyes and ears open. Now that Miss Hamilton and I are betrothed, I'm very much afraid my cousin will intensify his efforts to do me mischief."

Parks reached out and took the purse, hefted it, and tucked it inside his shirt. "That be true, yer grace. I'll keep an eye out and have all me friends on the lookout too, but ye watch yer back as well and that of yer lady."

"I shall, my friend. Believe me, I shall. I want nothing to happen to Miss Hamilton."

"Except a wedding and a bedding." Parks grinned. "I do wish ye well, yer grace. Ye deserve happiness and I'm thinking ye'll find it with yer Miss Hamilton."

James rubbed the back of his neck. "I hope so, Walter. I sincerely hope so."

James turned to Robbie as soon as the door closed behind Parks.

"I'm going out tonight to look for Dunlap. Do you want to come along?"

"Of course. I'd love to get my hands on the bugger."

"I have first dibs, Robbie. If there's anything left of him when I'm finished, you may have your turn."

Robbie shrugged. "All right, if you insist. I guess a betrothed's claim trumps a mere cousin's. When do we leave?"

"After the Hammershams' recital."

Robbie held up his hands as if to ward James off. "The Hammershams?" he said, a distinct note of alarm in his voice. "Ain't they the spotty, caterwauling twins?"

James laughed. "I'm afraid so. However, I know I can count on you, even at such a cost."

"But why the Hammershams, James? Take pity on my ears!"

"Because, as painful as the Hammershams' musical efforts are, the recital will be the perfect place to introduce Sarah as my betrothed. I want to make an immediate public appearance to scotch any rumors."

"I guess you're right. Don't want to give the tabbies any time to sharpen their claws." Robbie sighed. "Well, I'm off to rest up for the excitements of the evening. Gads, I never thought I'd willingly torture my hearing with the Hammershams." He paused in the entrance hall.

"New footmen?" he asked, looking at the two men standing there. One was over six feet tall, with shoulders as wide as a door and hands the size of melons. The other was shorter but beefier. His cauliflower-shaped nose looked as though it had been on the receiving end of one boxing punch too many.

"Temporary hires, I hope. Both are also connected with Bow Street."

"Runners, eh? So you finally convinced Bow Street to take you seriously?"

"No." James snorted. "They still think I'm an old soldier who sees phantom enemies behind every bush, but they are willing to humor me, for a price."

"Like the color of your blunt, do they?"

"Precisely." James shrugged. "But what they think makes little difference. I'm happy. Jonathan and Albert are both quite competent."

"Don't think I'd care to meet them in a dark alley." Robbie collected his hat from Albert. "See you tonight."

Sarah was coming down the stairs as Robbie was leaving. She froze when she saw James. She would have turned around and retreated to her room if Lizzie hadn't put her hand on the small of her back and pushed her forward.

James glanced up and saw her. "A moment, Sarah, if you have the time."

"Lizzie . . . " Sarah began.

". . . will see you later," Lizzie finished. She laughed and slipped past Sarah.

Sarah stood still, looking down at James. She remembered the touch of his hands so clearly her breasts tingled. He waited for her, and finally she descended. He gestured her into his study and closed the door behind them.

"We need to talk."

Sarah nodded. She stared at James's intricately folded neck cloth.

"Sweetheart, my cravat is not that interesting." The edge of his hand gently tilted her face up. Her eyes met his. He was frowning.

"Are you haunted by last night? Did you have nightmares?" His thumb rubbed lightly over her cheek. "I'm so sorry, love, that you had to endure Dunlap's attack. I won't let it happen again."

Sarah's hands twisted in her dress. "No, it's all right. I slept well last night."

The line between James's eyes deepened. "You aren't afraid of me, are you, Sarah? You must know I would never hurt you."

"No." Sarah could only whisper past the lump that suddenly appeared in her chest. "No, James. I'm not afraid of you."

James's hand dropped abruptly. "Do I need to apologize, then? Did my touch insult you?"

"No! I'm, I'm just a little . . . overwhelmed this morning, I guess."

He studied her face; then he nodded. "It has been a rather intense time, hasn't it? And you haven't even been properly proposed to."

Sarah flushed. "Well, the evening did end somewhat awkwardly."

James grinned. "I'll say. I thought Aunt was going to birch me. I can't say I relished feeling all of nine years old again. Did she give you a scolding?"

"Not really. I'm sure she didn't want Lizzie to know exactly what had been going on in your study."

"I should hope not!" James frowned. "Lizzie had better not allow such liberties or I'll be giving *her* a birching!"

"Oh? And so why is it all right for me to . . ." Sarah's indignation quickly died in embarrassment. "To . . . you know."

James grinned. "I do know, sweetheart. If I were your brother, I would probably lock you in your room. But I'm your betrothed, not your brother. It is my goal to take as many liberties as possible."

"James!"

"No, not now, alas. I'm afraid Aunt Gladys and Lady Amanda will be keeping a close eye on us until the wedding—though if we are clever and not *too* indiscreet, I imagine we can manage to steal a kiss or two."

He opened a drawer in his desk and drew out a little box. "As you say, last night ended a little awkwardly. If we hadn't been interrupted, I would have given you the Alvord engagement ring." He grinned. "Well, perhaps not. I wasn't thinking very clearly. I had too many beautiful distractions."

Sarah flushed as James's gaze traveled slowly from her lips to her breasts. Then he took her left hand in a strong clasp and slipped a ring on her finger. It was a simple band, a single emerald flanked by two diamonds. Beautiful. Elegant. A lie.

She should tell him that she couldn't marry a rake. She would tell him now, if only she could get the words past her lips.

"And I'm certain that even the strictest chaperone would agree it is appropriate for a newly betrothed couple to exchange a kiss, wouldn't you say?"

"Um?"

James did not wait for a more coherent reply. He brushed his lips across her mouth.

It was the lightest touch, but she felt it in her soul. An odd little whimper of need slipped from her, calling his mouth back to hers.

She was dying of thirst and he offered her moisture. She drank greedily, even dipping her tongue past his lips. He growled, sucking her deeper into his hot, wet mouth.

She was on fire. Flames lapped up her thighs, across her belly, over her breasts. She needed his mouth in those places too, though whether his touch would soothe or burn, she couldn't say. She just knew she needed him with a hunger she had never felt before.

His hands pressed her against his hardness. They slipped up her sides to cup her breasts. His thumbs teased her nipples through her muslin dress. It was not enough. She wanted to feel his fingers on her naked flesh.

There was a banging on the study door.

"James, if I come in there now, will I be scandalized?"

"Just a minute, Aunt."

"Only a minute, James."

Sarah gaped up at James. Even the threat of his aunt's appearance could not douse the fire in her veins.

He had turned her into a wanton.

She saw him swallow. His breathing sounded as fast and heavy as her own as he straightened the neck of her dress.

"Remember, a *short* betrothal," he whispered. "A very short betrothal."

His aunt rattled the doorknob.

"Come in, Aunt. Your sensibilities are safe."

James sat at his desk after Aunt Gladys had taken Sarah off shopping for her trousseau. He contemplated pouring himself a stiff brandy. How was he going to survive to his wedding? It wasn't Richard's plotting that concerned him now, but his own body.

He hadn't slept well. When he'd closed his eyes, all he had seen were Sarah's beautiful, creamy skin and her small, firm breasts with their slightly darker, delicate nipples. He had felt their gentle weight and warmth in his hands. When he had managed to get that image out of his mind, it was replaced by her flushed face, her small gasps of passion. He had wanted to taste her skin again, breathe her sweet smell, run his fingers over the silk of her shoulders. His blood had felt molten, heavy, ready to erupt.

It was a good thing that his aunt had interrupted them this morning, or he would have anticipated his wedding vows on the floor of his study. It was clear Sarah would not have stopped him—and he was afraid he could not have stopped himself.

Aunt Gladys and Lady Amanda had better prove to be very good chaperones.

Chapter 12

"The bloody bastard's *engaged* to the whore!" Richard threw the newspaper across the room. It fluttered to the floor at Philip's feet.

"There's a difference between engaged and wed," Philip said quietly.

"The only friggin' difference is time, which we seem to be running out of!" Richard glared at Dunlap. "*You* were supposed to take care of this, you incompetent ass."

"*I* did not spread the juicy rumor throughout Palmerson's ballroom that the duke had been cavorting naked with his charming American whore."

Richard pushed the remains of his breakfast out of his way. "How the *hell* could you have failed to rape that skinny bitch?"

Dunlap shrugged and picked an imaginary bit of lint off his breeches. "I'll not fail again."

"You'd better not. I'll be damned if James gets an heir before he gets a gravestone." Richard drummed his fingers on the table. "No, I think it is time to return to my original plan. It yields a more permanent solution."

"You want me to have the girl killed?"

"No, I was thinking of something more permanent than that."

Dunlap frowned. "What's more permanent than death?"

"Nothing, you imbecile. *Whose* death is the issue. Kill the girl and there is a chance that someday James will find another. Kill James and I become Duke of Alvord now."

"You want me to have Alvord killed?" Dunlap shifted in his seat.

"No, I want you to kill him yourself."

"Are you crazy?" Dunlap surged out of his chair. "I can't kill the Duke of Alvord."

Richard shrugged. "You have the reputation of being good at what you do. So far you have not demonstrated your competence, but I am willing to give you another chance."

"I'm good at being a brothel keeper. I am not a murderer, for God's sake."

"The word on the street says differently."

Dunlap shook his head, raising his hand in dismissal. "Exaggerations and lies, some fostered, I admit, to make my business associates think twice before crossing me."

Richard smiled—a cold, unpleasant expression. "Not quite. There *is* Chuckie Phelps. And Tom Bellington of New York City, Walter Cunningham of Boston, Pierre Lafontaine of Paris."

"You *have* done your homework." Dunlap ran a hand through his hair. "Chuckie was an accident. The others— those were in my early days, when I was establishing my business. I haven't murdered anyone in years."

"Well, then, this is your opportunity to brush up on your skills."

"No, I—"

"Yes," Richard interrupted. "You will dispatch James to the hereafter promptly or you will be seeing caricatures of Chuckie Phelps with your oh-so-distinctive drawers around his neck everywhere you turn in London. The Earl of Lugington will be most interested to discover the identity of the man who murdered his heir."

Dunlap scowled. "You need to give me some time."

"Some. Not much. I expect to be attending my dear cousin's funeral within the fortnight."

Sarah faced the front steps of the Hammershams' townhouse with a queasy stomach. She dreaded having everyone stare at her. Last night had been horrible. Tonight should be better—being a duke's intended had to be better than being a duke's whore. James had assured her that the ring on her finger would silence all gossip. Perhaps. Sarah suspected she would still be the subject of speculation.

"Courage," James whispered, putting her hand on his arm. She leaned gratefully into his strength for a moment and was rewarded with a warm smile.

"You don't think people will quiz me about the Green Man?"

"They don't dare. No one wants to antagonize the future Duchess of Alvord. If anyone is bold enough to ask, you must just pretend to be deaf or stare at them as if you cannot believe such an asinine comment came from their lips."

"We call it 'coming the dook,'" Robbie said. "It's quite a sight. Something will annoy James and just like that," Robbie snapped his fingers, "he'll turn all stiff and cold."

"His voice freezes you dead," Lizzie added. "You feel like a noxious, ugly, slimy sort of bug and you just want to crawl back under a rock."

"Lizzie!" James laughed. "I'm sure I have never behaved in such a way, and certainly not with you."

"Remember when I was fourteen? It was just after you got back from the Peninsula. I went riding one morning without telling you or Aunt Gladys."

"Hmm. I *was* a little angry."

"A little? Brrr. I'd hate to see you really angry, then. I stayed out of your way for days, James, truly."

"Well, you never went out without telling us again." James started up the stairs to the Hammershams' door.

"If you ask me, it's bred into him," Robbie said, following behind with Lizzie. "It's a natural reaction. He doesn't think about it."

"I don't believe I asked you, Robbie. And surely earls can be just as stiff-necked as dukes."

"No, you're wrong there, James. Got to be at least a duke. An earl can freeze some mushrooms, but it's a frost compared to an ice storm."

"Ridiculous!" James smiled down at Sarah as he stood aside for her to precede him into the house. "If I had such power, I'd turn Robbie into an ice sculpture."

"A donkey?" Sarah asked.

"That's the polite term."

Sarah handed her wrap to a footman and followed James to the music room. The place was exceptionally crowded. The smells of candle wax, perfume, and unwashed bodies hit Sarah in the chest. That, and the hundreds of eyes that turned her way as she stepped over the threshold on James's arm.

"My, my," Robbie whispered over Sarah's shoulder. "The Hammersham gals have gotten quite popular."

"Alvord!" A short, elderly man dressed in the height of last century's fashion yelled at James. "Good to see you."

"Hartford," James shouted back. "Let me make known to you my betrothed, Miss Sarah Hamilton from Philadelphia. Sarah, the Duke of Hartford."

"Your grace." Sarah curtseyed as best she could. The man had to be close to eighty years old and deaf as a post. Any conversation would be carried on loudly enough for the people in the far corners of the room to hear.

"Pretty, very pretty. Had to go to the New World to find a suitable female, hey, Alvord?"

"Sarah is also the cousin of the Earl of Westbrooke. She came to her family here in England when her father died."

"Westbrooke, you say? Here, ain't that young West-brooke hiding behind you? Well, that's good. Blood's blue—not Red Indian. Can't have the future Dukes of Alvord descended from savages, can we?"

There didn't seem to be much to say to that. James inclined his head. Hartford didn't take the hint.

"Lusty wench, too, I hear."

Sarah stood stiffly as the old man examined every inch of her.

"Looks pretty cool, but those are the best, ain't they, Alvord? Cool on the outside, hot-blooded on the inside. Had a mistress like that once. Looked like an ice queen till I got her between the sheets. Then she couldn't get enough of me. Never slept when I visited that piece, I tell you."

If Sarah's blood hadn't been hot before, it certainly was now. It roared in her ears and turned her face bright red. She wished the floor would open up and swallow her.

"Hartford, you forget yourself." James's tone did sound glacial.

"Don't go prudish on me, young fella. I got the same thing buttoned up in my breeches as you do. Ain't so old that I've forgotten what it's for." The old man chuckled. "Haven't forgotten at all. Why just last night . . ."

"Yes, well, excuse us, Hartford. Need to take our seats."

James headed for the chairs set up at the other end of the room, tugging Sarah along behind him.

"Got long legs," Sarah heard the Duke of Hartford say as she hurried after James. "I like long legs in a gal."

"Sorry," James muttered. "Hartford thinks that age forgives all sins. Let's sit over here. It looks like the sisters are ready to begin."

Sarah glanced back at the Duke of Hartford. He was looking down some young girl's dress. "What do his children think of him?" she whispered.

"He hasn't any, though it sounds like he's still trying."

"At his age?" Sarah stared at James. She really was fuzzy on the details of procreation, but it certainly seemed that a man the age of the Duke of Hartford should be finished with such pursuits.

"He's old, sweetheart, not dead." James smiled in a way Sarah could only describe as wolfish. "I hope that I'm as, um, healthy when I face eighty."

Thankfully, the Hammersham sisters began to sing at that point. After a few notes, Sarah realized that their voices were nothing to be thankful for. Not only could they not carry a tune, they couldn't find one between them. The audience, welcoming a reprieve from the auditory torture, clapped enthusiastically whenever the girls paused.

"Not much longer before intermission," James whispered. "We'll drink a glass of punch and then we'll go. I think we've accomplished tonight's objective of silencing the gossips."

Sarah smiled up at him as though he had promised her salvation. He had to admit as Miss Elvira Hammersham hit a particularly sour note that the quiet of his waiting coach did seem like heaven.

He was proud of Sarah. It had been a trial for her to

come out after last night's horror. She had shown true courage.

He was also proud she was his. Hartford was an idiot, but James had felt a jolt of satisfaction that the old man envied him his woman. God, how primitive! But he felt primitive when he thought of Sarah. The possessiveness and protectiveness that he had always felt for Alvord, he now felt for her. He needed her in his bed, yes, but he needed her in his life as well.

The people around him were clapping. The Hammershams must have finished. He took Sarah's elbow and helped her to her feet.

"Shall we seek the refreshment room and then gather Robbie and Lizzie and escape?"

"Yes, please."

Sarah's eyes were green tonight, he noted, and her skin was cream-colored in the candlelight. He wanted to kiss her right in front of the entire *ton*. He leaned forward slightly, imagining the splendid scandal it would cause.

"James?" There was a slight note of alarm in Sarah's voice.

He straightened and placed her hand on his arm. "Let's go and see if the punch has been worth this punishment."

Sarah sipped her drink. If she had to face one more fawning male or simpering female, she was going to be violently ill. It was a wonder the *ton's* heads didn't fly off their shoulders, they spun their faces so quickly. As Miss Hamilton she had been met with condescension, suspicion, or indifference. The duke's whore was greeted with horror and disdain. Now, as James's betrothed, she was receiving a heaping dose of toadying.

She didn't know how she'd managed to be civil to

Lady Palmerson. At least Lady Felicity and her friends had had the sense to stay away.

"Sarah!" Major Draysmith greeted her with a grin. "I was delighted when I read the announcement in the papers this morning. I'm so glad you and James worked out your differences."

"Thank you, Charles." This was definitely not the place to go into the details of her hasty engagement.

Charles moved on to congratulate James. Sarah felt a light touch on her shoulder and turned to face Lady Charlotte Wickford.

"Hello, Lady Charlotte." Sarah thought her voice sounded pleasant enough, if a little cautious. The other girl smiled.

"I just wanted to congratulate you on your betrothal."

"Thank you."

"There was a time when the betting had Alvord offering for me."

"Oh?" Sarah couldn't see any signs of heartbreak in the other girl, but perhaps Lady Charlotte just hid her feelings well. "I'm sorry if you've suffered a disappointment."

Lady Charlotte laughed. "Oh, dear, don't worry that I nurse a broken heart! I confess I would have loved to be a duchess, but I had already decided that the cost was too high."

"The cost?"

Lady Charlotte stepped closer and lowered her voice. "Sharing the Monk's bed. I decided I couldn't do it."

"Lady Charlotte!" Sarah looked around quickly. No one was close enough to hear.

"They say Alvord doesn't keep a mistress, because no one woman can satisfy him. He picks his partners from the rougher brothels to find enough variety for his taste."

Lady Charlotte's eyes had a hot glint in them. She moistened her lower lip. "Is it true? Is he insatiable?"

"Lady Charlotte!" Sarah's head was beginning to throb.

"What's your secret? Did you learn it from the American savages? Is that how you got Alvord to offer for you?"

It was clear Lady Charlotte did not think Sarah's magic lay in her looks or personality.

"Whatever it was, it must have been quite spectacular to capture the Monk's jaded interest."

"Lady Charlotte, I don't know what you are talking about. I'm sure James has always behaved as a gentleman." Sarah would not dwell on the episode in Lord Easthaven's garden or the activities in James's study. "I hope you are not spreading malicious lies about him."

"Oh," Lady Charlotte said, smirking, "it's a love match, is it? On your part at least. I don't believe dukes marry for love." With that, she nodded and moved off into the crowd.

Sarah stared after her. She wanted to tell the little brat that dukes did too marry for love, but she knew that would sound extremely childish. And she was very much afraid that the other girl was right in this case.

"Sarah."

James was smiling down at her. He frowned and studied her face.

"Are you all right?"

"I'm just a little tired."

"We can leave now, if you like."

"That would be wonderful."

Lizzie and Robbie shared the carriage home with them, so there was no opportunity for private conversation. Sarah was relieved. She closed her eyes and rested her head against the squabs—and saw Charlotte Wickford's cold little face again. She squeezed her eyes tighter and shook her head slightly, rubbing it against the smooth leather of the seat.

She could not imagine James in the same room with the whores she had seen on the Philadelphia docks or in her father's infirmary—the thought of him in the same bed was inconceivable. But then, what did she know? Nothing. No, less than nothing. She could not imagine any man touching the painted, pox-marked women who sought help in her father's office, yet obviously many men had touched them. She swallowed a hysterical giggle. They had done much more than touch, though what exactly they had done was still a mystery to her.

Sarah turned her head to gaze out the window. She twisted the Alvord engagement ring so that the emerald dug into her palm.

How could she marry a rake?

How could she not marry James?

James watched Sarah climb the stairs to bed. Something was bothering her, that was clear. However, he had no time tonight to discover the problem. Tonight he intended to locate Mr. William Dunlap.

When he and Robbie climbed into a hackney a short time later, they were no longer attired in eveningwear. They would still pass for gentlemen, but their boots, dark breeches, and dark cloaks blended into the shadows and enabled them to move at a considerably faster pace than that required to cross a dance floor or fetch a glass of lemonade.

They headed east, along the Strand and Fleet Street toward the City. Shortly before they reached Bridewell Prison, James directed the jarvey to turn into Red Lion Court. They clattered down the narrow street and stopped in front of a rundown building. The weather-worn sign proclaimed it the "Spotted Dog."

"Ye want I should wait, yer lordships?" the jarvey asked as James and Robbie climbed down.

"Come back in an hour," James said, throwing the man a coin.

"You think we'll find Dunlap here?" Robbie sounded skeptical.

"No." James surveyed the battered door. "But I'm hoping we'll find the trail that leads us to him." He shoved open the door and stepped inside.

The smell hit him first—the smell of ashes, spilled ale, and too many men crowded together. It could have been the Dancing Piper, and he could have been sixteen years old again.

But he wasn't sixteen, and after the initial shock, he certainly felt the difference. The women surveyed him with speculative interest, even those who were already entertaining a customer. He could feel their eyes moving over his face, his shoulders, his chest, his hips, and his legs. At sixteen he had blushed like a maiden. Now he let his eyes return their looks.

"Here, yer lordships, come sit with Bess and Jen, and we'll get ye a nice tankard of ale—or gin if ye like."

"Ale is fine, thanks," James said as he sat down at a table. The madam was a thin, tired-looking woman, not at all like the buxom Dolly.

The girls were not so different from Fanny, though. They looked a little more desperate—or perhaps it was just that now he could see their desperation. He guessed Bess, the girl who had attached herself to him, was a few years younger than he. She might have only a year or two left in the relative comfort of the Spotted Dog before she was forced to move into the streets to ply her trade in doorways.

"Ye want to go upstairs, yer lordship?" she asked. She leaned close, putting her hand on his crotch. The combined smell of her breath, her body, and her last customer's semen made James's stomach roil.

He gently removed her hand. "No, thank you."

Bess pouted, but James saw the relief in her eyes. Relief warring with worry. If he didn't buy what she was selling, she would be that much closer to the streets.

"Some talk is all I need tonight," he said. "I will pay your going rate and then some. It will be the easiest money you've ever earned. Same for Jen, right, Robbie?"

Robbie nodded.

"Yer sure ye don't want to go upstairs?" Bess tugged her already low bodice lower. "I can make yer cock crow, see if I can't."

"I'm sure you can, Bess, but I really do only want to talk. I need some information."

Bess pulled back. "Information? What kind of information?"

"Information about an American named William Dunlap."

"Gawd!" Jen choked on her ale.

"We don't know nuttin' about no Dunlap," Bess said quickly, her face suddenly pale.

"Are you certain?" James dug into his pocket, pulling out a handful of coins. He put them on the table—bright, gold sovereigns—and slowly, almost idly, began to separate them into two piles.

"Aye." Jen's eyes followed the track of James's index finger as it slid a coin across the old, gouged table.

"Nothing?" Another coin clinked against its fellow.

Bess moistened her lips. "What do ye want to know?"

"Where I might find him."

"Why?"

"I don't like him."

Bess and Jen exchanged looks. Then Bess glanced over her shoulder and lowered her voice. "Ye might try the Broken Dove," she said. "Or the Red Lady."

"Or the Rutting Stallion by the river," Jen added.

"Aye, that's another of his houses," Bess said. "He's gots lots of places to hide in Lunnon. Best take yer friend and watch yer back when ye go looking for him. He don't fight fair."

"I didn't think he did."

James and Robbie finished their ale.

"Thank you for your time, ladies," James said as he and Robbie got up to leave.

The girls' hands flashed out to collect their piles of coins.

"Thankee, yer lordship," Bess said, her eyes growing wide when she saw how much money was in her hand. "Come again, do."

"Aye, and ask fer us," Jen shouted after them.

"Gads, the girl—Jen—was crawling with livestock," Robbie said as they stepped outside. "I doubt she'd bathed in the last week."

"Last month, more like. Bathing is a luxury for the rich, my friend. And rich we are, especially for this neighborhood. I think you are going to get a chance for some exercise, but of the pugilistic rather than amorous variety."

"What?"

"I may be wrong, but I believe two—no, three—large fellows are following us. I don't suppose you see any sign of that hackney, do you?"

"No, blast it. Are you sure we're being followed?"

"Don't look! And yes, I'm sure. You don't by chance know how to use a knife, do you?"

"No, I don't by chance."

"Pity." James slowed his steps. "I think we'll do better facing them now, before we reach that dark alley up ahead where they might have reinforcements. Help me over to the gutter and we'll see if they are really following us or just out for a stroll on their own."

James staggered and leaned into Robbie. He stumbled to the gutter and bent over as if to empty his stomach. He glanced back as he lowered his head to his knees. If the men behind them weren't a threat, they should give the sick man and his companion a wide berth. Instead, they hurried towards them.

"Be ready," James muttered to Robbie. "I don't see any clubs or sticks, but they're sure to have a knife or two."

The one in the lead made a grab for James. Robbie stepped back instinctively, clearing James to swing out of his crouch and connect his right fist to the fellow's jaw before the other man knew he'd been noticed. The man's head snapped back, slamming into the second fellow's nose. The first man crumpled to the pavement.

Ordinary street thugs would have fled at that point— one man down, another injured, the odds now even. Unfortunately, these were not ordinary street thugs. They had obviously been hired to do a job that they hesitated to leave undone.

Robbie was holding his own with thug number three. His science wasn't textbook, but for street fights, dirty was best. The second fellow, his nose dripping blood, had slipped a knife from his boot. James freed his own knife, sidestepped the man on the ground, and slashed at Bloody Nose's knife arm. His knife clattered to the pavement. James kicked it away and lashed back with his boot, hitting the man squarely on the knee. He howled, grabbed his leg and fell on the first attacker. At this point, Robbie's opponent decided flight was in order and took off at a run.

"I don't suppose the Watch is around when you want them, are they?" James wiped his knife on his breeches and slipped it back into his boot.

"What do we do with them?"

"Ask a question or two. Hey, there." James hooked Bloody Nose's good leg with his boot as the man tried to get to his feet, sending him crashing back to the ground. "Don't hurry away. Your friend here isn't much of a conversationalist, but I'm hoping you have something of interest to say." He pulled a gun from his pocket and pointed it at the man. "Perhaps this will aid your memory."

"I don't know nuttin', guvnor. God's truth." The man's eyes kept darting back and forth, looking for an escape.

"I doubt if you could recognize God's truth if it bit you on the arse. I suggest, however, that you try to come up with some truth if you want to keep your miserable hide intact and out of Newgate. Who hired you and what was your task?"

"Nobody hired us, guv. We're just poor men, trying to make ends meet."

James said a very short, very vulgar word. Bloody Nose scooted back, but James took a quick step forward and put his boot on the fellow's bad knee.

"You know," James said conversationally, "I've broken a man's knee this way. Knees, in case you don't know it, my friend, are designed to bend only one way. They can be made to bend the other, but it is not very pleasant—at least for the person to whom the knee is attached. I, for example, would not suffer a whit if I stepped down here."

James leaned a little of his weight on his foot and the man screamed.

"God's balls, he said we was to jump a nob. Them knows how to prance around a ring, not really fight. He niver said we was to jump the likes of ye!"

"I will take that as a compliment. Now, tell me who 'he' is and where we may find him. If I like your answer, you will be free to go and take your slumbering friend with you."

"I can't. It'd mean m'life." The man was obviously afraid, but James felt little compassion for someone who would gladly have sliced his liver out just moments before.

"It means your life if you don't. I'm here and your employer is not. You've already felt how sharp my knife is." James put a little more pressure on the knee. "Shall I step closer and let you feel it again? I wouldn't want you to worry that it's grown dull with disuse."

"All right, all right!" Rivulets of sweat poured down the man's face. "It was Dunlap that hired us. Now let me go, guv, like ye said ye would. I don't know nuttin' more."

"Not even where we can find Mr. Dunlap this evening?"

"No! I swear it. We just gets the word that a job needs doing and when the job's done, we gets our coin. We niver see Dunlap hisself. Don't want to see him!"

"I imagine you don't." James sighed. "I really am sorry to have to ruin a perfectly good knee. However, you do have another, so perhaps you won't miss it so much." He leaned forward. The man screamed again.

"Stop! Stop! I'll tell ye, just stop!"

James eased off. "I thought you might change your mind."

The man swallowed. He looked around quickly, then whispered, "The Rutting Stallion, by the river. He's usually there when he's in Lunnon. But I can't swear to it, guv. He could be at one of his other houses."

James nodded. "Very well, I believe you have done your best." He lifted his boot. "Good evening to you."

The man scrambled to his feet and vanished into the alley up ahead before James finished speaking.

"He left his friend behind," Robbie said.

James nodded. "An associate only, I'm afraid. I didn't really expect him to take the body along. The dead weight would slow him down."

"So what do we do with him?" Robbie eyed the man worriedly.

"Leave him. He's starting to come around. I suggest we remove ourselves from the vicinity and find our way to this Rutting Stallion."

"You're very good with that knife. Where did you learn to fight like that?"

"On the Peninsula. Not all the fighting was on the battlefield. I found it paid to be prepared." James scanned the street on both sides, looking for any movement in the shadows.

"Can you show me some of those moves?"

"Yes, if you want. But fighting is always the last resort, Robbie. The first rule is to pick your battles. Know your escape routes at all times. And be aware of your surroundings so you don't walk into trouble." James steered Robbie toward the curb, skirting a dark doorway. "Walk as if you know where you are going and are eager to get there. And, if you can ride, do so."

They reached Fleet Street and James hailed a hackney.

Dunlap poured himself a brandy. Certainly by now Alf and his companions had dispatched the duke. How thoughtful of Alvord to deliver himself so tidily. A pity about Westbrooke—Dunlap preferred three to one odds over three to two. However, Westbrooke wasn't much of a fighter, so his presence was negligible. And Alf had taken his best crew.

No, Dunlap thought as he leaned back in his chair and propped his feet on his desk, if you are going to be foolish enough to visit the stews of London, you have to expect some unpleasant surprises. If he looked out his window now, he might even see the dark forms of two bodies bobbing down the Thames. He had told Alf not to weight the corpses with stones. Runyon wanted proof that the job was done, and the best proof was Alvord's very dead body. Just to be safe, Dunlap had made arrangements for a boatman to find it in the morning. No use taking the chance that sun and water and the river birds would make Alvord's corpse unrecognizable.

As soon as he knew Runyon was satisfied, he was leaving. He would not be coming back. He'd quite lost his taste for England.

There was a commotion in the hall. Dunlap frowned. It sounded as though Belle was yelling. Belle never yelled during business hours. After hours, when he licked through the layers and folds of her luscious flesh to the pearl hidden within, *then* she yelled. God, she yelled loud enough to wake the Watch, if the Watch were stupid enough to venture into this part of London. He took a sip of brandy. He would miss Belle, but then the world was littered with Belles. Clarisse in his Paris house, for instance, was a lusty wench. She had quite an assortment of entertaining bed tricks.

There was the noise again. It was definitely Belle.

"Yer grace! I told ye, Mr. Dunlap is not here. No, ye cannot go into that room."

"Madam, I am going in there now. Please step aside. I will remove you by force if I must."

Dunlap bolted out of his chair, sending brandy flying. Shit! Alvord was just outside his door.

He opened the window behind his desk and threw his leg over the sill as he heard the doorknob rattle. It would take even Alvord a moment to break that lock. By then he would be gone. He climbed down the sturdy vine he had planted years ago when he'd first purchased this brothel.

A wise man always had an alternate exit.

The room was empty, of course. James looked out the window, but there was no sign of Dunlap.

"A pity, Robbie, but I believe the bird has flown."

"Damn. Shall we look at one of his other places?"

"No, I think not. I'm sure Mr. Dunlap is too wily to go to ground in an obvious location." James nodded at the distraught madam. "I don't suppose you know where your employer has headed, do you?"

"Oh, no, yer grace. I don't know nuttin'."

James sighed. "As I thought. Let's go home, Robbie."

They hailed a hackney. James was tired and sore. It had been a while since he had been in a street fight. A nice hot bath was what he wanted.

Unbidden, the image of Sarah flashed into his mind, Sarah with her hair down and her clothes off. Another part of his anatomy suddenly became stiff and sore.

He fervently wished he could relieve that ache as well tonight.

Chapter 13

"Lady Gladys, may I have a moment of your time? I wish to discuss my future."

"Again? There's nothing to discuss, miss, unless you want to discuss wedding plans."

Sarah stared down at the sunlight streaming over the green and gold carpet of Lady Gladys's sitting room.

"I'm not sure . . . I don't think . . . I really can't marry his grace."

She heard two teacups clatter into their saucers.

"Lud, girl, you can't jilt the Duke of Alvord."

"Amanda is right, Sarah. The announcement has appeared in all the papers. It is too late to change your mind."

Sarah swallowed. "Perhaps we could let the engagement stand until the end of the Season, and then—"

Lady Amanda snorted. "The way you're going, miss, you'll be *enceinte* by the end of the Season."

"Amanda!"

"Well, it's true, Gladys. The girl can't keep her clothes on around James."

Lady Gladys frowned at Sarah. "Amanda is correct on that score, Sarah. You have allowed my nephew shocking liberties."

Sarah's whole body burned with mortification. "I am sorry. I never meant . . ."

"Oh, don't apologize. I'm certain James was extremely persuasive."

"Extremely."

"Amanda!" Lady Gladys looked back at Sarah. "Your, um, activities with James are beside the point, dear. Even if you had done no more than discuss the weather, you would still be committed to this marriage. The engagement has been made public. To cry off now would ruin your reputation."

"If it weren't already ruined by your scandalous activities at the Green Man," Lady Amanda interjected.

Lady Gladys sighed. "There is that. And don't think the *ton* will forget, Sarah. A broken engagement will burden you *and* James for the rest of your lives."

"It can't be as bad as that!"

"Yes, I'm afraid it can." Lady Gladys patted the spot next to her on the settee. "Come sit down and we'll discuss this rationally. I'm sure you're just suffering from a case of bride nerves."

"Hard to see how the girl could have bride nerves, Gladys, after that last interlude in James's study."

"Amanda, you are not helping!" Lady Gladys turned to smile at Sarah. "It's natural to be slightly agitated at this time, dear."

"Pshaw! Slightly agitated? James is so agitated he can barely button his breeches."

Lady Gladys shot Lady Amanda a glare and then turned back to Sarah. "It's true, dear, that I've never seen James so attracted to a young lady." She rushed on before Lady Amanda could squeeze in a word. "And in England, it is vastly more comfortable to be a duchess than a governess. As James's wife, you'll have wealth and position."

"And plenty of children." Lady Amanda stared at Sarah over her teacup. "You obviously don't find the man repulsive, so what is the problem?"

Sarah shrugged. How could she tell these ladies that she couldn't bear to marry a rake? They would never understand.

Lady Gladys leaned over and touched her arm. "If you've had a falling-out with James, dear, you need to patch it up. I may never have married, but I've spent years observing couples. I'm afraid men rarely take the first step. That's the woman's job."

Lady Amanda nodded. "If you leave it to James, Sarah, the problem will never be resolved."

"But . . ."

"No, Sarah." Lady Gladys's voice was firm. "You must marry James. So if there's been a misunderstanding, talk to him."

Lady Amanda snorted. "Just be sure that's all you do."

Sarah mulled over the ladies' words. How could she possibly discuss such a topic with James? It certainly was not a proper subject for the breakfast table. Nor was it more palatable over a cold collation, cakes and tea, or roast pheasant. Since the ladies had suddenly become exemplary chaperones, there was never a moment for a private word. And really, what would she say? Fornication was expected of English peers. British lords spent more thought on their neck cloths than their bed partners.

But she was not a British lady. She could not ignore James's amorous pursuits. She had to speak to him. The ladies were right about that. But when? And where?

When she got home from the opera that night, she was too disquieted to sleep. She dismissed Betty, curled up with a blanket by the fire, and faced some home truths.

She loved James. She wished that she didn't, but she did. She could no longer imagine living without him. He had awakened something in her that was not going back to sleep. She ached for his touch—but she also ached for his fidelity and his love.

If she could have only his touch and not his love, could she bear to marry him?

She did not know.

She rested her chin on her knees and stared into the yellow and orange flames leaping in the grate. She was not going to find the answer here. She had to talk to James. Tonight. Now. She could not bear the uncertainty any longer.

She began to pace the length of her room. The thought of seeking James in his bedchamber made her stomach flutter like a hummingbird's wings. She grabbed her sides, folding her arms tightly under her breasts, and took a deep, calming breath. It didn't help.

Could she go to his room? His chamber was just down the hall. It would take her only a moment to reach it. She knew which door was his.

It was scandalous, but they *were* engaged. According to the *ton,* her reputation was already shredded.

She paused at the corner farthest from the fire. What if he wasn't there? He hadn't come to the opera with them. What if he were spending the night at a brothel or with an accommodating lady of the *ton?*

Now her stomach housed a flock of hummingbirds.

Enough. It was clear she was not going to be able to sleep, so she might as well seek him out tonight. If he wasn't in his room—well, she would just try again. She

would wait an hour—give the house time to settle down.
Then she would go.

Sarah cracked open her door and peered out. The hall
was deserted. She took a deep breath and let it out
slowly. Facing James in his room had seemed like a
good idea earlier, but now she could think of a hundred
reasons why she should stay safely where she was. Yet
hiding in her bed would not solve her problems. She
looked down the hall again. The distance to James's
room seemed enormous, but she knew it was not. She
just needed to get her feet to move. She forced herself
to step over her threshold.

She hurried down the corridor. Thankfully the other
doors stayed firmly closed. She did not want to face the
ladies or Lizzie. What if Harrison was in the room,
waiting up for James? She'd die if James's proper valet
caught her creeping into his master's bedroom.

She reached the door and put her ear to the wood. She
couldn't hear over the pounding of her heart. She held
her breath, closed her eyes, and concentrated. No
sounds. She glanced up and down the corridor. No one
coming. She grabbed the doorknob. She needed two
hands, she was shaking so badly.

The door opened soundlessly and she slipped inside.
No sign of Harrison, thank God. A banked fire glowed to
her left; moonlight glimmered through a window across
from her. The bed—huge and high, like a medieval king
might have slept in—stood next to the window, the bed
curtains drawn back. In the dim light she couldn't be certain whether James was there or not.

She moved quietly across the floor, hardly breathing. Yes, he was there, on his back, bedclothes down to his waist.

The shadows played over his face, over the long lashes against his cheeks and the hollow at the base of his throat. He still didn't wear a nightshirt. She could see the fine dusting of hair that covered his chest. It was golden, she remembered. Was it soft? She had wanted to touch it at the Green Man, to trace its path over his flat nipples, down his belly, to his navel and the narrow line that disappeared under the sheet. Could she touch it now? He was asleep. If she were very careful, he would never know.

The intimate light and quiet made her bold. She reached toward him.

His hands shot off the bed, grabbed her upper arms, and lifted her, throwing her down hard onto her back. He loomed over her, his weight pinning her to the mattress.

"James!"

His grip loosened. "Sarah?"

"Yes," she croaked. She stared up at him, but his face was lost in the shadows. Was he angry?

"Just a moment." He turned away. She heard a tinderbox creak open, a flint scrape. A candle flared to life.

His skin glowed warm. So much skin. Shoulders, lovely broad shoulders, and a strong back that tapered down to a narrow waist, still hidden by the blankets. He turned toward her and she saw his chest again. She had forgotten how his muscles rippled when he moved. It was truly amazing what was hidden under shirts and coats and cravats. Her eyes traced the sinuous line from his neck, over his shoulders, down the muscles in his arms.

"Like what you see?"

"What?" Her eyes flew back to his face. He had that intent look again. Very intent.

"I never knew a woman's eyes could torture a man."

"What?" She shook her head, trying to clear her senses. She knew she sounded shatterbrained, but the husky tone of James's voice was quite distracting.

"Don't look and not touch, sweetheart. Please. I can feel your eyes on me, but I would love to feel your beautiful hands or, better, your soft lips."

She would love to touch the golden stubble outlining his jaw and the muscles bulging in his upper arms. Her hands ached to touch. She frowned and sat up, edging away from him toward the other side of the bed. A little more space between them would definitely help their discussion.

James woke when he sensed someone reaching for him. He should never have let his assailant get so close. He wouldn't have, if he hadn't been deep in a delightfully erotic dream.

He would almost have rather died than give up his dream. He'd had Sarah naked in his bed with no blankets or pillows to obstruct his view—and he had been enjoying the view. He'd let his gaze explore every inch of her—from her hair, her lips, her throat to her lovely small breasts. Her waist. Her thighs. He had an extremely active imagination, but he could not decide the exact shade of the lovely hair nestled between those thighs. Would it be the same reddish hue as the rest of her hair? And would it be as soft? He'd been just about to find out when he'd felt the man reaching for him.

As soon as his hands closed around the intruder's arms, he knew it was not a man.

It was Sarah. What was she doing in his room? In his bed? He blinked. No, he was not still dreaming. She had on a high-necked white nightgown. She would never be wearing so much clothing if this were his dream.

He turned to light a candle. He could hardly focus long enough to strike the flint.

He had Sarah in his bed with only a nightgown between his skin and hers. Just a few buttons, so conveniently placed under her chin, over her slender throat, and down her lovely breasts. It would take only moments to slip them free. He had many moments—hours—before any of the maids would be up.

Blood rushed from his head to another part of his body.

Sarah had his ring on her finger. She was in his bed. Aunt Gladys and Lady Amanda were asleep, but even if they woke, they would not poke their noses into his chamber. He was safely tucked up in his own bed. With Sarah.

He should have locked his door—but then, of course, Sarah would not have found her way in. Why was she here?

Frankly, he didn't care why. She was here. Surely his dreams were about to be fulfilled.

He turned—and found her studying him as closely as he had been examining her in his dream. God, it was exquisite torture. His skin burned everywhere her eyes looked. He needed to feel her hands, her lips on him. He was desperate for her touch.

He would beg if he had to.

Somehow James had managed to close the space between them. His face was only inches from hers. He looked . . . hungry.

"James, stop that."

"Stop what?"

She could feel his breath on her lips. If she raised her hand, she could touch his chest. His very naked chest. Did he have no shame? Certainly he could find a nightshirt to put on. But then he would have to get out of bed, and she would see every muscled inch of him. Unless she closed her eyes—which, of course, she would.

Maybe.

"Stop looking at me like that," she said. "We need to talk."

"Are you certain? I can think of much more interesting things for our mouths to do."

He leaned a little closer, and she leaned back. Any farther back and she would fall onto the floor.

"And anyway, you are the one looking at me, love. Not that I mind, of course. I'd be happy to show you any part of my body you would like to see." His hand cupped her cheek.

Sarah moistened her lips, and saw James's gaze drop to her mouth.

It would be so easy to be seduced from her purpose.

It would be so easy to be seduced. Being alone with James in his warm, shadowy bed, surrounded by his scent and heat, was wonderful.

"We need to talk about our future," she whispered.

"Ahh. I would love to talk about our future, sweetheart." His fingers moved to play with the buttons on her nightgown. "Why don't you come under the covers and get comfortable?"

"I don't think so." Sarah eyed the blankets. "Do you have breeches on under there?"

He grinned. "Care to look?"

"No, I think I'll stay right where I am, thank you."

"You're not cold?"

"I'm rather warm, actually."

"Really? Then you shouldn't be buttoned up to your chin, love."

He slipped the first button free. Sarah raised her hand to stop him, but somehow she ended up tracing the curve of his muscles and the tendons in his arms. He kissed her fingers as they brushed over his skin. She dropped her hands back to the bed.

Another button slipped free of its hole.

He touched the end of her braid. "I remember your hair from that night at the Green Man. It was red and gold silk."

Sarah blushed. "It was a mess. I was too tired to braid it."

"Hmm?" He loosened the plaits and ran his fingers through the strands. "It's beautiful like this."

He pushed her hair back from her temples. His hand moved slowly down her cheek to her throat and the next button on her nightgown. She grabbed his wrist. She had to remember he was a rake. A libertine.

Apparently a very successful one. He was certainly making her mindless.

"James, do you make all your women feel this way?"

Another button slipped free. "What way, love?"

"Hot and . . . restless."

"That sounds like a fever." Another button opened.

"But I'll tell you a secret." He leaned close and let his lips brush her cheek. "You make me feel hot and restless, too. Maybe we have the same illness." His lips grazed her mouth and she turned her head instinctively to follow them as they retreated.

"Maybe we can cure each other." He moved to her neck, to the sensitive place just below her ear. "I think so." His voice was a trifle unsteady. "I definitely think so."

"But, James." Her voice was a trifle unsteady as well. Every time his mouth moved to a new spot, a new jolt of heat shot through her. Still, she had a vague—rapidly growing vaguer—sense that she needed to say something important. She couldn't let this lovely fire consume her.

"James. Oh!" His lips found the base of her neck. Her breasts ached; the lower half of her body throbbed. Another button slipped free. She wanted to tear the blasted nightgown off. She needed to feel his hands and his mouth everywhere.

No! She had to say what she had come to say. She wetted her lips and tried again.

"James, about the other women."

He opened another button. One more and he would reach her breasts. All hope of rational conversation would be gone when that happened. She pushed at him and he raised his head. She looked him in the eye.

"I've thought a lot about this, James. I know I can't change your past. But I'm an American, not an English-woman. It would kill me to think you were doing this with other women once we are married. I don't want to share you."

One corner of his mouth crooked up. "And I don't want to be shared."

"You don't?" She tried to keep hope from flooding her until she was sure she understood. "So you'll give up your other women? Give up the brothels?"

"Give up the brothels?" James seemed quite shocked. "*And* my other women?" He sat back.

Sarah frowned. Had she misinterpreted his words? "I know I'm asking a lot. I know it's not the English way. But I'll make it up to you, James, I promise. You just need to show me. I don't know anything now, but I'm willing to learn. Just show me what you like. I want to please you."

"That sounds lovely, sweetheart, but you're not making a great deal of sense. Where did you get the idea that I've had hordes of women?"

Sarah studied his face. He looked puzzled, not angry. "Isn't that why you're called Monk?"

James frowned and would have spoken, but Sarah rushed ahead.

"Richard told me first, but even your aunt and Lady Amanda know. Lady Charlotte said it was common knowledge that you frequent brothels." She flushed. "She said you didn't keep a mistress because you needed variety."

James stared at her. "Charlotte said I needed variety?"

She nodded.

He looked stunned. He slid down onto his back and covered his face with his hands. Sarah felt her stomach plummet.

"I can't share you, James." She touched his shoulder. He was shaking. "I'm sorry, but I just can't do it."

An odd little noise escaped through his fingers. She stared at him suspiciously. "Are you laughing at me?"

"At you, at me, at the whole damn situation," he gasped. He leaned up on his elbow. "Sarah, it's true I used to be called Monk by some people. Richard gave me that name back at university. I knew you didn't like it, but I thought you knew what it meant."

"It doesn't mean what Richard said?"

"No. At least it didn't. I really thought no one used it anymore. No one calls me it to my face." He grimaced. "I certainly didn't think Aunt Gladys and Lady Amanda knew the blasted name."

"And Lady Charlotte. She thought we, um, that is, she thought we had already been in bed together."

James grinned. "Well, we had."

Sarah made a face at him. "You know what she thought! And I think she wanted me to tell her all about it."

James gave a low whistle. "Maybe old Charlotte isn't as cold as she's made out to be."

Sarah grabbed his wrist again. "You leave Charlotte alone. She is quite disgusting."

"Oh, I will, sweetheart, I will. But it's a bit of a shock to discover I have a reputation for being quite the devil between the sheets."

"Well, aren't you?"

"I have no idea. I, my love, am as virginal as you."

It was Sarah's turn to be stunned. "You are?"

James nodded. "My lamented nickname means exactly what it suggests."

Sarah stared at him. His lips were quirked in a half smile and he looked faintly embarrassed.

"I thought, I mean it seems . . . Well, from what everybody says—the *ton,* that is—men climb in and out of bed with any woman who will let them."

"I grant you, I may be the only virgin duke above the age of fourteen."

"But how can that be? You certainly seem to know how to, um, you know."

"Do I? I guess you must inspire me. I certainly feel inspired now, don't you?" James reached out to cup the side of her breast through her nightgown.

"Um." She certainly felt hot. If only his hand would move.

James lifted her left hand and kissed the inside of her wrist. He stroked her thundering pulse with his thumb.

Candlelight winked over the emerald in the Runyon engagement ring.

"Before I compromise you . . ." He grinned. "Before I *thoroughly* compromise you, I need to be certain. You have no more doubts about our marriage, do you?"

The wonderful physical sensations receded slightly as Sarah focused on James's face. "Why? Why do you want to marry me?"

"Why? Being in my bed isn't enough? No," he put his finger on her lips when she would have protested. "It's not just that. It's not that the story of the Green Man got out or that I need a wife and heir or even that I lust after your beautiful body, though it's all of that." He kissed her wrist again, sucking lightly on her skin. "God, I haven't been able to sleep for wanting you since that night at the Green Man. But it's more than that."

He looked directly into her eyes.

"I need you, Sarah. Somehow you've woven yourself into my heart and my soul. I cannot imagine life without you beside me—in my bed, yes, but also at my breakfast table, in my drawing room, on the grounds of Alvord."

"Really?" Sarah studied his face. What she saw swirling in his amber eyes reassured her.

"Really. Say you'll marry me, Sarah." He brushed her lips with his. "Say yes."

She sighed. All the agonizing, all the reasoning and rationalizing she had done were like a summer rainstorm—intense, but forgotten once the sun broke through the clouds. It didn't matter that James was an English duke. He was James and he was vital to her happiness.

"Oh, yes," she said.

His face lit up. "Then, my love," he whispered in her ear, "I would dearly love to lose my virginity." He kissed

her. "Of course, you will have to lose yours as well."
Another kiss. "But I shall try to make it up to you."

His fingers slipped open the last of the buttons.

"You look slightly flushed, sweetheart. I'm certain
you will be more comfortable without this annoying
nightgown."

She didn't know if she would be more comfortable or
not. Comfort wasn't the issue. Survival was. If she didn't
feel his skin on hers soon, she would go up in flames.

He slid her nightgown slowly up her leg. From her
ankle to her calf, his palm moved over her skin, stopping just above her knee.

Sarah squirmed. She desperately wanted his fingers to
move an inch or two higher. Her hands fluttered over his
shoulders. She whimpered.

"Please."

"Please? Love, anything for you when you ask so
nicely."

His hand moved, his thumb brushing the spot that so
burned for him as it slid up her thigh to her hip. Then
both hands grabbed her nightgown and pulled it over
her head. It went sailing off into the shadows.

"God, Sarah. You are so beautiful." He just looked at
her, his gaze traveling from her breasts to her belly to
her thighs. She moved to cover herself, but his fingers
brushed hers away. He sighed, his broad hand warm and
heavy on the patch of springy curls she had tried to hide.

"Red," he breathed. "Just like your other hair."

He scooped her up and deposited her under the covers,
pressing her up against the length of his naked body.
Flames licked over her skin. He turned her on her back
and gently stroked her breasts, lightly touched her nipples.

She arched into his hands. A wildness surged through
her, stripping away all shyness. She needed him. She ran

her hands over his hair, his back, even his muscled buttocks. She panted, sobbed. His touches were soft, too soft, teasing.

"Shhh, sweetheart. Easy." He was panting, too. He gave a breathless laugh. "I think we won't try to go slowly this time, hmm?"

Sarah shook her head. She barely heard him. The hunger was consuming her. There was a gaping emptiness in her that she needed him to fill.

"Please," she whimpered again.

One of his long fingers touched her gently in the wet, dark aching place between her legs and she exploded. She gasped and clung to him. Wave after wave of sensation racked her, sweeping away the fire, cleansing her, leaving her body limp and at peace. She looked up at him.

"Now it's my turn, sweetheart." With the madness washed out of her, she heard the tension in his voice.

He rose above her and she opened her legs to welcome him. She ran her hands over his shoulders and back. All his muscles were tense, just as hers had been.

Something warm and firm touched her where James's finger had been before and then it was bearing into her. Her body stretched. She wasn't sure it could stretch so wide, but she held still because she knew it was James coming to her.

"This may hurt," he gasped. He eased farther into her, filling her. "God, Sarah." His voice was only a hoarse whisper. "You are sweet. So sweet."

Sweat made his back slippery. She slid her hands down his spine and tilted her hips. His breath caught and he surged into her. She felt a burning deep inside where he was. His hips moved under her hands, once, twice, and stilled. A warmth pulsed into her; then his body relaxed and lay heavy on hers. She held him close as she felt his heart slow and steady.

She could barely breathe for the weight of him. She couldn't quite comprehend what had happened, but she felt a deep contentment. She didn't want him to move. When he did, the air was cold against her sweat-slicked skin. He gathered her up and held her close. She laid her head against his chest.

"I'm sorry I hurt you." His breath stirred her hair.

"It was nothing." She laid her palm flat against his chest.

"It was your maidenhead breaking. It won't hurt like that again." He tangled his fingers in her hair. "I'm getting a special license today. I want us married as soon as possible."

Sarah felt herself blushing. What would James's family think about such a hurried wedding?

"Do we need to be married so quickly?"

"Yes." James ran his hand up and down her spine. She stretched into his body. "There are at least three reasons for the rush, sweetheart. First, I don't plan to sleep alone again, and Aunt Gladys may object to my moving you into my room without the blessing of clergy. I am *not* going to sneak down my own corridors."

Sarah stirred. "I should be sneaking down those corridors, James, back to my own room. What time is it?"

James pulled her more securely against his side. "You are not going anywhere."

"But what will the servants say? Harrison or one of the maids will be in soon."

"The servants will be overjoyed to find you in my bed, Sarah. They don't want Richard to be duke. Before you came into my life, Harrison regularly threatened to

look elsewhere for employment if I didn't do my duty
and secure the succession."

"Well, I should at least put on my nightgown."

"You're fine the way you are. I don't expect you'll
have much use for a night rig in the future."

"James!"

"The second reason for the hurry," he said, ignoring
her outburst, "is actually more important. Remember
when you wondered at the Green Man if you might be
with child?"

Sarah buried her face in his side. "I didn't perfectly
understand the matter."

James chuckled. He put his hand on Sarah's flat stomach. "Well, it is certainly possible that you're pregnant
now."

"Really?" Sarah didn't feel any different. She put her
hand down next to James's. He linked their fingers.

"Really."

"After only one time?"

"Yes. It doesn't usually happen the first time, but it
can. Richard knows that, too—as I'm sure he knows
that I don't intend to limit myself to just one time. And
that is the third reason we need to marry quickly—I
don't know what Richard will do. If something happens
to me, I want you taken care of. If you should be pregnant, I want our child recognized as mine."

"Hmm." Sarah supposed she should feel worried, but
she felt too warm and relaxed in James's arms. She was
having a hard time bringing her thoughts into order. Just
a short time ago she had been in her room gathering her
courage to confront James, and now she was naked in
his bed, having just gone through the most wonderfully
intimate experience of her life. She, who had spent her
life virtually alone, was on the verge of acquiring a hus-

band, a sister, an aunt, and possibly a baby. A new life that she and James had made together. She was surprised by the fierce warmth that flooded her at the thought. She hoped she was pregnant. She wanted a boy with James's amber eyes.

James's hand stroked slowly through her hair. She felt his broad fingers slide over her scalp to the nape of her neck. She felt so warm and relaxed. So safe. Her eyes drifted shut. It had been a long day. In a few moments she was asleep.

Chapter 14

James listened to Sarah's even breathing. He felt a deep physical relaxation and a profound peacefulness, but he couldn't sleep. The memory of what had just happened was too vivid.

He had expected the physical release, though the reality had been a thousand times more satisfying than he had imagined—and he had imagined the event in minute detail too many times to count. God, it had been heaven—the smooth silkiness of her skin; its sweet, heated smell and slightly tangy taste; her soft sighs and whimpers; the creamy beauty of her breasts and belly. And then he had felt her long legs, her soft thighs around his hips and her delicate hands sliding over his back. When he had come into her tight, wet body, he'd felt he had come home.

That was what he had not expected. The spiritual release that had come with the physical. He had pumped his life into her—not just his seed, but his soul. The feeling of loving and being loved had overwhelmed him. He had not wanted to leave her, even though he'd known his weight was crushing her. He had buried his face in her hair and neck and had breathed in the musky smell of sweat-slicked skin and spent sex, mixed with the familiar clean scent of his linen sheets.

He hoped that they had made a child, here in the bed where Alvords had been conceived for generations, a son to carry on his line or a daughter with Sarah's sunset-colored hair. He smiled and ran his hand down her back. She mumbled and snuggled closer.

James felt himself grow hard again. It seemed a shame to waste the night sleeping. Sarah would be too sore for another joining, but there were other ways to make love. He moved his hand from her shoulder to her breast.

And froze. All his senses snapped into heightened alertness. He held his breath to listen better. Yes, there it was again. He hadn't imagined it. The faintest sound in the corridor outside his door—the scrape of a boot on the floor. It was still too early for the servants to be up.

"Sarah," James whispered. He put his finger over her lips so she would stay still as she woke. "Get under the bed *now*."

She stared up at him for a moment and then nodded. He watched her vanish over the side before he turned to welcome his visitor.

It took Sarah a second to understand what James meant. Then she too heard a step in the hall. She nodded, slid across the sheets and dropped to the floor.

She scooted under the bed. She did not want the chambermaid to see her—just as James did not, no matter what he'd said. Now that she wasn't drugged by his presence, she was shocked by her behavior. How could she have been so wanton? She had just about begged him to take off her nightgown.

Where *was* her nightgown? She shivered. Goose bumps prickled her arms. She couldn't see a thing in the thick shadows under the bed. She reached around blindly. Her fingers collided with something hard and round—an old chamber pot, by the feel of it.

The bed creaked sharply and the mattress sagged towards her. She heard muffled grunts, a thrashing sound. Certainly the chambermaid could not be causing this commotion. Something was very wrong. She grabbed the chamber pot and scrambled out from under the bed.

James was locked in a wrestling match with a cloaked, masked man.

She had no time to think. She lifted her makeshift weapon high and slammed it down onto the back of the intruder's head. He grunted and fell forward onto James. James pushed the body to the floor, and then reached under his pillow to pull out a gun.

"Well done!" He grinned at her.

She stared at him. "You keep a gun under your pillow?" She swallowed, feeling slightly faint. "You could have shot me when I came in earlier!"

"I would never shoot you, love."

"Well, you should have shot him." She pointed to the man on the ground.

"Oh, I don't think so. Guns can have such permanent results, and this fellow may be of more use to us alive than dead." He climbed out of bed and pulled away the scarf that had partially obscured the man's face. "Hmm. It looks like we have finally found our friend Dunlap."

The door crashed open.

"Ah, Harrison! Just the man we need. Come in and give me a hand, will you?"

Harrison stepped in and closed the door firmly behind him, shutting out a gathering crowd of footmen. He managed to look decorous even with his nightcap askew and his hairy ankles sticking out from under his nightshirt.

"Good evening, your grace, Miss Hamilton." Harrison kept his eyes firmly fixed on the ceiling. "If I might, your grace, may I suggest Miss Hamilton borrow your dressing gown?" He reached into the wardrobe and pulled out a long, blue robe. He held it out in their direction.

"Splendid, Harrison." James took the robe and draped it over Sarah's shoulders. She scrambled to get her arms in the sleeves and belted it tightly around her waist. "Miss Hamilton has misplaced her nightgown."

"Indeed." Harrison took a quick glance in her direction and was visibly relieved to find her decently covered. "I'm certain it will turn up." He looked at James. "You might wish to don some clothing yourself, your grace."

"Good point."

James scooped his breeches off the floor. Sarah's eyes were drawn to the part of his anatomy usually covered by that item of apparel. It didn't look the way it had felt. As she watched, it stirred and thickened. She looked wonderingly into James's face.

"Later, sweetheart," he muttered as he almost jumped into his breeches. He pulled on his shirt. "I don't suppose you have any rope, do you, Harrison? I'd like to secure Mr. Dunlap's hands before he comes to."

"I'm afraid I don't, your grace, but we might use a few of your second-best cravats."

"Brilliant. Hand them over."

Sarah watched James truss up Mr. Dunlap. He tied Dunlap's hands behind his back and then looped the other end of the cravat around the man's neck.

"You're quite good at that."

"I've had a little experience, on both sides of the rope. Fortunately, the Frenchman who tied me was not an expert in the art." James pulled the last knot tight. "There we go—and just in time, too."

Dunlap's eyes fluttered open. He rolled over on his side. "Alvord. How the hell did you manage to hit me on the back of my head?"

"Miss Hamilton did the honors. I believe she had a score to settle with you."

Dunlap looked at Sarah. His eyes focused on her oversized robe and bare feet.

"How handy she was nearby," he said dryly.

"Yes, indeed. You might also be interested to know that Miss Hamilton has agreed to wed me, and we expect to enter that blessed state today."

Dunlap shifted his weight on the floor. "My felicitations."

James inclined his head. "I believe that I have heard unpleasant rumors that marriage to me might have an adverse effect on Miss Hamilton's continued good health. I am sure that such rumors are unfounded. Wouldn't you agree?"

Dunlap shrugged. "Rumors are like wheat—a small kernel of truth and much chaff."

James jerked on the cravat and Dunlap's arms moved higher on his back. He winced.

"There had better be no truth to these rumors, Dunlap. Do you get my meaning?"

"Completely."

"Good, then I suggest you spend the next few minutes telling me everything you know about my cousin's actions."

"I can't."

"Oh, I think you can. Candor is certainly in your best interest. You may not be totally familiar with the ways of British society, but a duke wields significantly more power than a mere Mr. Runyon. I could have you hung for trying to kill me. However, provide me with the right information, and I'll consider other options for ridding us of your presence."

"Like passage from this benighted island?" Dunlap snorted. "I would love to be quit of your hell-born cousin."

"As would I. Tell me what I need to know and you can sail back to your homeland. For example, what hold does Richard have over you?"

"There was an unfortunate accident in Paris a year or so ago . . ."

"You mean Chuckie Phelps?"

"Exactly. It wasn't quite what it seemed, but I couldn't very well go to the authorities and explain things."

"No, I don't suppose you could. So Richard's been blackmailing you."

"Yes, he had some of my letters. Chuckie and I had a rather, ah, intense friendship."

"Yes, yes." James looked over at Sarah. "No need to go into the details. I'm more interested in my cousin's plans."

"He flat doesn't want to see you married, ever. He's a bit unbalanced over it."

"I noticed."

Dunlap tried to shrug. "There's no reasoning with him. You don't suppose you could loosen these ties, do you? I'm losing circulation to my hands."

"What a pity. Think of it as penance for your treatment of Miss Hamilton at the Palmerson ball."

Dunlap looked over at Sarah. "My apologies, ma'am. My heart truly wasn't in it."

Sarah pulled James's robe more tightly around her. "You, Mr. Dunlap, are a disgusting, spineless parasite."

Dunlap inclined his head. "I didn't expect you to understand."

"Lord Westbrooke and I encountered your men outside

the Spotted Dog," James said. "Why did you undertake the task in person tonight?"

"Your cousin insisted. I prefer to subcontract this kind of work. As you can see, I'm sadly out of practice."

"You weren't doing so badly. I was quite happy for Miss Hamilton's assistance." James leaned back against the bed. "So here's my proposition. You will write a confession—"

"You'll have to loosen these damn—pardon." He shot Sarah a look. "These *blasted* bonds if you want me to write anything. And you'd better hurry or my fingers will be so numb it'll take 'em days to get back feeling."

"Don't worry. You'll be able to write. You will also be carefully guarded. You will write a confession detailing your involvement and Richard's. In exchange, I will see you loaded on the next ship bound for America with the understanding that you are never to darken England's shores again."

"No danger of that. I can't wait to shake the British dust off my boots. I've found the climate doesn't agree with me."

"Exactly." James lifted his pistol and pointed it at Dunlap. "Harrison, would you invite two of our most burly footmen to join us?"

"Not the Runners," Dunlap said as Harrison left the room.

"Ah, you know about them. I wonder why they haven't broken the door down by now."

"I think perhaps they aren't feeling quite the thing. I had to encourage them to take some much-needed rest."

"Really? I would hate to think you had deprived us of two of Bow Street's finest."

"Not permanently," Dunlap said quickly. "They will

awake in the morning with aching heads. I slipped them something in their wine."

There was a noise at the door. "Sarah, love, you look quite fetching in my dressing gown, but you might want to fade into the background now," James said.

Sarah moved to the far corner of the room as Harrison came in with two footmen. They hauled Dunlap over to the desk and pushed him into the seat. James loosened his bonds while the footmen held him in place.

"Please make your recollections very detailed," James said. "You might find your accommodations on your trip to America slightly more appealing if you satisfy me that you have written all that you know. Do not, however, embellish."

"I wouldn't dream of it." Dunlap scratched away for considerable time. "Done," he said and sat back. James retied his hands, then perused the confession.

"This should do." He gestured to Harrison and the footmen. "Would you be so good as to escort our guest to the wharves? Tell Captain Rutledge of the *Flying Gull* that Mr. Dunlap requires passage to New York. He'll know what to do."

"I assume I'll not have to spend the journey trussed like a Christmas goose?" Dunlap asked as the two footmen hustled him toward the door.

"No. Rutledge will see that you don't jump ship before she sails, and then he'll probably put you to work. You should have a tolerable crossing. Better than you deserve."

Sarah came out of the shadows as James closed the door behind Dunlap. "Do you really think he will go quietly?"

James gathered her into his arms. "Yes, he seemed

genuinely anxious to leave England. And Rutledge is
good man. He won't lose track of him."

She rested her head on his shoulder. "I'll be happi
once I know Dunlap is gone."

"Rutledge will send word as soon as they set sail." I
rubbed his hands up and down her back. "But I tru
don't expect anything to go wrong."

"Too bad we can't stick Richard on the same ship.'

"Yes." James combed one hand through her ha
"Though I'm not sure we should curse your homelan
with my evil cousin."

"True." She sighed. James's fingers felt wonderfu
"Will Dunlap's confession be enough to get Richard
leave us alone?"

"I don't know. I'm happy to have it for my own sak
There were times, many times, when I wondered i
wasn't imagining Richard's role in this. But whether t
word of an American brothel keeper will be enough
stop Richard . . ." James shrugged. "We'll see. Fir
though, I'm getting a special license." He held Sarah
hair away from her neck and kissed the spot just und
her ear. She tilted her head to give him more access. I
laughed and held her away from him.

"This will have to wait. When Harrison comes bac
I need to get dressed and start things in motion for o
wedding tonight."

"What should I do?"

"Go back to bed—your own bed, unfortunately." I
pulled her close again and kissed the other side of h
neck. "I hope this will be the last time you sleep ther
He grinned. "I hope it will be the last time you sleep
all for quite some time. So get your rest." He let her
and turned toward his bed. "Now, let's see if we can fi
that elusive nightgown."

It took a few minutes, but James finally put his hands on it. It had sailed halfway across the room and landed near the door.

"It's a wonder Dunlap didn't trip on it," he said.

"It's a wonder the footmen didn't notice it," Sarah said.

"Well, if they did, they are probably cheering about it in the servants' quarters." He held the nightgown up. "You had better put this back on. I doubt you want to be traipsing down the corridor dressed only in my robe."

"I certainly don't." She reached for the nightgown, but James held it away.

"No, no. I'll give you your nightgown when you give me my robe."

Sarah blushed, suddenly shy. She took a deep breath. *This is ridiculous,* she told herself. After what she and James had done together, standing naked before him was nothing. She untied his dressing gown and shrugged her shoulders, letting the robe slide down her arms to pool at her feet. She glanced over at James.

"God, Sarah." He reached out to touch her shoulders, her waist, her hips, her breasts. "You *are* beautiful." He gathered her hair in his hands, bringing her body against his, and kissed her.

Sarah lost herself in the heat of that kiss. Her knees gave out and she sagged into him. She stretched, wrapping her arms around his neck, putting her skin, her breasts, and her legs, against the firmness of his body, the roughness of his clothes. His hands spread over the curves of her bottom, settling her against the hard ridge of his breeches. She moved and he groaned in the back of his throat. His tongue stroked into her mouth.

"Your grace?"

Sarah heard a faint scratching at the door.

"Your grace? It's Harrison."

She leapt back as if scalded. Harrison was on the other side of the door, a door he might open at any moment. She grabbed her nightgown out of James's hands and threw it over her head. She scrambled around in the voluminous garment.

"Here, slow down," James whispered. "You're trying to put your head through an armhole. Let me help you."

"Mmzpt!" she said through the folds of cloth.

James grabbed her thrashing arms and held her still. "Stop panicking." He found the neck opening in the tangle of cloth. "Stick your head through here."

Sarah's head popped out of the fabric. She threw a frantic look at the door.

"Harrison won't come in until I tell him, sweetheart. I think he has a good idea of what may be going on in here."

"How embarrassing!"

"Then I guess I'll just have to make you so lost in passion you can't think to be embarrassed. But not now, alas." He turned towards the door. "Come in."

Sarah was afraid she'd see a smirk on Harrison's face, but he looked reassuringly normal, as if there were nothing irregular about frantic whispering and scrambling sounds coming from behind his master's closed door.

"Did Mr. Dunlap get off as planned?"

"Yes, your grace. When Thomas and William loaded him into the hackney, he jumped right in. I believe he was happy to have his way back to America taken care of."

"I hope you're right. It will certainly make things easier. Has the staff returned to their rooms?"

"Yes, your grace, but the maids will be up shortly."

"So I had better get Miss Hamilton back to her room."

"That might be best, your grace."

"Very well. Could you get my gear organized? I've got a busy day."

James stuck his head out into the corridor to check for servants before he extended his hand to Sarah and pulled her along to her room. Once there, he ducked inside, closed the door, and kissed her again.

"Dream of me, sweetheart, and I'll see you when I get back. We'll tell Aunt Gladys and Lizzie and Lady Amanda our news then, shall we?"

"I certainly don't want to tell them by myself." Sarah felt a little ill thinking about it.

"You won't mind being an English duchess too terribly, will you, Sarah?" James was suddenly serious.

Sarah laid her hand along his jaw. "I want to be your wife, James. If that means I must be a duchess, then so be it. I just hope I won't disappoint you."

He pulled her to him in a quick hug. "No chance of that. Now get some sleep if you can."

He opened the door and moved back down the hall. Sarah watched him go. She could not believe that he was hers—or would be hers in a few hours. She yawned and closed the door. She didn't think she could sleep a wink. Her bed seemed small and cold now. Lonely.

She climbed under the covers and laid her head on the pillow. She was certain she'd relive the amazing events of the night, but she was more tired that she knew. In moments, her eyes closed and she was asleep.

Chapter 15

"Oh, miss, I hope I didn't wake ye!"

Sarah lifted her head from her pillow and squinted at the sunlight streaming in the window. She could tell it was much later than she usually slept.

"What time is it, Betty?"

"Almost noon, miss. The house is abuzz, though no one except Harrison knows why and he isn't saying. That one wouldn't tell his dying mother the time o' day if his grace had told him not to."

"Hmm." Sarah took inventory of her body. She had a definite ache and a wet stickiness between her legs. Other than that, she felt the same as she had the day before. The same—yet profoundly different.

"Here now, I've brought ye some tea and a few biscuits."

Sarah pulled herself to a sitting position. Could Betty tell she wasn't a virgin anymore?

Apparently not. The maid chatted away just as she did every morning.

"There's flowers all over the drawing room, miss, and all sorts of food being delivered. I've had to beat Lizzie away from yer door twice, she was that eager to see if ye knew the cause of all the bustle. Even Lady Gladys and Lady Amanda don't know. It's all his grace's doing."

"Is his grace at home?" Sarah was aware of a familiar fluttery feeling in her stomach at the thought of James.

"No. If he was, ye can be sure his womenfolk would have had the secret out o' him by now."

Sarah sipped her tea. She was quite certain that she knew what all the fuss was about, but she'd rather wait until James was home to face everyone.

"Do you suppose I might have a bath, Betty?"

Betty grinned. "His grace left orders for just such a thing when ye woke. I'll tell the footmen to bring up the water."

Sarah stayed in bed finishing her breakfast as the footmen readied her bath. She recognized one of the men from last night. He gave no indication that he had seen her in James's room. Either she had truly managed to stay in the shadows or he knew to keep James's confidence.

"No, thank you, Betty," Sarah said when the bath was ready. "I don't need any help."

She waited until Betty had left the room to climb out of bed. Her nightgown had a red stain on the back. Perhaps when the maid collected the soiled laundry, she'd just think that her courses had come early. James would have a harder time explaining the stain on his sheets. But if they were married tonight, it wouldn't really matter.

She climbed into the tub and felt the warm water lap around her body—her breasts, her arms, her legs, her . . . her mind skittered away from that thought. She wasn't even sure what to call it, this part of her that ached for James whenever he touched her.

She had given some attention to her face and her hair before—plenty of anguish over that red mop—but little thought to the rest of her. She was tall and thin. She put clothes on and took them off. She was hardly ever completely naked except during her quick baths, and then she never looked at what the clothes covered.

But she had been naked with James. Completely and shockingly naked.

She soaped her hands and slid them up her ankle to her knee, remembering the feel of James's hands traveling the same path. She dunked her head and felt the water roll off her breasts as she raised her arms to lather her hair. Her nipples tightened as the cooler air brushed them. Her body was so sensitive, as if it had been dormant all these years and now, like the crocus after the cold winter, had burst into bloom. Her skin didn't just cover her body, it connected it in the most amazing way. When James's lips touched her throat, her knees wobbled. When his clever fingers brushed her breast, her breath caught. And when he touched her *there,* which even now had grown hot and needy, she came apart.

She rinsed her hair and squeezed the wetness out, then wrapped a towel around her head and a robe around her body and went over to the fire.

Just thinking of James warmed her. When he had come to her, when she had felt him inside her, when she had felt his warm seed flow into her, she had felt a connectedness she had never known before. She put her hand on her stomach. Could she be carrying his child now?

She rubbed her hair with the towel, feeling the warmth of the fire begin to dry the red mass. She wished she had known her mother. She had only vague impressions left, wisps of sounds, traces of smells. For a long time she couldn't separate the pleasant memories from the horror of her mother's death: the darkness, the smell of blood, the screaming, the desperate whispering. And her father—had he been different when her mother was alive? She had scraps of memories of him, too, of laughter, a rough cheek, strong hands carrying her high. But maybe those were dreams rather than memories.

Her children—hers and James—would know beyond any doubt that they were loved.

The door banged open. "There you are!" Lizzie said.

Sarah laughed. "Where else would I be?"

"Anywhere else! It's past noon, you know, and you're just drying your hair." Lizzie flopped down in the other chair by the fire. "I've been dying to get in here to ask you what was happening, but Betty wouldn't let me past the door until you were awake. She said James said to let you sleep. Now, why would James say that?"

Sarah flushed and turned quickly toward the fire, hoping Lizzie would attribute her heightened color to the heat. "I'm sure I don't know."

"I'm sure you do. James was too busy to accompany you to the opera last night and this morning he leaves directions for you to sleep late and have a bath when you get up. Add to that the armloads of flowers appearing in the drawing room, the parade of delivery boys from Fortnum and Mason's, and Harrison's knowing smirk, and I'd say something significant happened between the time I left you last night and now."

"Maybe you should ask Harrison."

"I *did* ask Harrison. Aunt Gladys asked Harrison. Even Lady Amanda 'Ferret' Wallen-Smyth asked Harrison. Harrison isn't talking. 'His grace will be home shortly' is all he'll say. He won't even say where his charming grace is or when he'll deign to stroll back to Berkeley Square. So I'm asking you, Sarah. Come on, tell all. What's going on between you and my brother?"

"Um . . ." Sarah smiled at Lizzie. "His grace will be home shortly?"

"Arghh!" Lizzie threw a pillow at her. Sarah laughed and caught it.

"Am I interrupting?"

Sarah's head snapped around. James was leaning on the doorpost, smiling at her. She was sure she was grinning like a bedlamite, but fortunately Lizzie's attention was focused on James.

"There you are!" Lizzie knelt on the seat of her chair and leaned on the back to face her brother. "Where have you been all morning?"

"Here and there." His glance slid over to Sarah. Her breath caught. She was very conscious of being naked under her robe. Thank God Lizzie was in the room, otherwise she was afraid she would just have untied the belt and opened the sides wide to James.

"That's no answer. Tell us why there are so many flowers downstairs and why the kitchen is bursting with food."

"Oh, I think Sarah knows." James smiled slowly.

Lizzie grabbed another pillow and flung it at him. "Well *I* don't know, so tell *me!*"

James laughed. "Patience, sister." He sent the pillow spinning through the air to land on Sarah's bed. "Why don't you go down and join Aunt Gladys and Lady Amanda in the drawing room? Sarah and I will be down in a minute and I will tell all then." He looked at Sarah and grinned wider. "Well, maybe not *all.*"

Sarah felt her face flame.

"I'm not leaving you here alone with Sarah," Lizzie said. "She has only her robe on, James."

"I noticed."

Lizzie got up and grabbed his arm. "Come on." She tugged him toward the door. "If I get you downstairs, I'm sure Sarah will come along shortly. Do hurry, Sarah," she said as she pushed James out the door, "or

Aunt Gladys and Lady Amanda and I may tear James apart to get the story out of him."

"I'll hurry," Sarah said, laughing as she closed the door behind them.

Sarah was amazed, when she came downstairs a few minutes later, at how the house had been transformed. There were indeed flowers everywhere—by the front door, on the bannisters, on the tables. She drew in a deep breath. The air smelled like summer.

Aunt Gladys sat by a large vase of red roses in the drawing room. "There you are. Maybe now we'll find out why James has emptied every hothouse in London."

"I thought you would have guessed, Aunt." James moved a vase of violets on the mantle.

"These many flowers—must be a funeral or a wedding," Lady Amanda said.

"Precisely. And since, despite Richard's wishes, I'm not planning on dying any time soon, the conclusion is obvious."

"Not so obvious." Aunt Gladys frowned at him. "Exactly whom are you marrying? When we came home from the opera last night—I don't need to point out that you didn't see fit to accompany us—I believe Sarah was still intending to be a governess, not a duchess."

James brushed a speck of lint off the sleeve of his coat. "Yes, well, we've worked out our differences."

"Don't see how you could have. She's been in bed the whole time since, hasn't she?"

"I believe the question is, Gladys," Lady Amanda said, "*whose* bed?"

"Hmm." Lady Gladys's eyes surveyed James and then

Sarah. Sarah kept her chin up, though she knew her face was redder than her hair.

"Well I don't care how it happened, I think it's wonderful!" Lizzie said, hugging first James and then Sarah. "When is the wedding?"

"Tonight." James grinned.

The wedding was very small, which suited Sarah perfectly. Only the people she cared about were there—Aunt Gladys, Lady Amanda, Lizzie, Robbie, and Charles. She remembered certain things clearly. Proper Wiggins actually breaking into a wide grin as he opened the door to the drawing room for her. Her hand on Robbie's arm just before he gave her to James, the emerald in her engagement ring glowing in the candlelight. Aunt Gladys's face, her eyes sparkling with unshed tears, her lips wobbling in and out of a smile. And James, blond hair gleaming in the candlelight, amber eyes swirling with humor and love.

She had tried to listen to the minister's words, but her mind kept wandering to James. She smelled his soap. She felt the heat of his body all along her side. If she looked out the corner of her eye, she could see him, dressed elegantly in proper eveningwear, listening to the minister. But if she closed her eyes, she saw him in different candlelight, without the civilized coverings of coat and breeches. She knew now the strength and beauty of the body beneath the clothing. She knew what it was to be surrounded by the heat and the smell of him. Her knees shook as his hand came up to cover hers. The touch of his fingers was both a reassurance and a promise.

Afterwards they sat down to a lavish dinner. Sarah touched James's hand when he led her to the seat at the foot of the table.

"That's Aunt Gladys's place."

"Not anymore. You're my hostess now, sweetheart."

"But I don't know what to do!"

"Wiggins does. Just nod yes to all his questions, and if he looks odd when you say yes, smile and say no."

"As if it were that easy!"

It turned out to be that easy. The problem was realizing when Wiggins was addressing her.

"Shall I have the footmen serve the second course, your grace?"

Sarah waited for James to answer. James smiled down the length of the table and lifted his eyebrows.

"Your grace?" Wiggins was right at her elbow. She turned to look at him.

"Am *I* 'your grace'?" she whispered.

Wiggins nodded.

"Well, then, yes, Wiggins, if you think it's time."

In the drawing room after dinner, Aunt Gladys smiled and leaned towards Sarah.

"James looks so happy, dear. I've never seen him so content."

Sarah looked to where James stood by the mantle with Charles. He *did* seem happy. Some strain, some tension that had been a part of him was gone. He must have felt her eyes on him, because he glanced over. His lips turned up in a slow smile. Sarah looked down at her hands.

"I believe he's more than happy, Gladys," Lady Amanda said. "I don't expect you'll be lingering downstairs tonight, hmm, Sarah?"

Sarah was saved from answering by the arrival of the tea tray. She leapt up to pour.

"Richard will not be very pleased to read about your wedding in the paper tomorrow, James," Charles said as he took his teacup from Sarah. "I assume you've sent the notices to the papers?"

"Don't need the papers." Robbie leaned back in the settee and stretched his feet out in front of him. "You'd have to be blind and deaf not to notice the hubbub around here today. Wouldn't take more than a question here and there to get all the particulars."

"True. Though even if he gets wind of it tonight, seeing it in print will give him indigestion with his breakfast." James stayed by Sarah as she finished pouring. "If that were the end of it, I wouldn't care, but I'm afraid the notice will spur him to desperate action."

"Surely Richard will realize his cause is lost," Aunt Gladys protested. "You're married. What more can he do?"

"That's the question, isn't it?" James said. "Last night, William Dunlap almost strangled me in my bed."

"Good God!" Charles's tea sloshed into his saucer. "How the devil did that happen?"

James shrugged. "He drugged the Bow Street Runners I had engaged to help guard the house."

"How did you stop him, James?" Lizzie asked. Sarah kept her eyes firmly fixed on the teapot.

"Let's say his head had an unfortunate encounter with a chamber pot."

"Conked him over the noggin, did you? Well done!" Robbie saluted James with his teacup.

"You always were a light sleeper," Charles said. "Always the one who heard the enemy sneaking into camp when we were on the Peninsula."

"Yes, well, I managed to get a confession out of him. I hope it will persuade Richard to give up his obsession with the dukedom."

"Good luck," Robbie said. "I imagine you'll have as much success at that as you'd have getting the Thames to flow backward. The man's a lunatic."

"And he's getting bolder." Charles leaned forward, his elbows on his knees. "I don't believe you have time to try to persuade him, James. He must know that his role in this is exposed. He'll act quickly. I think you need to trap him now, just as we used to do when we had a soldier we suspected of treason. Catch him in the act. You can do it. You just need the right bait."

"I don't think that will work, Charles. Richard's tried to kill me many times, but he's always hired someone else to do the job."

"Perhaps he's desperate enough to try himself now, especially with Dunlap gone."

"I don't know." Robbie shook his head. "I agree with James. I don't think Richard will take him on directly."

"Maybe—" Sarah swallowed, trying to clear the sudden dryness in her throat. "Maybe there's other bait besides James that would lure Richard out of hiding."

Charles frowned. "What do you mean?"

Sarah heard James's sharp intake of breath even before she spoke. "He's not afraid of me."

"Absolutely not!" James almost shouted the words.

"But it might work. I'm certainly not a physical threat to Richard."

"I'll not allow you to put yourself at risk."

"I don't know, James," Charles said. "If we took the proper precautions—"

"No. Do not even think of it. It is totally out of the question." James slammed his teacup down on the table. The sound of china clattering against china made everyone cringe. "Now if you'll excuse us, I think we shall retire for the evening."

* * *

James pulled Sarah up the stairs. The thought of her having anything more to do with Richard made him want to jump out of his skin.

"James, could we slow down to a run? I'm afraid I'll trip."

James stopped. "I'm sorry. I'm a little upset."

"I noticed." She ran her finger down his cheek. "Let's sleep on the problem. Maybe a solution will come to us in the morning."

"An excellent idea." James started back up the stairs at a slower pace. "Only, I don't intend to sleep tonight."

"Not at all?"

"Not at all. I have too many years without you to make up for."

Chapter 16

"He's married!" Richard threw his newspaper down on the breakfast table, knocking over the cream.

"Yes." Philip tried to stem the white flow with his napkin. He'd been expecting this outburst. One of Lord Eversly's footmen had told him about the activity at Alvord House the night before.

"He's supposed to be dead."

"I know." Philip dodged the teapot that Richard flung across the room. A spray of hot liquid burned his hand. He flinched and wiped it on his dressing gown.

"Where the bloody hell is Dunlap?"

"On his way back to America."

"On his way to America!" Richard's eyes narrowed as he leaned over the table. "I thought you told me he could do this job," he spat between gritted teeth. "You swore he was competent."

"I thought he was. Apparently he attempted to dispatch James the night before last, but failed. The rumor on the servant grapevine is that Miss Hamilton bashed him over the head with a chamber pot. James got a confession from him and then arranged for his passage early yesterday morning."

"A confession?" Richard surged to his feet, upending

the breakfast table and sending the dishes shattering to the floor.

Philip brushed steak and kidneys off his lap. "No one will believe the word of an American whoremonger."

"Perhaps not, but I am sick to death of waiting for this to be resolved. I will not wait any longer. Today, Philip. We will settle this problem today."

"Richard, think. You need a plan."

"No, Philip, I need results."

Sarah hovered by a large floral arrangement in Lady Carrington's ballroom. It had taken hours of argument, but James had finally agreed to the scheme. She couldn't say she enjoyed playing cheese to Richard's rat, but if her role led to Richard's entrapment and removal from their lives, it would be well worth it.

James had lived in the shadow of Richard's obsession too long. Even the short time Sarah had been the object of his machinations had been too long. But the coal in her gut that kept her determination burning was the thought of what her life would be like if she and James had a child. She would never be able to relax. Every night when she put the infant in his crib, she would worry that the babe would be gone when she came to him in the morning. She would scrutinize every servant, suspect every visitor, search every room, and every quiet landscape for potential danger. It would be hell on earth.

James had worked to reduce the risk. He had insisted that she dress in bright yellow and wear a yellow plume in her hair so she would be easier to trace in the crush of the ballroom or the dim light of the garden. He had Walter Parks alert his extensive network of associates. There was a street urchin by the front door and another at the back gate. A coachman leaned against one of the many vehicles lined up outside. A hackney driver idled halfway down the block, and at the street corner a man in livery chatted with a maid. Even inside the ballroom there were people alert for trouble.

Yet James still could not let go. Sarah had forced him to retreat to the card room, but he kept reappearing at her side at the end of every set.

"James," she finally hissed. "Nothing will happen if you keep hovering over me like an anxious nursemaid."

"I don't *want* anything to happen." His face turned stony.

"I know." Sarah sighed. Her next partner was approaching. "We've gone through this over and over, James. We agreed to try this plan. Now go play cards." She gave him a little push. He glared at her, then at poor Viscount Islington, but he did finally turn and stalk back to the card room.

When the viscount bowed at the end of their set, Sarah was certain she would find James at her elbow again, but he'd managed to stay where he'd been sent. Now she was waiting for Lord Pontly, one of the more brainless specimens of the *ton,* to claim her for a country dance.

"Ah, Miss Hamilton—or, I should say, *Duchess.* How is my new cousin?"

Sarah turned slowly. Richard was standing just behind her.

"Mr. Runyon." She swallowed sudden fear. "How nice to see you."

Richard chuckled. At least that is what she assumed he intended the noise to be. It sounded more like icicles splintering against the pavement to her.

"You don't lie well, *your grace.* Since you have allied yourself with my cousin—much against my advice, you will recall—you cannot be glad to see me. Where is James, by the by? He's been standing guard over you like a dog with a new bone."

"I believe he is in the card room. If you look, I'm sure you will have no trouble finding him."

Richard took her arm. "Oh, I've found what I'm looking for."

"Mr. Runyon, I have promised this dance to Lord Pontly."

"Pontly graciously gave up his dance to me. Now, come along."

Sarah had no choice—the pressure of Richard's hand on her arm forced her across the dance floor. She scanned the room, looking for Robbie or Charles, but didn't see either of them. She hoped the other watchers had noted Richard's entrance on the scene.

Richard steered her toward a set forming near the doors to the garden. At least it might be cooler on that side of the room. Mr. Symington was to be one of their group. He was partnering a mousy-haired girl who kept her eyes on the floor. He certainly had wasted no time in finding his next victim.

The orchestra struck the first note.

"Shouldn't we move a little quicker, Mr. Runyon? We'll miss the set."

"So eager to dance with me? Too bad. We aren't heading for the dancers, my dear, but for the doors just beyond."

"Well, yes, I guess a bit of fresh air might be nice." Sarah's eyes skittered over the ballroom as the door loomed closer. Was that Robbie in the corner? She couldn't tell. And Charles? He might be over by the ficus plant, but unless he had eyes in the back of his head, he would be of no help.

Richard swept her out the door and down the steps. A bulky shadow loomed out of the darkness. Sarah opened her mouth to scream, but a rough hand slapped across her face. Someone jerked a bag over her head and someone else threw a cloak around her, binding her arms to her sides and hampering her legs. Thick arms grabbed her and hoisted her into the air.

"There's the back gate," she heard Richard say. "Load her into the carriage and let's get the hell out of here."

"I believe you just trumped your partner's card, old man," the Earl of Eldridge said.

"For the fourth time!" Viscount Paxton threw down his hand. "My fault for playing with a newlywed."

Eldridge leered at James. "Mind on other matters, hmm?"

Eldridge's partner, Baron Tundrow, grinned. "We should raise the stakes. Maybe that will sharpen Alvord's wits."

"No, thank you. I don't care to go home a pauper." Paxton leaned across the table. "Alvord, get your mind out of the bedsheets or give your seat to another player."

"Surprised you're here at all." Tundrow laughed. "Thought we wouldn't see you for at least a week."

Eldridge nodded. "Too horny by half, Alvord. Go home and take your lovely wife to bed. Let poor Paxton here play with a man whose mind is on his partner's aces, not his wife's arse."

James stood. "Then, if you'll excuse me?" he ground out.

"Definitely." Paxton gathered up the cards. "Have an enjoyable evening."

"Very enjoyable!" Tundrow chuckled. He called after

James. "We'll be looking for an heir in nine months, Alvord."

James ignored him.

He knew he had done Paxton a disservice in agreeing to play with him. The cards could have been written in Sanskrit for all the sense he was making of them tonight. He had not wanted to be in the card room. He had not wanted to be at Carrington's bloody ball.

He scanned the ballroom for Sarah and saw her yellow plume waving by a mass of flowers. He relaxed slightly.

He hated this plan. Why the hell had he let Sarah persuade him? He had tried to devise every possible safeguard, but he knew that nothing was without risk. Well, this was the first and the last night he was going to allow this insanity. Tomorrow he would hunt down Richard and have it out with him, as he should have done months ago.

James watched the yellow plume move across the ballroom. There were too many people in the way for him to identify Sarah's partner. He shifted position so he could get a better view.

"Your grace, let me congratulate you!"

"Mrs. Fallwell, how nice to see you." Melinda Fallwell, one of Lady Amanda's particular friends and a formidable gossip in her own right, blocked his path. She would talk his ear off if he let her. He tried to see around her elaborate headdress. The forest of purple feathers sprouting from her green turban made it impossible for him to see the other side of the room. Was the yellow plume heading to a set by the garden doors?

"Couldn't wait for a proper wedding, could you?" Mrs. Fallwell chuckled. "Never knew you were so hot-blooded. Take after your father. He was quite the buck in his salad days, I'll tell you. I spent an evening touring the shrubbery with him. Oh my!" Mrs. Fallwell's fan increased its tempo in front of her suddenly flushed face. She nodded her head and her feathers bobbed in agreement.

"But then he married your mother," she said. "Such a cold girl, she was. Beautiful, but icy. No one could understand what he saw in her. Guess it was just time to start his nursery. Figured he didn't have to worry she'd sow a cuckoo in his nest." She folded her fan and tapped James on the wrist. "But it looks like you didn't make your father's mistake. From what Amanda told me, your bride has blood hot enough to match you own."

That caught James's attention. "Excuse me?"

"You know." Mrs. Fallwell threw him an arch look and fanned herself again. "That inn. What was it called? The Green Man? Amanda told me all about it at the Palmerson do. Wondered why it took you so long to get a ring on the girl's finger."

"I see." James considered strangling Lady Amanda. He looked around for her—and saw the yellow plume disappear out the doors to the garden.

Bloody hell! He might have said the words aloud— he registered Mrs. Fallwell's sharply indrawn breath as he charged onto the crowded dance floor.

"Alvord, watch where you're going!"

"My hem!"

"Have a care, man!"

James ignored the complaints as he pushed his way to the garden. He would flatten anyone who tried to stop him—fortunately no one did. He reached the doors and pounded down the stairs.

He was too late. All that was left of Sarah was a broken, yellow plume.

* * *

"James, what happened?" Robbie and Charles hurried down the garden steps.

"They've taken Sarah." James studied the ground. Two, no, four men—four men against one woman. He pushed aside his terror and thought quickly. "I'm going after them. They must be in a coach—the crush of traffic outside should slow them. I'll catch the hackney driver Parks has waiting down the block."

"I'm coming with you."

"All right, Charles. Robbie, will you see the ladies home?"

"I'll make arrangements for them, and then I'm coming after you."

James nodded and took off at a run to the back gate, Charles at his heels.

The gate stood open. The alley was deserted; Parks's boy, gone. Laughter and music drifted faintly from the ballroom; the rattle of carriage wheels, the creak of harnesses, and the clopping of horses' hooves came from the street. James ran down the cobblestones toward the main thoroughfare.

"Yer grace." A small boy darted out of the shadows, chest heaving. He pointed down the street. "If ye hurry, ye can catch Rufus—he's goin' after 'em."

"Well done, lad." James tossed the boy a coin. "Tell Parks."

James ran up to an old, broken-down hackney and grabbed hold of the driver's seat just as Rufus started to pull away.

"Hey!" Rufus raised the butt of his whip, aiming it at James's hands. "Let go, if ye knows what's good for ye."

"It's Alvord, Rufus. I'll take over now."

Rufus squinted down at James. "Oh, sorry, yer grace. Didn't know it was ye."

"No offense taken. Hurry down, man, and let me go after them."

"Sure, yer grace." Rufus jumped down from his seat. "Keep your eye on the coach with the wide scratch on the back."

James glanced ahead and nodded. "I see it. My thanks."

"Good luck, yer grace."

Rufus stood aside, and James swung up to take the reins. Charles climbed up beside him.

"Not exactly what you're used to," Charles said.

"No." James urged the nag into motion. Her ancient feet shuffled forward. "We don't want to overtake Richard's coach anyway, nor get close enough to let them know they're being followed. There's no telling what Richard would do to Sarah then."

"True. Let's just hope this sorry specimen of horse-flesh can manage to keep Richard's equipage in sight."

James nodded, weaving between the carriages waiting to take their wealthy owners to the next entertainment. The horse had a mouth of iron. The only blessing was that Richard was also stuck in traffic. If only he had his own rig—but then any of his own carriages was distinctive. If Richard or his henchmen happened to glance back, they'd know immediately who was following them. A hackney was much less obvious.

"There—they turned right," Charles said.

"I see." James yanked on the reins and the nag reluctantly responded. Patience, James counseled himself. Patience was bloody difficult.

Richard continued east. They followed him through the broad streets of Mayfair down Piccadilly to Haymarket. The streets got narrower and more cluttered as they made their way toward Covent Garden, but they managed to stay close. Richard's carriage was just ahead of them as they approached the intersection with Henrietta Street.

"Hey, yer lordship, what's a nob like ye doing drivin' that hack?"

James glanced over for a split second to see the sorry drab who had called out to him. Then he heard the pounding of horses' hooves coming too fast. He swung his head back to see disaster barreling down on them from Henrietta Street.

Richard's coach got clear, but the poor animal hitched to their carriage never had a chance. She stood in the intersection and screamed as two matched grays and a fashionable curricle crashed into them.

Chapter 17

No one bothered to take the bag off Sarah's head. That was a mixed blessing. It was hot and she could barely breathe, but the men in the coach ignored her. She curled up tightly in her corner and held very still, listening and hoping she would learn something that would help her escape.

"We did it, Philip!" That was Richard. "We got the bitch. You're sure James can't find us?"

"I'm not sure of anything." Philip's voice was low and hoarse. "But your cousin should have no way of knowing where we are. We should have time, time enough for you to send the note."

Sarah smiled to herself. They obviously didn't know that Mr. Parks's associates were following them.

"Ah, yes, the note." There was a pause, then Richard continued. "I'd say there was no rush to send the note."

"What do you mean?" Philip's voice was sharp.

"That we should take time to amuse ourselves."

"Finishing this is amusing enough." Sarah thought she heard a thin whine of panic. "You've—we've—waited for this for years, Richard. This is it, do you understand? Half the *ton* saw you leave the ballroom with the girl. You can't hide any longer. When this is over, either you or Alvord will have won."

"I'll win, Philip, never fear. With the girl, we've got James by the balls. A pity Dunlap didn't manage to kill him, but this may actually be better. He won't want to lose the only bit of tail he's ever gotten. He'll acknowledge my claim to the dukedom. I'll finally get what is mine. I'll be Duke of Alvord."

"I don't think it will be that easy, Richard."

"You can't tell me that the man will give up swiving now that he's finally figured out how to do it?" Richard laughed. "I don't think so. He'll do anything to get her back."

The coach lurched to the left. Sarah heard the clatter of carriage wheels and the sound of two vehicles colliding. Then pandemonium. Horses screamed and men shouted. She hoped Mr. Parks's men had decided that now was an excellent time to free her.

Richard knocked on the roof of the coach. "What's going on, Scruggs?"

"Nuttin', sir. Some drunken bucks crashed their curricle into a hackney, that's all. Just missed us, sir."

"Good." Richard laughed. "That was close, heh, Philip?"

"Yes, it was close. Allow me to point out, Richard, that we have just had demonstrated the fact that no plans are perfect. You cannot delay sending the note to your cousin."

Sarah listened to the noise fade behind them. Her hope of immediate rescue faded with it.

"I don't think we should just hand the girl back to James."

"Richard." Philip's voice was icy. "We have discussed this."

"You're just an old maid, Philip."

"It will be difficult to kill her and escape hanging. And if she's dead, you'll have nothing to bargain with."

"I won't kill her, though she may wish that I had." Richard chuckled. Sarah's heart leapt to her throat.

"Richard! You are losing sight of the main goal."

"No, I'm not."

"You are. The goal is the dukedom, not revenge."

"*Your* goal is the dukedom. Mine is the dukedom *and* revenge." Richard's voice grew louder with enthusiasm. "God, can you picture James's face when he finds out his precious wife has been ridden by half the British navy? If she ends up pregnant, he'll never know if the brat is his or some drunken sailor's. And if she doesn't get a babe, she's bound to get the clap."

Sarah thought she was going to vomit. She bit her lower lip.

"Richard, your cousin is not powerless. He has many friends, in both high and low places. See how easily he got rid of Dunlap? I'm quite certain he would kill us or have us killed if we injure his wife in any way."

"I'm not afraid of him." Richard was silent for a few minutes. "Maybe I'll have her myself."

Philip grunted.

Sarah thought quickly. Her hands and feet weren't tied. If she could get the bag off her head, she could shake off the cloak and run when the coach stopped. The carriage was slowing. She readied herself to take advantage of any opportunity.

"I don't think so." The words were whispered in her ear as Richard's arms came around her. She twisted and he tightened his grasp, making breathing difficult.

She heard the carriage door open and smelled the familiar stench of the docks. Rough hands grabbed her and dragged her out of the coach. Someone hefted her

over his shoulder and carried her through a narrow door
Here she smelled smoke and ale. She heard the low
drone of male voices, punctuated by curses, the scrape
of chairs, the clink of heavy glass mugs.

She struggled, and the man carrying her tightened his
hold, grinding her stomach against the point of his
shoulder. He started up a flight of steep, winding stairs
He wasn't careful with his burden. Sarah had her head
knocked against the wall twice before she was carried
into a room and dumped onto a soft surface. She heard
the sound of booted feet retreating and the scrape of a
key in a lock.

She lay still for a moment, listening. She heard
nightmarish noises: deep, drunken voices; the rhythmic squeaking of a cheap bed; a woman screaming
and somewhere, thin, hysterical crying. But all the
horrible noises were muffled, like they were being
heard through doors and walls. She shrugged off the
cloak and lifted the bag off of her head.

She was alone in the most garish room she had ever
seen. Everything was blood red—the walls, the
draperies, the bed she was on.

She leapt up. She didn't want to have anything to do
with a bed in this place. She tried the door. Locked, as
she had anticipated. Maybe she could escape through
the window. She pushed the heavy draperies aside. She
had expected to see thick, iron bars, but the window was
clear. It even opened easily. She leaned out and looked
down into blackness. There was enough moonlight to
see the oily glint of the Thames far below. Only a bird
could escape this way.

She turned back to the room. She made a careful cir-
cuit, looking for anything that might help her escape. It
was an educational, if nauseating, tour. The paintings on

the wall, which she had taken for still lifes and pastorals were, on further inspection, pornographic in the extreme. There were peepholes in the wall across from the window—fortunately all closed at the moment—and broken handcuffs on a table. She found a chamber pot under the bed and picked it up, hoping she might have another opportunity to hit someone over the head.

She studied the red drapes. They certainly were ugly. She tore one down and dropped an end over the window sill. Maybe someone would see it and wonder why a red curtain was hanging down the side of the building. Maybe James would see it.

How long would it be before he came? Would he come? She could not rely on it. Something must have gone wrong.

She eyed the bed. No, she couldn't stomach it—she would sit on the floor. There were probably bugs in both locations, but the floor's fauna seemed more appealing than whatever might be lurking in the bedding. She spread out the cloak, sat down with the chamber pot by her side, and tried to formulate a plan.

James held on to one gray's head. Charles had taken charge of the other. The drunken idiots in the curricle were useless. At least the hackney horse stood still. It was too stupid to bolt.

"Daisy!"

James looked over his shoulder to see Rufus and Robbie running toward the melee. Rufus reached for the old horse's bridle and started whispering in her ear.

"Need a hand?" Robbie asked.

James nodded. "How did you find us?"

"Ran into Lord Dervin, or is it Devin? You know—the old soldier with the bald pate and hairy ears?"

"Lord Dearvon."

"Right. Saw him just after you left. He said he'd see the ladies home, so I hurried after you. Got to the street just as you pulled away. Rufus and I—I don't think Rufus really trusted you with Daisy—grabbed another hackney and trailed you."

"Good. See if you can get those two in the curricle—who *are* they, anyway?"

Robbie looked over. "Viscount Wycomb and the Honorable Felix Muddleridge."

"Oh, God. I should have known. Get them to take charge of these cattle, will you?"

Robbie pulled the two drunken men out of the curricle. The drab who had called to James obliged by bringing over a large bucket of liquid which Robbie dumped over the gentlemen's heads. It was sufficiently cold or noxious to shock them out of their alcoholic stupor.

"I say," Wycomb sputtered. "What the hell are you doing, Westbrooke?"

"He's waking you up," James said. "Come take charge of your horses."

Wycomb peered at James. "Alvord, is that you?"

"Yes, it's me. You ran me down with your cow-handed driving."

"Sorry. In my altitudes, I'm afraid."

"I'd say so. Take this horse and have Muddleridge take the other."

"Well . . ." Wycomb scratched his head.

"*Now,* Wycomb."

The man finally moved. James dropped his hold on the gray.

"Rufus, I'll leave you with Daisy. We're taking the

other hackney. Tell Parks . . ." James raked his hand through his hair and looked at Robbie and Charles. "Any suggestions as to where Richard might be taking Sarah?"

"How about the Rutting Stallion?" Robbie said. "It's in this direction."

"As are most of the brothels of London." James closed his eyes. God, he wished he had something to go on. Sarah could be anywhere. Every second counted. If he guessed wrong, Sarah paid a horrible price.

"Let's try the Rutting Stallion."

James prayed he had guessed right.

Chapter 18

The doorknob rattled. Sarah grabbed the chamber pot and leapt up, ready to smash it over Richard's head.

"*Duchess,*" Richard said from the hall. Malice dripped from his voice. "So kind of you to greet me." He lunged, grabbing her wrists and twisting them down. "You're not going to play the same trick on me that you did on Dunlap."

Sarah struggled to free herself, but Richard's hands were like manacles. He squeezed tighter, and she gasped in pain, certain her bones would splinter from the pressure. Her fingers opened, and the chamber pot shattered on the floor. Richard kicked the shards out of the way and slammed the door shut behind him with his foot. He smiled.

"So here we are, Duchess, just you and I. I wonder how we shall pass the time." He jerked her up against his body.

Sarah swallowed, trying to clear the roaring from her ears. She could see the pores of Richard's skin, the stubble of his beard. She breathed in his stench, the musty smell of oily hair, dirty linen, and dried sweat. She tried to pull back, but his hands trapped her body against his.

"I have an idea. This *is* a bedchamber." He twisted her arms behind her back, gripping both her wrists in one hand. He grabbed her chin and forced her to face the bed with its gaudy red sheets. "Why don't you show me the games James likes to play? I imagine you've taught my little cousin quite a few tricks."

"No."

Richard jerked her hands up and a sharp pain shot between her shoulders. She bit her lip to keep from moaning.

"Does that hurt?" He laughed. "It's nothing compared to what you'll feel in a moment." He dragged her to the bed.

"Don't do this. You don't want me."

"Of course I don't want you, you red-haired whore. This isn't about wanting." He thrust her back up against a bedpost, holding her still with his body. "Not that kind of wanting, at least."

He pulled the remaining pins from her hair, and ran his dirty fingers through it. "Does James spread your whore-red hair over his pillow when he rides you, Duchess? Or does he like it feathering his chest while you ride him? Does he wrap his hands in it like this?"

He twisted his hands roughly in her hair, pulling it so tight she was sure it would come out from its roots. She grabbed his wrists.

"Let me go."

"Oh, no." His eyes moved from her hair to her throat. "I've waited too long for this day." He yanked her hair, forcing her chin up. "I bet your fair skin bruises nicely, Duchess." He put his mouth on her neck, just under her jaw line, and sucked hard on the tender skin there. Sarah tried to lean away from him. He laughed and bit her. She felt a bead of blood trickle down to her collarbone.

"That's my first mark, Duchess—the first of many."

"Stop. Please stop."

"No, I won't stop. I won't stop until I am finished." He yanked her hair again, causing her eyes to tear. "Do you know what my very first memory is, Duchess? The image I most remember from my childhood? It's my father thrashing me in his study. I was only four years old. He birched me on my bare ass. And do you know why?"

Richard paused, clearly expecting a response.

"No," Sarah whispered. He had her head bent back so far her neck and shoulders ached.

"He birched me because I'd pushed my snotty little cousin down and made him cry. 'James is the Marquis of Walthingham,' he said, 'and will be the Duke of Alvord. A peer of the realm.' God. *He* should have been the duke, but he didn't have the guts to challenge his brother and take the wealth and position that were rightfully his. He didn't want them. He was happy with his dusty old books and smelly dogs. He didn't care that he was giving away my birthright as well."

Richard loosened his grip and Sarah straightened slightly. Would he get so caught up in his story she could escape?

"At Cambridge, there was a girl I wanted, but the only way I could get her into my bed was to promise her James. You should have heard the bloody bitch. Even when I was screwing her, all she talked about was him—his shoulders, his legs, his goddamned ass. Well, she never made it to James's bed. I broke her neck and dumped her in the river."

Sarah straightened a little more. She could see the door. It wasn't that far away. If she could knee Richard as she had Dunlap . . .

He was holding her too tightly.

"So no, I'm not going to stop, not now that I have revenge in my hands. I'm going to enjoy every minute of this night. When I rape you, I'll be raping James. When I drag your skinny body downstairs and watch thirty lusty fellows take their turns with you, it'll be James's face I'll see."

"James will kill you."

"I don't think so. I think he's going to have an accident. It's very rough on the wharves, you know. Or perhaps he'll be so maddened to find your bloody body covered by seamen—do pardon the pun—he'll take his own life."

"No!" Sarah shoved at his chest and tried to jerk her knee up. He blocked her easily.

He laughed. "You have only yourself to blame, Duchess. I tried to discourage you from marrying James, but you were blinded by lust. This is where your lust has led you."

He flung her onto the bed. She scrambled for the other side, but he came down on top of her, pressing her into the mattress. She bucked and thrashed, but she could not move his weight. She clawed at his eyes, but he batted her hands away as if they were no more than irritating flies at a summer party.

"Yes, Duchess, fight me. I love it when you bitches fight. It's so much more fun."

Sarah heard the excitement in his voice. She felt his erection digging into her thigh. He leaned up on his elbows, pinning her to the bed with his body, and pulled a length of rope from his pocket.

"Silk would be kinder on your delicate flesh, Duchess, but I suspect raw wrists will be the least of your pains come morning."

He tied her hands to the bedposts and then straddled her, running the tip of his index finger slowly along the low neck of her ball gown.

"Tell me about your husband, Duchess. Is James all that is proper in bed? Does he fumble your skinny body with the candles snuffed and your nightgown buttoned up to your chin?"

Sarah swallowed her terror. "Let me go, Richard. I'm sure we can work something out if you let me go. James is a reasonable man."

"Is he?" His finger dipped lower, tracing the swells of her breasts. "I doubt he is reasonable about you. And I don't want reason, I want passion. Passion and pain. James stole what is mine, now I have what is his. I want him to feel what I have felt all these years."

His fingers curved under the delicate fabric of her dress and pulled hard, ripping it to her waist. He stared at her breasts. She tried to move her arms to cover herself, but the rope just cut deeper into her flesh.

He ran his filthy fingers all over her skin, molding her flesh, touching her nipples. She closed her eyes to shut him out.

"Look at me, Duchess."

Sarah shook her head, turning her face away.

"Do not defy me, bitch." He slapped her hard. She tasted blood. "Look at me."

"No." If he hit her hard enough, she would be free. Oblivion offered her the only escape from this nightmare.

Richard might well have read her mind.

"I'm an expert at this game, Duchess." He squeezed her breasts hard. She gasped. Hot tears ran from the corners of her eyes to trickle over her ears. "I will give you more pain than you have ever known, but not quite enough to give you peace."

He laughed and slid down her body. She tried to kick him, but she was hampered by her skirts and his weight.

He spread her legs wide, tying her ankles to the posts at the foot of the bed.

"And now I shall see where the Monk has worshiped." He took out his dagger and slit her skirts, ripping them up to her waist.

Philip Gadner sat in the shadows of the common room and took another swallow of ale. God, he hated this place. He looked over at a nearby table. Alf and Scruggs each had a tankard and a whore to entertain them. They'd been willing to stay till this was finished. They wanted a chance to rearrange James's face in payment for the beating they'd taken from him outside the Spotted Dog when they'd still been working for Dunlap.

Richard needed to send that letter. One would think he could keep his breeches buttoned long enough to get that single task done, but no, a little blond whore with big tits had caught his eye. He was upstairs now, plowing the piece. Philip hadn't complained too much. It was better than having him plow the Duchess of Alvord.

He leaned back and drummed his fingers on the table. Surely Richard was done now. He never took very long with women. Philip glanced over at the stairs. Yes, there was the whore now—with a big, beefy sailor following her, a broad smile of satisfaction on his ugly face.

Damn! Philip surged to his feet. Where the hell was Richard?

James, Robbie, and Charles left the hackney with a sailor lounging by the waterfront.

"James." Charles pointed at the Rutting Stallion. "Look, there, over the river."

"I see it." A red length of fabric fluttered from a window. James counted. "Third floor, end room."

"Do you think that's where Sarah is?" Robbie asked.

"I hope so." James pushed open the door.

"You!" The madam recognized James and Robbie from their earlier visit. She was not pleased to see them.

There was a roar from a nearby table. James looked up to see Dunlap's thugs spilling women and ale on the floor in their rush to get to his throat. He also saw Philip Gadner's shocked face. There was no sign of Richard.

"Robbie, Charles, I leave you to entertain our friends." He nodded at the two men bearing down on them. Philip had not moved. "I have to find Sarah."

"Go, James," Charles said. "We'll be along shortly."

James took the stairs two at a time.

Sarah had never felt so exposed or so humiliated.

"Look at me." The sharp edge of Richard's dagger pricked the underside of her breast. "I want you to see who it is between your legs. I want you to know whose seed will be planted in your belly."

She felt the dagger scrape across her stomach and down to the curls at the apex of her legs. She tried to flex her knees to shut him out, but the rope was tied too tightly. She felt him touch her, felt his dirty fingers pry her open, and then pain shot into her belly as he thrust one finger inside her. A hot tide of shame surged over her. She swallowed tears and opened her eyes. Richard looked back at her. There was no mercy in his cold, blue gaze.

"Still young and fresh, Duchess," he said, running his free hand over her. "Sweet. And tight. So tight. A treat for me—and the first few of the men downstairs who will have you. By tomorrow morning, you'll be as loose as the oldest, cheapest slut in the London stews."

He withdrew his hand to fumble with his breeches.

The door slammed hard against the wall before Richard had worked the first button loose. He whirled to face James striding over the threshold.

"Richard!"

Sarah saw the shock and pain in James's eyes just before she felt Richard's knife at the entrance to her womb.

"Come a step closer, James, and you'll see my blade buried in your whore."

James froze. "What do you want, Richard?" His voice was calm, but Sarah saw how intently he watched his cousin. This was not the inn yard at the Green Man. They both knew that this time Richard would not back down.

"Too bad you arrived so early, James. I was just about to enjoy your whore." Richard ran his left hand over Sarah's leg. "Shall I continue? Perhaps you would like to watch? You might learn something."

James did not rise to the bait. "What do you want, Richard?" he asked again.

"I want what is mine."

Sarah felt the cold metal move as Richard shifted to face James. The dagger rested against her thigh now.

"I want the dukedom."

"It's yours—just put the knife down."

"Just like that?"

"As long as you put down the knife and don't hurt Sarah."

"You care so much for your whore?"

"Put down the knife," James repeated.

"Perhaps I'll carve my initials into her white thighs first. Shall I? Then every time you kneel between her legs, you'll remember that I was here, too. You'll remember how I beat you."

Richard turned back to Sarah and in that instant, James moved. He dove for Richard's knife hand and grabbed it, twisting it up and away from Sarah's body.

"No!" Richard screamed. He would not let go of the knife. "You bloody bastard." His free hand swung at James's face. James deflected the blow with his forearm, and Richard swung lower. James blocked that punch with his thigh.

"Richard, stop," James panted.

"No, you whoreson. I won't stop until you're dead."

Sarah strained against her bonds, but none of them loosened. She could do nothing but watch the men struggle between her legs. James had grabbed Richard's other hand, and the two men were locked in a horrible parody of the waltz, with the grunts and pants of their exertion as their music. James was taller and stronger, but he was trying to control Richard, not kill him. Richard was wild with the strength of madness. Death shone in his eyes.

"Richard!" Philip appeared in the doorway. "What are you doing? Stop it, now!"

"Philip . . ." Richard glanced toward the other man, and in that instant, the knife flashed down. James jerked his arm back, but it was too late. Blood spurted from Richard's chest.

"Richard." The knife clattered to the floor as James put both his hands over the wound. He tried to staunch the bleeding, but the damage was too great. Blood pulsed out, turning Richard's shirt and James's hands bright red.

Richard gaped down at the spreading stain. His face was white as if all the color in him was draining out through the gash in his chest.

"You've won," he whispered. Sarah heard a rattle echo

in his throat. "God damn it, you've won." His eyes closed and he crumpled, falling facedown between her legs.

The thick smell of fresh death filled the room.

"You've killed him." Philip stared at Richard's body.

"It was an accident." James took his own knife and cut the rope holding Sarah, pulling her away from Richard's corpse, off the bed and into his arms. She clung to him, burying her face in his shirt and breathing deeply. His familiar scent, the feel of his body against hers, the strength of his arms around her and the steady beat of his heart all calmed her and gave her solace. She dared to think that the nightmare was over.

"You've killed him," Philip repeated, his voice dull with shock.

"I didn't mean to. His grip slackened when he saw you. I didn't anticipate it and I could not compensate."

"He's dead." Philip walked slowly over to the bed. He gathered Richard's body into his arms, pulling it tightly against his chest and smearing his own clothes with Richard's blood. His cheeks were wet with tears. Sarah looked away as the first deep sob tore through him.

"Sarah." James smoothed back her hair, talking quietly by her ear. "Are you all right, sweetheart?"

"Yes." She felt her own sobs clog her throat. "I'm so glad you're here, James. I'm so glad you came." She tightened her hold on him, remembering the terrible things Richard had said and done to her. "It was awful. He hated you so much."

"Shhhh." James rocked her against his solid body. "It's over now. Richard can't hurt you any more."

"He can't hurt either of us any more." She tried to feel relief, but the smell of blood and death, the harsh sounds of Philip's grief, and the pain in her own body all kept her tethered to the nightmare. "Let's go home, James. Please, let's go home now."

"All right, love." James kissed her gently on her temple. "Robbie and Charles will be along in a few minutes. They can clean up here."

Sarah glanced at Philip. He had sunk to the floor, his face buried in Richard's neck. "What will happen to him?"

"I don't know. He helped abduct you. He should be punished."

"He also tried to keep Richard from hurting me, James. He only wanted Richard to send you a ransom note."

James nodded. "I believe you. I'm not eager to bring charges against him. If he were to stand trial, the whole sordid story would come out."

Sarah's stomach twisted. Surely she would not have to revisit this night? She clutched James's arm.

"I want this over, James. I don't want to have to talk about it or think about it again. Isn't Richard's death punishment enough for him? Can't we just leave it at that?"

"Perhaps. I doubt Philip's a danger to us or to anyone, though I don't relish sharing the same city with him. I don't even want to share the same country with him." James cupped the back of her head, kneading out a little of the tension in her neck. "I'll have him held for a few days while we decide where best to send him. There's nothing tying him to England—I doubt he'll object to an extended journey, especially when he considers the alternative might be the hangman's noose."

"All right." Sarah relaxed slightly. She didn't care where Philip went as long as she could put this evening firmly in the past.

"Your poor dress is in tatters, love. Can you bear to wear one of these hideous sheets wrapped around you?"

"There's a cloak on the floor, James, on the other side of the bed. They wrapped me in it to bring me here. It will cover me."

James went to fetch the cloak. Sarah wrapped her arms over her breasts. She didn't mind James seeing her this way—he had seen her with much less on, of course—but she wanted to be covered before Robbie and Charles arrived. She glanced nervously at the door. They should be there any minute.

And she didn't want to be exposed to Philip either. His sobs had finally subsided. She looked back to where he knelt with Richard.

He had moved. He had put Richard's body aside and was rising, teeth bared like a vicious dog, with Richard's bloody knife in his hand. His eyes were on James's back where he bent to pick the cloak off the floor.

"James!" Sarah screamed and threw herself at Philip. He started to turn towards her. She aimed for the knife. She hit him on the side, and he twisted, falling heavily to the floor, his knife arm caught under him.

That was when Robbie and Charles finally reached the room.

"My God." Robbie stopped at the open door.

Charles pushed past him. James helped Sarah up and wrapped her in the cloak as Charles knelt to examine Philip.

"Dead," he said. "Knife pierced straight through his heart."

Chapter 19

After reassuring Aunt Gladys, Lady Amanda, an
Lizzie that they were all right, Sarah and James went up
stairs, leaving Robbie and Charles to fill in the details.

"I need a bath, James," Sarah said when they en
tered his bedroom. "I have to wash the filth of tha
place off me."

The footmen brought up the tub and filled it. As soo
as the door closed behind them, Sarah stripped off he
clothes and sank down into the warm water. She wa
afraid she would never feel clean again.

Then she felt James's hands, large and firm, on he
back, soaping away the despair with the dirt.

"Dunk your head, sweetheart."

James's fingers massaged her scalp and slid throug
the long strands of her hair. His palms brushed her nec
and his knuckles skimmed her earlobes. His mouth, s
gentle, touched the bruise Richard had put on her throa
His tongue caressed it. Her body woke in response.

She had feared that she would never want to b
touched again. Now she knew that James's touch wa
what she needed to heal. She needed his body in hers t
wash away the final horror of the night. She needed hi
love flooding her, drowning all the ugly memories. Sh
needed to love him to feel alive again.

"You'd better finish the job, Sarah. I don't trust my-self to wash your front."

Sarah raised her hands, wrapping them around James's wrists. She slid them up his forearms and heard his sharp inhalation.

"It's all right, James. I'd like you to do it."

"Uh, Sarah." His voice was strained. "Are you sure that's a good idea? Are you ready for where it might lead?"

"Yes. I need you. In every way."

She heard his breath release and felt the tension drain out of his arms. "Okay, sweetheart." His voice shook slightly. Then his hands slid over her shoulders, down her collarbone to her breasts. It was what she needed, what her body ached for—his fingers, his palms, there on her skin. She breathed in his scent and knew it was James who touched her. She felt her body grow soft and welcoming.

His hands left her breasts, hugged her sides, smoothed her stomach and thighs. His fingers tangled in the hair at the juncture of her legs and touched her where she most ached for him. She shuddered and looked up at him. He looked back, his face intense and needy.

"I love you, James."

He bent his head and brushed his lips over hers.

"And I love you, Sarah." His voice was husky. "I think I'd better get you out of the tub now."

He wrapped her in a thick towel and held her against him, letting his lips graze her jawbone, her eyes, her lips. She could feel his erection with her belly, and she rubbed against it. He moved back.

"Not yet, sweetheart. I want to wash the filth of this night off me, too."

"Shall I wash you?"

"That would be lovely, Sarah, but I'm not under the best control at the moment."

"I don't mind. I want to touch you that way. Please?"

He kissed her deeply. "When you ask so nicely, love, I can't say no."

She started with his back, just as he had with her. She soaped her hands and slid them over his broad shoulders. She pushed him gently and he leaned forward, so she could reach all the way down his back to his buttocks. She moved her hands forward along the sides of his hips. His breath sucked in and he jerked in the tub, sending water over the side.

"Careful, sweetheart, or you'll get soaked." His voice was strained and breathy. Sarah smiled. She put her hands back on his shoulders and let them slide down over his arms, over the hard ridges and slopes of his muscles.

She needed this. She needed to feel this power after her nightmare of powerlessness. She let her towel slip as she leaned forward. She reached around to run her hands over the planes of James's chest, brushing her naked breasts against his back.

"God, Sarah." He tried to turn toward her, but she stilled him with her hands.

She needed to feel this power to give. Now she wasn't a victim. She wasn't even the recipient of James's protection and love. She was the giver. She was strong. She felt her love for James flood her, washing away the very last dregs of the fear and hate she had felt in Richard and in herself.

She shifted position so she could further explore James's chest and that tantalizing line of hair that ran from his chest to his navel and below. He reached for her breasts, but she pulled back.

"Not yet." She placed his hands on the sides of the tub and held them there a moment. "No touching yet. Keep your hands right here until I tell you that you can move them."

"God, Sarah, I don't know if I can. Your touch is killing me."

She grinned at him. "Then prepare to die, James, because I have many other places to touch."

"Many?" he croaked. He took a deep breath and closed his eyes. "I shall try to endure, but remember, I am only a man."

"Yes, I can see that."

He chuckled.

She bypassed that part of his body to wash his feet. Slowly she moved up his ankles to his knees and thighs. He slid forward and up in the tub, and she ran her hands over his buttocks. She circled around to his inner thighs and cupped the heavy round sacks that hung between them. He inhaled sharply and jerked. More water sloshed onto the floor.

"The servants are going to wonder what we've been doing."

"Huh?" James looked at her, his eyes glazed with passion. She smiled and let her fingers move up the smooth length of him. He closed his eyes and bit his lip. His knuckles showed white where he gripped the side of the tub. She stroked again and James moaned.

"Please, Sarah, can we go to bed now?"

"When you ask so nicely, I can't say no."

James's hands flew off the sides of the tub and grabbed her shoulders, pulling her forward. His mouth covered hers. Water cascaded over the sides of the tub.

She started laughing. "The servants are definitely going to wonder what we were doing."

"The servants are going to know exactly what we were doing. Now come to bed before I explode."

The sheets in James's big bed were white, not red. The only sounds were James's—and her—whimpers of pleasure. The only thing tying her was her love, and that was a knot she never wanted loosened. She opened willingly for James and he came to her, filling her body and her spirit. She reveled in the tension he built in her, and when their release came, she spiraled off into a deep peace.

"Do you think we made a baby?" she whispered when his body relaxed onto hers.

"Hmm?" He seemed pleasantly mindless. She ran her hands over his back and hips.

"Do you think we made a baby?"

He leaned up on his elbows and blinked down at her. "Maybe." He grinned. "A baby would be wonderful, but I'm in no rush. I'm happy to work at it for quite a while."

"At least now our baby will be safe."

"Yes." A shadow crossed his face. He slid out of her body and lay down next to her.

She leaned up on her elbow. "Are you upset about Richard's death?"

"I didn't mean to kill him." He looked up at her. "We were struggling. When he saw Philip, he stopped, just for a second. Without his resistance, my hand flew forward. I couldn't catch myself in time."

"I know." She cupped his cheek and looked into his troubled eyes. "You had no choice, not really. You both could not have lived—Richard would not have allowed it. He would have fought until one of you was dead."

James closed his eyes. "I know. He was a problem with no solution, but he was also my cousin." He looked back at her. "I should be appalled that I killed him, but mostly I'm relieved."

"So am I." She laid her hand on his chest. "There is still one thing that I don't understand, though. Why did Richard spread the rumor about us at the Green Man? He must have known it would force you to wed me."

James grinned. "I don't think it was Richard who spread that rumor."

"Who else could have?"

James pulled her down onto his chest. "My bet is that it was Lady Amanda."

"Lady Amanda? Why do you think it was Lady Amanda?"

"Because her bosom bow, Melinda Fallwell, told me that's where she got the story."

Sarah thought back to the horrible night at the Palmerson ball when the story had spread like wildfire through the *ton*. She remembered Lady Amanda talking to Mrs. Fallwell and Mrs. Fallwell's reaction.

"Maybe you're right. But why would Lady Amanda spread the tale?"

"Perhaps," James said, running his hands down her sides and cupping her naked breasts, "she realized that we belong together."

Sarah shivered. It was so hard to concentrate when James's clever fingers did such things to her. "I always thought Lady Amanda was quite astute."

"Quite." He leaned up to nuzzle the sensitive skin behind her ear. "And loyal. I'm sure she is hoping for an Alvord heir in nine months' time." He flipped her over so that he was now on top.

"Shall we get back to work on that, sweetheart? We don't want to disappoint Lady Amanda, do we?"

Sarah wound her arms around James's neck.

"No, we certainly don't want to disappoint dear Lady Amanda."

About the Author

Born in Washington, D.C. and raised in suburban Maryland, Sally MacKenzie ventured west in 1972 to help co-educate the University of Notre Dame. Graduating with a B.A. in English, she spent a short time at Cornell Law School before returning to the D.C. area where she lives with her husband and, depending on the time of year, some combination of her four sons. She's written federal regulations, school newsletters, auction programs, class plays, swim league guidance, and the annual MacKenzie family newsletter, but *The Naked Duke* is her first published novel. Readers may visit her in cyberspace at www.sallymackenzie.net.

More Regency Romance
From Zebra